MW00764044

Tales of the Eastern Indians

by Geoffrey Girard

All tales spin out
from the same web...

Say Sird 10/16

Copyright

Tales of the Eastern Indians. Copyright ©2008
by Geoffrey Girard. All rights reserved. Printed in the United
States. No part of this book may be used or reproduced in any matter
whatsoever without written permission from the publisher except
in the case of brief quotations embodied in critical articles and
reviews. For information, please write to: Middle Atlantic Press,
PO Box 345, Moorestown, NJ 08057.

Middle Atlantic Press books may be purchased for educational,
business, or sales promotional use. For information, please
write to: Special Markets Department, Middle Atlantic Press,
PO Box 345, Moorestown, NJ 08057.

Middle Atlantic Press website www.middleatlanticpress.com

First edition

1 2 3 4 5   09 08 07 06 05

Cover and interior illustrations by Brian Rappa.
Cover and interior designed by Desiree Rappa.

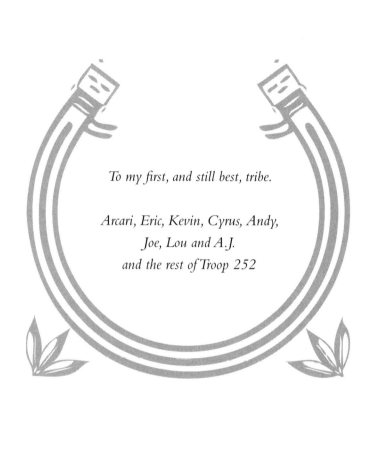

To my first, and still best, tribe.

Arcari, Eric, Kevin, Cyrus, Andy,
Joe, Lou and A.J.
and the rest of Troop 252

ACKNOWLEDGEMENTS

Special appreciation to the following individuals and organizations who contributed greatly to the writing of this book:

Chief William Little Soldier, of the Munsee Delaware Indian Nation-USA, who generously shared his time, rich knowledge and personal experiences. Special thanks for hosting me and my son Erich on our visit to the tribal land.

Alex Koehler (Ojibwa), Morningstar (Ramapough Lenape and Cherokee), and Joseph Rising Sun (Cherokee), who provided additional personal insights and memories.

The American Indian Education Center, American Indian Library Association, Cumberland County Historical Society, Cradleboard Teaching Project, Lenni Lenape Historical Society, Native Languages of the Americas, and The National Museum of the American Indian.

Additional research materials were also offered (I didn't even have to ask!) by the ever-supportive bookseller Linda Keller from her private collection, gracious librarians Mary Dees and Kathy Poulton, history men Dave Faller and Bob Tull, art teacher Greg Stanforth, and young scholar Douglas Girard via his weekly library visits.

The gang at Middle Atlantic Press including the editorial eye of Kathy Brock and the superb design team of Brian Rappa and Desiree Rappa.

To friends and family who supported the process throughout.

CONTENTS

Introduction

When European explorers first arrived in North America in the late 1400s, there were (it is generally estimated) about one million people already living here in at least a hundred distinct tribal groupings, many who'd been thriving for 10,000 years, some who'd become powerful nations. These people became collectively known to the world as "Indians," later "Native Americans" or "American Indians."

Today there are more than three million American Indians in the United States with an estimated twenty million partial descendents. In short, after several centuries of devastating disease, territorial wars, and government-forced relocations and assimilation, there are more Native Americans in the United States today than when the "two worlds" collided some six hundred years ago.

"We are still here!" boasts many tribal websites, t-shirts, and bumper stickers. Absolutely! From the reemergence of hundreds of once lost tribes, to the return of native languages long thought dead, the Native American culture is currently experiencing a revival of tradition, global appreciation and strength that will surely thrive another 500 years. There are now more than a thousand organizations dedicated to the protection of Native American history and culture and its continued development and recognition. Each year, several thousand events are held across the country towards the same goal, including more than a thousand public powwows. Some three hundred CDs of traditional and modern American

Indian music have been recorded in the past year alone. While writing this book, the Seminole Indian Tribe of Florida purchased the famed Hard Rock Cafe restaurant franchise for $965 million.

The tales you're about to read are based on the actual history and legends of the many tribes who once lived, and still live, in the eastern United States. This unique group represents each phase of our country's growth and success while undergoing unique challenges and triumphs all their own. Like all cultures, Native Americans hold closely to tradition, perhaps even more than most because theirs is a culture that had been under assault for so long. These stories are written with respect to that larger tradition.

For more information, I have included brief historical notes at the end of each story. Also, at the back of the book you'll find a short list of sources used during my research for further reading. The telling of history often changes with each age, and this is especially true with the complex history of the American Indian. Always seek a balanced account, as that's where you'll find real people.

THE HUNTERS
23,000 B.C.E.

Miksa had always been a skilled hunter, maybe the best in his clan. So, he knew.

Something was hunting him.

What that something was, exactly, he had no idea. Not yet. Only that he and the others had been followed, *stalked*, for two days and nights now. That some creature was watching them from afar and patiently awaiting the best time to attack. Even now, perhaps, somehow leading them towards a trap.

He knew all of this because that's also how he hunted.

The cool wind often carried faint scents and sounds, clear visions of grazing herds or lost calves from around the next hill. With these mental images, he moved easily around his prey, always taking in the full story of the land to patiently shape the hunt as he wished. Eventually, he would direct the animal to the exact time and place of his own choosing and then, and only then, strike. This was the true mark of any good hunter. The thing hunting him, whatever it was, understood this. It, too, was being patient. It, too, now waited to attack.

At first, he'd thought it might simply be the others. One of the men from his clan sent to spy on them, to see how the three were doing. If they were truly worthy to join the Hunters. He knew now, however, this thing was definitely not from his family.

It sounded quite large and moved strangely as it crept in the tall grasslands far behind them. Very strangely. Two legs like The People, but at a gait and size he could not yet understand. Its marks, which he'd backtracked one morning to find, were heavy and split almost like a bird's. A giant bird, he'd first thought, then shook off the notion as too absurd. No bird was that big. Not even the great eagles his grandmother told stories of.

Just the night before, he'd heard it kill one of the deer. A startled, half-choked, squeal. Then another sound…

Thump, crunch. Thump, crunch.

He shook away the memory, tried focusing only on their task. Their own prey.

The Long Hair, the *a'tix*, marched ahead, no break in pace, its massive shape dark and strangely alive against the endless grasslands.

They'd followed it for three days now, as it led them further away from the north mountains, away from the others. That morning, the three had made noises together and Saghani lit a small fire to make some smoke. The Long Hair then turned to follow the sun as they hoped it would, moving towards the half-empty riverbed they'd found. Where it would eventually stop to drink.

A male, it had just left the herd days before to roam alone for the rest of its life. The Long Hair herds were only for the females and calves, and this one was certainly no longer a calf. It stood taller than two men already, weighed as much as two hundred.

They'd been told only to hunt one of the *a'tix* calves, to wait until it had mistakenly separated from its mother. Or perhaps one of the other smaller grassland animals, an elk or sloth. But the three had come across the young Long Hair first and took it as a sign from the Keepers. Surely, this was the kill they were meant for.

Miksa watched it stop again to pull free another clump of tall golden grass with its long snout. He'd never seen something eat so much in all his life. *Eat well, Long Hair,* he thought. *Soon it will be our turn.* He wondered if that was all the Long Hair was doing, looking for food. Or maybe even, like himself, it was on some sacred mission. Some calling only the Long Hairs knew about.

After they'd captured it, he or one of the others would run back to guide the rest of the clan. Then, they would all camp near the kill for many, many nights, living off the animal's almost-infinite meat and crafting tools and weapons from its bones.

He would take one of the Long Hair's giant teeth or even its tail as a prize. At last, the *Okraserk* would cut across his forehead with one of the stone daggers. Miksa would then be marked.

Finally, to be a real Hunter. *Tomorrow, for sure.*

The Long Hair had stopped to sleep for the night and the three hunters set down the fire they carried and built it again against the imminent cold and darkness. Crouched by the flames, he and the others finished the last of the slick rabbit meat, a catch from the morning before. While they ate, Saghani recounted the story of the monster Long Hair who'd eaten many families.

Miksa didn't mind hearing the tale again. The *Okraserk* had just told the exact same to all three boys before they'd left, but Saghani told good stories and would probably become the new *Okraserk* one day. Miksa gnawed at the last meat on the bone and listened as the monster again chased the woman with her baby through the endless woods and how the people had broken holes in the frozen lake so that the heavy beast would fall through. Still, the monster came.

Saghani spoke now of the boy, the one whom no one had paid any attention to. "Even the old women stepped over him," he said. Yet, as the rest of the family collapsed in fear, he'd struck. One spear right through the animal. Then he jumped to the other side and stabbed another. "The people were thankful," Saghani ended. "And gave him two girls to be his wives." Miksa and Tuktu blushed, laughed. "But he accepted only one of them," Saghani finished, smiling playfully. "Then, then they made him chief."

They considered this last bit together, quietly. Miksa wondered some what role he would ultimately play in his family, then carefully passed over the small rabbit bone. Saghani collected it with the others into a blanket of grass they'd made, and dropped the packet of bones into their small fire while the three hunters thanked the animal masters once again. Miksa pulled his jacket closer against the chill and watched the smoke lift away on the cool wind and smiled. The animals they killed did not truly die, but only discarded their husks of fur and meat. Their spirits continued, of course, and were eventually steered back to earth by the heavenly animal masters, the Keepers. As long as they properly honored the spirits that had passed by respecting the remains, those same spirits would always return again in a new husk. Whether a small rabbit, or the mighty Long Hair now snorting in sleep like distant thunder, there would always be another hunt.

Miksa turned suddenly to the darkness behind them. And wondered with a chill how many other hunters were even now watching their prey.

The Long Hair came to the creek in the morning, just as they'd planned. The water was low, both embankments muddy and soft. The morning sun burned bright behind Saghani and Tuktu as they moved in slowly with the torches and spears.

Miksa waited alone, flat and still, upwind and across the creek bank. He inspected his own spear tips again, pressing his thumb forcefully against the sharp meticulously narrowed sides to expose any potential break. The fluted rock tips shattered easily and often, and Miksa sometimes felt half his time on Earth was spent simply recrafting crumbled knives and spearheads. Most broke while being made. But these spears were made from good rock, he decided. Strong. And, he carried five of them. Surely, one would find the Long Hair's heart.

The giant moved ever nearer, lumbering towards the creek's trickling sound and promise of fresh water.

Straight towards Miksa.

It was, quite simply, the largest thing he had ever seen. He'd helped skin and cut other Long Hairs, of course. But none so big as this. And certainly not one so *alive*. It breathed like a hundred men, and each step rumbled the earth like thunder. The tusks lifted up and down, taller than any man, broad and curved, sharpened at the ends like gigantic spears. Miksa knew the scars the other Hunters had harvested over the years, knew the story of each and every one. He knew that none of the men had any such scars from an *a'tix* and now suspected why. Such men did not return to the clan.

Miksa scrunched closer to the ground, willed himself even more invisible. He now wished they had four more Hunters with them.

The beast had lowered one leg halfway down the embankment to get closer to the low water. Dropped its neck to drink, the strange long snout slurping the water up and then blowing it out again into its mouth. The foot had sunk deep and the mud curdled over its immense hairy paw. *Now*, Miksa thought. *Now we will take him.* He held up his arm in signal when it dipped again for another drink.

Saghani sprung from the cover of the horizon, shrieking and waving his torch. The Long Hair lifted and whirled, its huge head turning towards the sound. As it turned, the tips of its tusks gleamed in the early morning sun.

Tuktu appeared now in the open, also carrying a fire torch, as the two hunters closed in together towards the Long Hair from opposite directions. The Long Hair moved to flee, but its half-sunken foot slipped in the mud with the pivot. Saghani and Tuktu pressed closer, fire jumping. The *a'tix* strained backwards, pushing its great shoulders. The huge eye grew white with surprise. Fear, maybe. Again, the heavy paw sunk deeper, its whole body now suddenly threatening to tumble into the creek.

You have one choice now, mighty Long Hair, Miksa thought. *Just one.*

It stepped purposefully into the creek. Its surest escape from the approaching enemy. Forward. The great body moved into the creek in just two steps. Then, lifted its paw on the other side.

There, Miksa stood waiting.

He was above their prey now. Not much, but enough. The beast pushed up the embankment towards him. Two steps were all Miksa had if the mud didn't slow the giant down. Two steps before he was crushed into the ground and killed.

He stabbed out at the huge shape, shouting, and the Long Hair stumbled backwards, snorted in confusion, or something more like anger now.

Miksa tossed his first spear at the briefly exposed chest, but the beast swung away and the spear bounced harmlessly off its side. The Long Hair turned back and charged again, its dark shape moving like solid night, stamping up the side straight towards Miksa.

Two steps away…

The dirt collapsed. Feet sunk again, the embankment giving way to the Long Hair's great weight.

Saghani and Tuktu had reached the opposite embankment and, as the three planned, had already lit the dry grass they'd carefully laid along the creek, trapping the Long Hair between the growing flames and the two embankments. The wafting smoke spun in the wind around them all, stinging Miksa's eyes and lungs. Tuktu dropped his torch and now tossed one of his spears at the beast's side.

The spear struck.

The Long Hair bellowed in agony and the strange roar sounded like crashing thunder striking only a few steps away. It literally shook the ground. Miksa's first thought was to crouch in fear, holding his hands to his ears to fend off the terrible sound. Instead, he stood even taller and drew back his spear for the killing blow.

Food for weeks. Enough hide and fur for dozens of new coats and blankets.

His prey reared back onto two legs, Tuktu's spear still hanging from its side, its front paws kicking freely in the air mere feet away as if leaping towards a final attempt up the embankment.

Chest exposed again, even more so than before. Miksa could picture its heart perfectly under the long dark fur. He'd seen the other men do it on smaller *a'tix* and knew his throw would not miss. He stepped forward, squeezed the spear tightly…

It was then that Tuktu screamed.

Miksa stopped mid throw. He'd never heard his friend make such a sound before. It was not a yell filled with pain or even fear. This was something else.

Then came another sound, one he had heard only once before. A sound somehow even worse than that of his own friend screaming. One he'd hoped never to hear again.

Thump, crunch. Thump, crunch.

His first view of the creature came only in brief flickers as the giant Long Hair still shifted and kicked just in front, continually blocking his view of the opposite embankment.

But, Miksa was thankful of that. What he could see was more than enough.

He saw something large and dark, a terrible shadow backlit against the rising sun just behind. Twice the size of any man. He saw two legs. A crown of feathers. *Feathers?* A monstrous bird of some kind. Tuktu kicking and flailing in midair as if carried by the wind.

He saw its mouth. Snout. More like a huge golden beak, its points as sharp as the tusks of the Long Hair, and it made up almost its entire head. It was as if someone had simply stuck two dark eyes and some feathers atop a chomping set of giant jaws. *Hungry* jaws.

He understood finally that Tuktu was caught between those same jaws. His terrible screams had stopped, yet Miksa somehow missed them. He knew what the sudden silence probably meant.

Thump.

Over the dancing Long Hair, Miksa watched in horror as his friend was slammed into the ground. Miksa saw the stumps of half-formed wings along its back.

Crunch.

He heard the jaws again snap tight.

The Long Hair turned. It crashed over the patchy flames up the creek, and now charged unevenly back up the far embankment. The ground broke way under its huge weight again, but it lifted with each step and its head and right leg soon crested the top.

The new creature jumped back from the approaching giant, and the plume of long blood-red feathers which ran along the top of its head danced like fire. Miksa did not know if the red along the side of its face was only blood. Tuktu dangled loosely in the horrible mouth like one of the girls' grass dolls, no longer moving.

With a bellow that erased all other sounds, the Long Hair clambered over the top with back legs scaling the last bit in an explosion of dirt that even landed on Miksa's side of the creek.

The bird thing jumped back from the giant. Screeched back at the Long Hair in a strange short bark only half muffled by Tuktu in its mouth. The *a'tix* paid no attention, and continued straight towards the beast and the promise of sunlight and open field waiting just behind.

Saghani stood frozen halfway down the far embankment, spear in his hands. Miksa found he hadn't moved either.

My friend, he thought. *I am a coward.*

The hideous bird tossed Tuktu aside, and sidestepped to safety as the giant *a'tix* stampeded past. The thing squawked, a shrill deafening sound, and snapped its jaws angrily. The Long Hair turned, grumbling like one of the angry Winter gods, its long snout and tusks swiping at the creature. The monster shrieked once, then dashed in the opposite direction. Miksa waited for it to lift into the sky, but it stayed on the ground and vanished instead behind the drifting smoke as the Long Hair rumbled away in the opposite direction.

Miksa found he'd somehow crossed the creek and now stood beside Saghani, whose eyes were almost as big as the moon. Miksa helped him to the top of the embankment where they watched the Long Hair's dark shape grow smaller and smaller on the horizon. All the while, Miksa kept an eye towards where the creature had run, knowing that it might easily strike again now that the Long Hair had fled.

They stood quietly for some time, the smoke slowly fading as the fires burned out.

The Terror Bird, at least for now, was gone.

He and Saghani moved slowly towards Tuktu. His body still on the ground, Miksa kneeled beside his friend. He already felt cold. Too cold. *What have we done,* Miksa thought.

"We go back," Saghani said. "Tell others of Tuktu."

"Yes," Miksa said, patting his still brother's arm. He recalled their games as children tossing sticks and rocks at imagined sabertooths. *We were to be great hunters together.* "Tuktu go back to others," he said aloud.

"We — "

"You take his body," Miksa stopped him. "Miksa follow the Long Hair."

"Long Hair is too great. Three were not enough. You only one."

"Tuktu's spear in the Long Hair. It is hurt. It can die."

"Miksa, please. You do not — "

"I am a Hunter, Saghani." *Like Tuktu,* he thought.

"What of the…" Saghani looked after the creature.

"I watch. You watch, Saghani."

"You are brave, Miksa. Or stupid."

"Bring Tuktu to the others," he said. "That just as brave. The Great Bird may come for you too." He stood, shook out the strange shiver in his bones, then pointed his spear towards the trail of the Long Hair. "I go," he said. "Good walk to you."

Saghani replied but his words were lost to the plain's wind as Miksa's ears had become lost in memory.

Thump, crunch.

Thump, crunch.

Miksa had followed the Long Hair's tracks easily, something all of the boys learned to do when they could first walk. Just show him a footprint half lost in the mud or long grass and he could tell you everything, from how old the animal was to how long ago it has passed by.

The marks he trailed now were thick and deep. They showed that the Long Hair moved quickly, but somewhat unbalanced. A slight limp in its gait. It was hurt. He pursued the footprints north towards the ice mountains. Soon he found Tuktu's spear, which had finally been shaken free. The tip was broken off, crusted in dark blood.

If you slow down, great one, Miksa thought, catching his own breath in the cool air, *I can end your suffering.*

It had taken him most of the day to catch up, though he'd jogged until the sun started to fall from the sky again. When it was finally in his sight again, he walked just behind it and downwind. Each step another test for his exhausted legs.

The ice mountains, an endless and ever-shifting island of ice, loomed like storm clouds on the north horizon. He knew from the stories that once, long before, the same mountains had covered all of the world. As Miksa walked towards them, he'd found his thoughts turning again to the strength of the Long Hair. Its wound and pain had not yet slowed it down and he wondered for the first time if it ever would. It had known he was following, had even turned a few times and snorted loudly in warning.

For awhile, he imagined the Long Hair would simply lead him straight into the ice and he'd never be heard from again. The thoughts of turning back, of giving up the hunt, crept back into his head. More so, the darker the land had grown.

But, the Long Hair had not turned back. So, Miksa kept walking. "You are truly a great spirit," he spoke to it from afar. "I will walk with you as far as you wish." Only the tundra's wind whistled back in reply, and Miksa ignored the numbness in his legs to move forward.

Earlier he'd smelled the wetland, long grasses recently lost to some flooded lake or river born of the retreating ice mountains. Here, the Long Hair would slow again. Perhaps, even get stuck in one of the hidden drops

Miksa had found.

Even now, Miksa lurked in the tall grass. Crouched low in the shadows of the setting sun, moving slowly at an angle towards the approaching Long Hair. The cold murky water tickled up to his knees at steps. Five spears held tightly in both his hands as the Long Hair approached.

The hint of the new moon had appeared on the scarlet-tinged horizon like a faded giant eye. Watching him. One of the Great Spirits. Or even Tuktu, maybe. Looking to see if he were truly a Great Hunter.

At that same thought, he stole another look over the grass and listened carefully to the few sounds on the low wind. Searching for some sign of the creature.

Not the Long Hair. The Terror Bird.

He had never once forgotten that the monster was still hunting the same plains. He wondered what Saghani would tell the others. Would they even believe him when he described it? He wondered some, too, if Saghani has made it back to the Others to tell them anything at all. If the creature had chased after him instead…

He squatted low again, waiting for the Long Hair. Its steps were much closer now. The huge form loudly smashed through the grass. Splashing in low water as it stepped deeper into the low marsh. Its heavy breath now filling Miksa's ears.

He'd moved around to the side a bit, wholly aware of where several of the sinkholes where. Positioning himself with the best opportunity to somehow drive the Long Hair into one.

Miksa slowly sunk four of the spears into the ground at his side. The last he held tight.

The Long Hair was close enough to smell now. Miksa even could see its snout swishing back and forth in the water.

Still, he waited.

At last, the giant moved to almost just beside him. Leaned over to drink. Miksa could make out its huge black eye through the grass.

Its heads turned slightly. Eye narrowing.

Aware.

Miksa sprang from the grass. He'd already tossed the first spear and it struck against the Long Hair's shoulder. Shattered on impact.

The Long Hair roared in fury, water splashing across the short distance between them, shaking its head and tusks towards Miksa.

Another spear grabbed already, holding his ground. Miksa shouted loudly. Cursing at his foe with his own roars of fury and warning. Thrusting out at the living mountain of hair.

Monstrous feet crashed towards him. Miksa sidestepped the tusk. Stabbed out again. The Long Hair bellowed, shuffled sideways. Miksa pushed ahead. Ever driving him towards the hidden trap in the water.

Suddenly, the Long Hair turned back.

Clomping straight towards him again.

Miksa splashed backwards. It lunged, lowering its head and giant tusks, and Miksa fell back from the killing blow.

One of the tusks smashed against his spear and Miksa's hand exploded in agony as he fell. He'd crashed to the ground on his back, the death-cold water completely embracing him. Miksa reached out blindly for his remaining spears. Sputtering out water, the icy darkness running over his face. He fought up to his elbows. Pushed up with one arm while the other sought his weapons.

The Long Hair stamped forward.

Miksa felt something sharp slice into his side. A great weight pressing against his whole body as he vanished again beneath the water.

The whole world grew dark.

His hand latched onto something. Lashed out.

Felt the spear jam deep. The weight lifted. Miksa rolled up to his hands and knees. Felt the burning in his side and knew one of the tusks had ripped him open. He wiped the water and the retreating darkness from his eyes.

The Long Hair stood just steps away, head lowered to attack again. Miksa saw where he'd cut him.

He rose to his feet and took hold of the spear in both hands. Charged ahead, screaming. The Long Hair moved sideways, to swing its head and tusks around again.

Then it stepped oddly and stumbled in a spray of water.

The Long Hair struggled to rise again from the submerged hole. Miksa wiggled his own feet into the ground and found a stance to meet whatever ever happened next. The Long Hair eased back into the water, waiting.

The two stared at each other for some time while the cold water dripped of their bodies like rain. Miksa would never know for how long. The sun had almost completely vanished and the moon had grown bright and huge behind both of them.

"Now, friend," Miksa said aloud in the darkness. "You and I will end this."

The Long Hair moved to lift from the water and Miksa lunged towards it.

Another sound...

Miksa froze halfway. Knew immediately what it was.

The creature appeared from the tall grass as if it'd always been there. Miksa dove aside.

The Terror Bird screeched, the stump wings flapping. It looked even taller than the Long Hair. Miksa backed away, stabbing his spear out at the monster.

Its horrible beak, shining in the moonlight, was as large as Miksa's whole body, and pointed into a killing curve. It snapped at his head and warm, sticky saliva splashed across his face.

The Long Hair had stepped free again from the hole. Miksa felt its huge shape moving just behind him. Allowed that he would probably be crushed.

The cold black eyes of the bird were piercing. Fixed on Miksa with something he'd never really seen in an animal before.

Hunger.

I am now the prey, he understood. He shouted and stabbed out his spear again.

The beak snapped off the tip and Miksa's shoulder tugged violently. A terrible shriek filled the night. A combination of the bird's howl and his own screech.

He saw a flash of the red feathers again atop its head. Red like flames. Red like blood.

Thump, crunch. Miksa thought. Next, it will snatch me up and smash me to the ground.

He raced for the last two spears.

The creature followed. Its huge legs lifting high and splashing oddly in the dark water.

He dove for the spear, landed in the water and rolled into a kneeling position. Bringing the spear up. Struck the creature in the side. Its legs stepped down on the weapon, snapping it in half.

Miksa fell sideways, reached for his final spear.

The gigantic jaws opened wide, dripping. Dropping over him.

Then nothing.

The creature was gone.

Now, only the Long Hair crashed between in the space where the jaws had just been. He listened to the sound of retreating feet. The strange bird legs splashing away quickly in one direction. The Long Hair thumping away to the other.

He lay still for some time, half lost in the grass, listening to the others grow further and further away. Watching the brightening stars above. Each one, a spirit for one who'd passed before.

Eventually, Miksa stood. His knees were shaking.

The Great Bird had run after the sun and, though he could see where it had dashed through the grass, he saw no sign of the creature now.

To the north, the Long Hair again shuffled away slowly towards the bright moon and the glowing mountains of ice.

Miksa watched him for awhile. Breathing in the cool night air. Thinking.

Then, he picked up the spear from the ground, his last, and ran his finger along the sharp stone tip.

Slowly, he started walking again.

Hunting.

The clan was gathered around a small fire when Miksa appeared beneath the setting sun.

He moved slowly, dragging something towards them, while the smaller children ran to him, calling his name and laughing happily. Saghani ran with them.

Several of the older men followed when they saw what Miksa carried. Enough meat to last for weeks. The rest cut away and left for the wolves the morning before. The other Hunters nodded, then two grabbed hold of the heavy catch to haul back towards the fire.

Miksa pulled Saghani aside. Took one of the three prizes he'd collected from his kill and handed it to him. The other boy nodded, hugged his friend closely.

The second prize was for Tuktu. To lay with his body.

The last, equal in length and shade to the first two, Miksa kept for himself. To always remember.

A long red feather.

NOTES: The current belief by most anthropologists today is that the first North Americans appeared between 30,000 B.C.E. and 10,000 B.C.E., amid various Ice Age migrations across the Bering Strait (which once connected Asia to North America). Some argue that various clans had made an appearance even sooner via boat. Evidence of their hunter culture, in which small clans migrated with the herds as the Ice Age shifted and settled, have been found across the entire continent. These first people shared their plentiful "New World" with various now-extinct creatures, including saber-tooth tigers, huge dire wolves, giant sloths, and, the clan's favorite prey, the wooly mammoth. There remains debate as to whether the mammoths died out due to climatic changes, disease, were hunted to extinction, or, most accepted, some combination of the three.

Mammoth are named from the Russian word mamot, which means "earth digger," in the mistaken belief that the prehistoric carcasses found half-buried in the ground were of modern creatures that actually lived beneath the earth and died when exposed to sunlight.

"Terror Birds" were the dominant predator of South America for more than fifty million years. These ightless birds stood ten feet tall, weighed as much as a thousand pounds, and could run as fast as the modern cheetah. When Central America formed and the two continents connected (about three million years ago), the birds roamed north while North America's saber-toothed tigers visited the southern hemisphere for the first time. The giant birds, who couldn't compete with the new predators, ultimately died out.

SWAN SONG
800 B.C.E.

The men who would soon club and cut him had quietly lined up into two long, facing rows. There were fifteen on each side, mostly the younger warriors, but there were also some of the older men and a few boys taking part in their first initiation. Each held a wooden club in one hand and a stone dagger gripped tightly in the other. When he passed them, they would choose which one to use.

The rest of the village was gathered just outside the human gauntlet, jostling for a better spot to watch from. All other work had stopped for this, and the crowd's low murmur filled his ears. At dawn, they'd stripped him to his deerskin loin cloth and painted symbols across his face and bared chest.

The order was given and he took his first step.

He told himself again that's all it was. First step. One step. Again and again until it was all over. He dared not look down to the end of the line. One step.

The first warrior grunted low and clubbed him in the arm. Pain, like ice, shot down to his finger and up his neck. The man to his left lunged forward and cut his leg just above the knee. This felt more like fire. And, he marveled at how similar the two feelings were.

He took another step forward. One step.

A club slammed across his bare back. A warrior to his right shrieked like an angry demon. The next man also used his club against his leg. He felt his shin split open, more than the dagger had done.

Another step. A long cut across his shoulder. Someone yanked his hair and slashed at his temple.

Another step.

He saw the crowd. Watching him. He'd told himself their interest was the same for any prisoner walking the line. But he knew better.

They'd come to see the prince.

Ohiti, the youngest son of Queen Wiyu, ruler of the mighty Wolf clan. To these people, he was the enemy.

It seemed he was halfway now. He'd lost count. It was only one more first step. One step. His arms and legs were so very numb...

He'd stumbled and one of the warriors shoved him back to his feet, back to the center. Their screams had built up, each man continuing a torrent of angry threats and insults as he passed. They shouted at him to stop walking. Called him a child. An animal. Warned him to not take another step. Told him to die.

Something cracked. The club or his own rib shattered. He did not know which. He no longer cared.

He simply kept moving.

The two lines blurred, the men looking more like ghosts or smoke. Their many shadows, covering the ground at his feet, now seemed more real.

He felt something being done to his body. Knew he was being beaten and slashed, but could not really feel it anymore. There was simply too much pain to suffer the specifics.

Another step. He staggered forward.

The entire world went dark for an instant, and his eyes closed. Drifting back to his own village, to his people. The Great Spirit lifting him at last. His body felt light, thankfully cast off.

Then something warm ran down the side of his face and it shook him back to where he was. One knee on the ground, only a wavering arm to hold himself up from falling face first into the red-speckled dirt. The warmth of his own blood even now trickled down his neck and along his shoulder. The club's blow had gashed his head just above the ear. Muted shouts fell away to the beating sound of his own heart throbbing slowly in his ears. He lifted his eyes, the long dark bangs of his hair sticky with sweat and blood. Burning his eyes. The total blackness creeping in again at the corners.

He saw the boy then.

Where all else had become a blur, he saw the boy. One of the spectators behind the line. One of the Bear tribe. Five or six years old at most.

Watching him.

One day, Ohiti knew, this same boy might, himself, he captured and forced to walk a similar line. It is why Ohiti had not yet cried out, or cursed, or screamed, or begged for mercy. He needed to set an example of how a warrior endured such trials, even for the children of his own enemy. It was understood that these same warriors would do the same if ever tortured at his village. It was simply how the next generation learned.

He fought back to his feet.

The boy smiled, and vanished back into the crowd.

Ohiti suddenly thought of the games they'd often played as children. Tossing rocks and burning sticks at each other to see who could endure the most pain. Pricking their faces with porcupine needles. His mouth parted as if to smile.

His eyes were half-closed, his steps uneven and plodding like an infant. He felt hands roughly shoving him back. Something burning his chest.

Another step.

The world tilted. His body shifting this way and that like a tree caught in the fall winds. His whole body trembled, as if he had no control over it. As if his own body were no longer his.

It now belonged to them.

He stepped forward once more, and realized for the first time that their hollering and shrieks had ended.

She waited for him there.

Hands lifted out to catch him.

His mother. The queen.

No. Not his mother. His vision came only in spurts of color and shape.

The other queen, he realized.

Their queen.

Draped in furs and shell necklaces, so that she looked like a pretty bear. Though his life probably depended on it, his clouded thoughts could not shake the image.

"Ohiti," the bear said, and its voice carried so that the whole of her village could hear. "The son of our greatest enemy."

He started to collapse, then felt himself righted. Half noticed her hand holding him steady.

"You have walked the warrior's line," she said. "The line of brothers." She looked past him to the others. "And you have walked it well."

He felt her grip tighten on his arm. "Very well," she said. The grip stung and he wondered if the bear had claws or it was merely her hand finding his fresh wounds.

"We would call him brother now," she announced and he heard the murmur of approval from behind. "If he, himself, accepts his new family." The last spoken to him alone.

He looked up to where the bear's eyes were deep brown and almost beautiful. He felt the darkness again. Lurking just at the edges of his reason and consciousness.

To accept would mean that he had been adopted into their village, where he would be accepted as a mighty warrior. To deny them meant that he was still their enemy and immediate death or, worse, another opportunity of initiation would follow.

"I am a Wolf," he said. The voice was sloppy with spit and blood. "You are not my family."

The *other* queen studied his face, her eyes searching deeply into his own. The eyes were angry, but he almost thought she'd smiled when she shook her head.

"Ohiti," she said and let go of his arm.

He'd collapsed to the ground before she'd even taken her first step.

"It's too far to swim," Tehila said beside him. She'd known what he was thinking.

"Maybe," Ohiti eyed the lake and watched the dark water ripple at their feet. "It might take the whole night and into the next morning, but it could be done."

The girl huffed in disagreement.

She was right, of course. He knew it was too far without a canoe. The vast lake which had separated their two villages for a hundred years stretched further than his eye could see. Some nights, he half-convinced himself he could actually see the glow of his own village's fires at the far side of the darkness. Each sunrise, he knew he'd only been fooling himself.

"One could steal a canoe," he said.

"The guards."

"Yes," he looked into the distance and smiled grimly, "The guards." Another path of escape lost.

The territory and paths back to his own village were well patrolled. The two villages had been at war for as long as he was alive, and both sides had grown quite adept at securing their specific borders. *This* was the land of the Wolf, *that* was the land of the Bear.

Only the lake, dropped between the two tribes like a pacifying parent, was shared by both. Here, on their own shores, both peoples fished and cleaned. Hunted turtles and beaver.

It was the foundation of their village. The Life Giver.

Yet, to Ohiti, it had become only another barrier.

One more barrier keeping him from returning home.

Looking over the lake now, however, he wondered if physical borders were all that was holding him back. He admitted the possibility that there were more difficult obstacles to freedom. He turned to Tehila.

The girl sat beside him, her knees curled up beneath her chin, arms pulled tightly around them to keep warm in the cool early night air. She wore a light deerskin skirt with a sash that went up over only one shoulder. Her hair was dark and braided down her back with bright feathers. Around her neck, she wore a single bear claw.

How they'd ended up as friends, he would never know.

He smiled to himself. That she was the most beautiful woman he'd ever met probably had something to do with it. She, however, more often accused the stars and the very gods themselves who lived among them. Laughed softly and told him it was their fate to meet.

The queen's only daughter. Princess of the Bear Clan.

His enemy.

How had it gone from that to … to *this*?

Did it matter?

He'd passed her clan's first initiation. Then another, one in which he'd been held under water at the lake until he'd passed out. Revived. Again. Then another, in which his feet were burned. For each, he'd passed. He'd never begged them to stop. He'd never cried out in pain. Each time, he was then again invited to join their clan. Each time, he refused.

Tehila came to him one night, brought him some turkey meat and sunflower seeds to eat. She'd been scared, then acted arrogant to hide her fear. He knew then that she'd snuck to meet him. He also knew then that she may have been right about the stars and the gods.

He'd hummed a soft tune when they were burning his feet. Only something to ignore the pain. It had even worked a little. He hadn't even been aware he'd done so out loud. A song he'd whistled and made up silly words to for years. Something he thought he'd made up.

But she'd heard it, Tehila told him, and it was a song that she knew too. This girl. An enemy he'd never even met. From where, she did not recall either. But she'd recognized it, she told him, just the same.

Later, she would admit that she felt she recognized him, too. That she'd even known him before he'd been brought to their camp. He did not know what she meant by that. Not yet. But, he knew that talking to her that first night was as easy as talking to someone he'd known a hundred years.

The two had not been far apart since.

While Ohiti was not permitted to leave the Bear village, he had been given freedom to walk about the encampment as he chose. He could not have a weapon but he often helped the men fish, and had even helped build one of the new wood shelters.

At dinner, he ate with the other men. They were no longer cruel to him. The insults gone. The physical abuse abandoned weeks before. He'd already passed every test.

But, he was not one of them, he was still the other, and so they mostly ignored him as if he were a ghost as he ate in silence. Though he'd clearly won their respect, he remained their enemy. And always would be, he was made to understand.

And yet …

Tehila turned to him and lifted her brows to suggest she didn't understand why he was staring at her. But, he knew she did understand. It was not the first dusk they'd spent sitting beside the lake together. Her cousin, Kola, often helped distract the guards and Tehila's mother, so that the two might steal some time away.

If only to talk for a little while.

He shook his head and looked away from her, quietly viewing the lake again.

There were indeed many barriers to going home.

"The swampland is not well guarded. It's quicker too," he said.

"Dangerous," she said. "Sinkholes and snakes. And they'd surely suspect you went that way."

"They'd cut me off," he agreed.

"Imagine it completely covered in white," she said.

"The swamp?"

"No," she laughed. "The lake. Like a million flower petals floating for as far as any eye could see. The entire lake covered."

"You're a strange girl."

"My grandmother says it happened."

"Then your grandmother is a strange girl too," he smiled.

"Toad." She playfully nudged his arm. "It was the swans."

"Swans?"

"They'd molted. Thousands of them. More," she gazed in wonder over the empty lake. "The lake was once home to more swans than any single person could count."

He looked back over the dark waters and tried to picture the white feathers as she'd asked him to. "Yes," he said. "I'd heard that too. My mother told me so."

"It must have been very pretty once." She sighed. "I can almost remember seeing them on the lake. The sound of their long, sad call."

"I can't remember," he said.

"But the song!" she almost yelped. "The one you … Now I know why I recognized it. It sounded just like the call of the swans."

"I don't know," he shrugged. "It's just something silly that's always been in my ears, my head."

"I wonder where they all went? The swans."

"My mother said they left with the war."

"Oh." They sat quietly again for awhile, simply watching the tiring sun's orange rays wash over the lake's dark surface. "My grandmother also said …" Tehila started.

He turned. "What's that now?"

"That swans mate for life."

"Is that so?" His whole body had tensed, warming uncomfortably. He enjoyed being close to the girl, but now, he almost wished to vanish into the very ground.

"A pair will stay together for fifty years. And if one dies or …"

"Or what?"

"Or if one goes away …"

He lowered his eyes. "What?"

"They will not choose another."

The sound of her breath filled the whole of the shoreline. He could almost feel its warmth against his skin.

"We should head back," he said. "Kola can't keep them off our trail forever."

She laughed, but he could tell it was forced.

"Ohiti."

He looked up at her again. Her eyes were glossy with tears that had not yet fallen. Might not. She was to be a queen some day, after all.

"I … I will help you escape," she said.

He carefully reached out and ran his fingers across her hand. Then he looked back over the lake.

"I know," he said.

As ultimate ruler of the Bear clan, a tribal position she'd inherited to command some one hundred souls for most of her life, it seemed that Queen Huku was unaccustomed to being argued with. That it was coming from her own daughter, Tehila realized too late, was probably not helping any. Her mother's tent had quickly become the last place on Earth she wanted to be.

"He is our enemy," the queen fumed at her.

"He is not mine." Tehila's voice trembled some when she spoke.

Behind the smoke of the small fire between them, her mother's eyes were wide with fury. "You said he was a good man," she argued, fighting to keep her voice strong.

"It matters not," the queen replied. "He was never adopted by our clan, so he remains the enemy."

"Why?"

"'Why?'" the queen mocked her voice, fed the fire another stick. "You are clearly still too young for this world, Tehila. But I do not blame you. It is clear now that I have been lax in my own duties as a mother and as your queen."

"Why must we war with them? Our tribes are not so —"

Her mother waved the question away. "It is difficult to explain to a child. It goes back many years."

"I know," she pressed. "But, when does it end?"

"Tehila," Huku reached over and took her hand. "Listen to me, daughter. He is a noble man, a brave man. Handsome even, I suppose," she sighed. "But that is all. Whatever brief dream you had for him is just that. A dream. Now you must wake."

For just a moment, Tehila considered the words. Who was this boy to her, anyway? He was indeed handsome, the most amazing man she'd ever met. Brave, and kind. Artistic, and clever. And the brief weeks she'd shared with him had somehow seemed like a hundred years and a few moments all at the same time. The happiest weeks of her life. And perhaps that was enough...

She would hold onto to those memories, of what briefly was, and that would suffice. If they were truly meant to be together, it would have been so from the start. She would cling to those memories as one did when waking from a wonderful dream. Dreams that always burned away in the midday sun.

"And if I will not?" She'd pulled her hand away from her mother.

"My belief that you somehow helped him to escape is difficult enough. Now, I must hear this?"

"I've known him before," Tehila said.

"Before?" The queen's face hardened behind the wafting smoke. "How?"

"I don't know," she said, and she really didn't. But she knew anyway. "Long before, I think. His face is ... There was a song he knew. We knew."

The queen grunted. "Foolish child ..."

"We are to be married," she said.

It had come out in a single rushed word.

"What did you say?" The queen lifted from the ground to stand over her.

"We are to ... He said he will return for me. That he will speak to his mother. That they will bring gifts to honor you and — "

"Silence!"

Tehila shuddered, turned away towards the fire.

"You foolish girl!" her mother hissed, moving closer so that none outside could hear. "Do you have any idea what you have done?"

"I think I do. Yes."

"They will take the suggestion as a sign of weakness by our clan. That we should seek any alliance —"

"But —"

"More than a lake separates the two tribes, daughter."

Her mother glared at the top of her head. "The lie of love has ruined your mind, daughter. If he returns here, in any form, he shall not live."

Tehila's heart clenched in agony.

"Then I will go to him," she blurted.

The queen laughed. Yet, it was probably the most terrible sound Tehila had ever heard. "I thought as much ..." her mother ran her fingers across her daughter's hair. "It is exactly as I feared."

"Mother?"

"Tonight," she said quietly above her. "I shall send warriors to their camp." Tehila looked up, knowing her eyes were enormous with fear and confusion, but no longer caring. Her mother's eyes, however, had become only dark slits that gleamed like black daggers. "After," the queen finished, "There will be no more talk of this."

The queen stormed from the hide-sheltered teepee, her hunched form vanishing though the entry.

Tehila sat alone then, with only her thoughts, watching the flames dance in the small fire. Each separate flame had become a thousand flames in the fish-eyed view of her tear-filled eyes. She knew her mother well. The decision had been made. Even now, specific warriors were being sought and gathered. Akicita and Wakte probably. Their best hunters. Killers. Quiet and skilled beyond all the others. Assassins who'd soon be sent to kill their accepted foe.

To kill Ohiti.

She slid from the tent as quickly and silently as a passing shadow. Hugging the dark patches of her camp, she moved beyond the first circle of teepees and into the outer camp. There, she found Kola and revealed her intentions.

Her friend begged her not to go and was soon sworn to secrecy. There was no time to argue. There was no point.

Tehila knew what she was meant to do.

She also knew where the guards were, and escaping the camp was easy. The only problem now was whether or not she could get to the Wolf camp and warn Ohiti before her mother's assassins could get there. A young princess racing across the world against seasoned warriors.

There was only one chance.

The swamplands.

They wouldn't think to look for her there to cut her off. If Kola did her duty, the camp would believe Tehila was in her teepee crying all night. Besides, even if they knew she was gone, they would not think she'd taken that dangerous route.

As Ohiti had predicted, there was no one guarding the swamps. The water was cool and heavy against her legs as she worked slowly through the tall grasses. Mosquitoes buzzing and biting at every turn.

One step, she thought. Only one step more.

She'd tripped over a sunken log and spilled into the stale thick water. Her face was soon lined with sweat and the dark muck of the swamp's floor. Tall skeletal trees leered and swayed above her against the watching moon. The horrible chittering and squawking of unseen creatures, frogs she told herself, filled the darkness between.

Tehila pushed forward. Each step more determined than the last. The same tune Ohiti had once whistled came to mind again, and she found herself humming it to ignore where she was. An owl screeched somewhere in the night, its cry filled with such sorrow and loneliness. The rose-colored promise of morning stretched slowly across the treetops of the eastern marsh.

A splash!

Tehila screeched, barely choking back the sound.

Something large was moving in the marsh.

She turned with the sound, whirling about to see where it was. The tune, *their* tune, now came out barely as a whisper. Some unspeakably muck-slicked thing sliding back towards its black lair of rot and mire beneath the dark water, before the sun once again reclaimed the rustling grasses.

She raced forward, heard the sound again, then twirled around in the darkness, stumbling in the water.

She'd landed over a small tree, half-submerged in the mire, its water-soaked branches soft and gnarled beneath her back and legs. Across her neck and legs now. The water burbled around her. It hissed like a doused fire.

Then the tree moved.

Each branch suddenly squirming against her skin, pushing back against her straining muscles as she fought to rise. Holding her down, blocking her. Her hands sunk into something cold. Smooth branches which wriggled and surged beneath her, separated to run over, beneath and between her fingers.

One stabbed deep into her skin. Burning.

Another slashed her leg. She pushed herself up into a sitting position. And watched with horror as a snake swam just past her chest. Twisting and weaving across the surface of the water as easily as any fish swam below.

A water moccasin. Newborn.

She noted its yellow-colored tail, and could not see its eyes from the top. Small. It was no more than a foot long.

Then there was another.

Tehila felt something slip across her back just as fire stabbed into her shoulder. She leaned forward and lifted up to her knees, legs half sunk in the sludge below and the water up to her chest.

The nests surrounded her completely.

A hundred tiny bodies, a thousand, squirming as one, spilling over her.

She could not count them all.

The fourth and fifth bites burned and she'd screamed.

Ohiti!

She fought to her feet but stumbled back into the water, landing in the ever-shifting darkness that wasn't water.

The tiny mouths struck again. And again.

Tehila no longer screamed. She couldn't. Keeping her eyes open was now the hardest thing she'd ever done.

The swamp thrashed and fizzled around her, a raging storm of pain and fear. In her ears, however, was another sound.

A song she knew.

She closed her eyes to it as the snakes covered her completely.

Ohiti found her.

She'd been gone for more than a day, the sun already vanishing behind the western marshes. Her own people had not yet thought to search the southern swamps.

But he'd spoken to Kola the night before and learned everything. He'd come back for Tehila as he'd promised. He hadn't secured his mother's blessing either, but he'd decided to become a Bear.

His choice.

Not theirs.

What happened after, he could not say.

As long as Tehila was beside him, the rest would somehow fall into place. He learned then of her mother's plans and Tehila's desperate hope to warn him. The rest was easy.

He'd known she'd come here. That it was the fastest way. When he found her, Tehila floated peacefully atop the water, as if lifted by the hundreds of squirming snakes beneath and around her. In the setting sun, their many scales glistened like the rippling current of the lake.

He thought of Tehila and himself sitting by the lake's shore. Then, he imagined the glittering scales were nothing more than beautiful swan feathers.

Whistling a tune that had comforted him for years, he stepped into the water to free her.

The first bite didn't hurt. Much.

He'd carried her out of the nests and to a patch of dry land before the poison from fifty different bites took hold.

She was still in his arms when they found them.

Both queens attended the joint funeral together, and the clans mourned as one.

Ohiti and Tehila were wrapped and displayed beside each other on wood stands, then burned together beside the empty northern shores of the lake.

In the spring, swans returned to the same lake. Their haunting call lifted above the cool water's edge, and their distant shapes looked like enormous white flowers drifting upon its surface.

Two swans.

NOTES: Forced adoption was standard for most eastern tribes well into the 18th century. Prisoners of war were typically enslaved, then given painful tests to determine if they were worthy of being adopted (if not, they were killed). Tribes often carried out raids intended to seize captives from other tribes to replace lost and killed warriors. The Iroquois, among others, called these "Mourning Wars," meant to replace and avenge their dead. Men, women, and children were all victims, and beneficiaries, of this practice, for once adopted, the person was considered an equal to the rest of the tribe and treated as such for life. Adoption of other tribesmen was so rampant, in fact, that very often the vast majority of any given tribe was made up of men and women from other tribes.

Many Indian tribes, especially during the prehistoric era, were matriarchal societies, in which women were the tribe's prime decision makers, and most Native American religions (there are many varieties) include a belief in reincarnation and the notion that a soul may come back to Earth again as another person or even as an animal.

CITY OF THE DEAD
350 C.E.

He lay in his coffin and waited.

His hands were folded neatly across his chest, the wood casket pressing agreeably against his elbows. The crypt itself was black as night, blacker. Not a speck of light, buried beneath thirty feet of earth.

Yet, when he closed his eyes, he could see them.

Five men. Stepping slowly into the city.

They sought the same as most other men. From their dress and features, they appeared to be of one of the southern tribes. Along the ocean, perhaps. Not as far south as his own people. Those who'd driven him out a hundred years before.

He forced those heated memories from his mind and focused again on the intruders.

As they'd stepped fully into his realm, they each seemed unsure. Afraid, even.

Yes, he thought, pleased. He could almost smell the fear now through the embracing earth. It was always amusing to have such guests.

Then he smiled, and even in that absolute darkness, his fangs had somehow glistened.

The mounds were everywhere.

They covered miles of cleared forest in a myriad of sizes and shapes. Some were only a step off the ground combining to form unknown effigies or paths deeper into the city. Another, towards the center of the clearing, reached as high as sixty feet. There were circular mounds and others made of perfect squares. Some were covered in thick dark grass, others still bare. A few were only half built, half covered in dirt with ramps leading up to the yet-uncovered wood structures constructed within. The five men had certainly seen such mounds before, various ceremonial and burial structures that seemed to speckle these lands. Their own tribe, in fact, buried its dead beneath the earth. But, never so many mounds in one place, and never so large. Had these been mere lodges, they could have easily housed a thousand people.

"We must leave this place," Kishethwa said again, looking about warily. He had not yet shaken the feeling they were being watched. He was the leanest of the five men, tall and dark-skinned against the growing shadows of the forest, the multicolored beads and shell bits around his wrists and belt marking him as the most experienced hunter in the small group. His suggestion had not gone unnoticed by the other men.

"Are you mad?" Nikamu waved that very suggestion away. Though not a hunter, he was the chosen leader of the small team, elected by the medicine woman. "Just look what the earth grows here," he laughed and held up one of the silver figurines. "This is not mere squash, my brothers." In one of the open mounds, a two-story square lodge only half-covered, they'd found piles of freshwater pearls, copper ornaments, and shell beads. There were also baskets filled with tortoise shells and polished mica.

Treasures from across the whole of the world collected all in one place. Simply left laying in the crude wood coffins they'd found on every level of the building. It was as if the gods had laid the precious items out as gifts. *Or bait,* Kishethwa thought to himself.

"These are for burial," he said aloud. "They are not ours to take. We should take only what we have already and perhaps come back with more men later."

"There's no one here," Nikamu replied simply, coldly. "This place is deserted."

"The spirits remain," Kishethwa warned. "And, that mound behind you is just now being built. Look at the fresh dirt! This one, too, perhaps."

"And how do you know that, brother? Those ramps could have lain like that for five hundred years for all you know. It would take a hundred men a month to build that structure and move all that dirt. Yes? Where are they then?"

"I don't know."

"I'll tell you. They've fled. Moved on. Died from disease a hundred years ago. Like the other villages we've found."

"This is cursed land," Linto said, looking about. They'd found three other small deserted camps on their travels. Each one, half-filled with several smaller mounds. "Perhaps Kishethwa is right."

"There are enough riches here," Nikamu held up an ivory pipe carved in the shape of a turtle. "We could return to our own village before fall. We were sent to collect and trade for valued stones and wares. And so, we have. More than we ever imagined. I suspect that every mound in the city is filled with more of the same." His eyes flashed. "A little bit of digging, just imagine the finds. We shall each surely sit at the assembly as chiefs next spring."

"We should bless the gods," said Peyak, the youngest of the party. He'd leaned forward to touch the handsome pipe.

"Yes," Nikamu grinned. "Indeed, yes. Of course. Tonight, for our good fortune."

"That night is upon us now," Kishethwa said. His voice carried more warning. The sun was already setting when they'd first discovered the vacant settlement and it now dipped slightly behind the trees, casting the mounds in shades of purple and red. "We must make camp away from this place and then, perhaps, return tomorrow."

"There's an empty lodge not a hundred steps away." Nikamu pointed to the curved wood structure. "And enough room for the five of us."

"I'll start a fire," Ephit said, moving quickly from whatever further argument might ensue. It had been a long enough journey.

"Good, good. This blessed harvest shall wait until tomorrow. Let us rest a bit." Nikamu stood and clasped Kishethwa's shoulder. "But, we must also set watch all night, yes? Though, I do not know what has our brother so concerned."

"I'm concerned, *brother*, because I'm not sure which is worse," Kishethwa stepped away from the storyteller and adjusted the bow fixed along his own back. "The possibility that we're the only living beings for a hundred miles or…"

"Or, what?" Nikamu smiled.

"Or," Kishethwa steadied him with a cold stare. "The possibility that we aren't."

All who have died are equal.

It was a saying he'd heard often in his long travels, one held to by many of the tribes he'd come across over the years. It was a mistaken belief.

Death still held many forms, many positions.

There were those who slept below. Rotted and half-formed from ages passed. Harvested from the cold, endless earth. Called forward each night to escape from the darkest and oldest of holes, crawling and slithering like insects, to carry more dirt. All at his own bidding.

Then there were the ones who'd welcomed him when he arrived many moons before. So warm and receptive to his curious knowledge and powers. From the many burial mounds and death ceremonies, he knew immediately these people respected Death, worshiped its idea in a way even greater than what his own people had before. The rest had been simple. They now slept beside the others. These men, women, and children. Mindless shells slowly decaying in endless moonlights as they built new lodges or shambled about the land looking for more treasures, more brothers and sisters.

A third group he used for other things. Unspeakable things in all but the darkest of gatherings. Material to craft his darker magicks.

He emerged into the moonlight, almost oating on its wan glow. Several of his children had already gathered just outside the opening, eagerly waiting his arrival. His skeletal fingers dripped from the worn blood-red cloak to touch lovingly across bare skulls and knotted hair as they crawled and tittered in anticipation at his feet.

He then lifted those same hands to the stars and began speaking the ancient words. Felt the surging power.

It was time for the others to wake.

The mound was higher the next morning.

Or, at least, Kishethwa thought so.

The others were not as sure. How could it be?

He'd shown them what looked liked human footprints, fresh tracks leading up the side. Thousands of them. In fact, under the closer scrutiny of the daylight, he'd found that the same tracks seemed to run throughout the entire camp.

Yet, each step was faded. As if a soft wind had come down in the night and washed away what had really been. As if something had tried to hide them.

"They're faded because they're old," Nikamu shook his head. He inspected a mica pendant edged with lustrous shell beads. At his side were three pouches already filled with more precious rocks and carved figures. Enough for a king. "You're seeing things."

Seeing things.

Hearing them too, Kishethwa thought, but kept the comment to himself. The others were already looking at him as if he'd lost his mind. His sleep, however, had been filled with strange sounds and voices.

Dreams, no doubt, though the nature of those imaginings and the rest of the night were now lost from his memory. Strangely, he could not even recall taking his turn at watch. Hadn't realized he'd been that tired.

"What's this now?" he finally noticed one of the men, Linto, running towards them. "What's he shouting about?"

"I don't know." Nikamu stood and watched with him. "Peyak found an entrance into one of the older mounds. A tunnel of some kind. They were planning to explore the matter further." He tapped Kishethwa's shoulder. "Could save us weeks of digging, yes?"

"Yes," Kishethwa replied absently, watching until Ephit skidded to a stop before them.

"Peyak," the younger man gasped. "Something took Peyak."

"Calm, brother," Nikamu put a hand on his chest. "Took him? What are you talking about?"

"Where is he? Where's Peyak?" Kishethwa had already freed his bow and notched an arrow.

"Hurry." Linto waved them to follow. "He went into the mound!"

"Fool," Kishethwa cursed and the three men ran.

It was one of the longer and larger mounds. The end curved for a hundred paces or more in the shape of a stretched-out snake. At its "mouth" was the half-hidden entrance. "What happened? Is he in there? In that thing?"

"Yes," Linto said. "We saw something…"

Kishethwa crouched to look straight into the waiting blackness within. A blast of icy air from within raced across his face and up his back, and he shook off the strange feeling before looking again.

"What's that light?" he asked. "Did he carry a torch?" Likely not enough room, or air, for one. The smoke would choke him in minutes. But the rays of the sun revealed only to the first curve. Beyond, only the gods knew.

"No," Linto replied, his voice still shaken. "It … That light was already there. That's what we saw, I suppose. We thought it was sunlight from the other end or… We climbed in after it and then that glow got even brighter. And…"

"And what, fool?" Nikamu peeked carefully into the dark gap.

"And then Peyak started screaming. He wouldn't come," Linto covered his eyes. "I ran."

"Mother Bear!" Kishethwa shoved his bow and arrows at him, and stepped quickly into the darkness himself.

Peyak was somewhere within. Probably hurt. He'd certainly explored such places before to chase out hares and beaver. Had even stumbled upon a sleeping bear once. Who knew what animal might have made this place its home? Or, what other grave robbers had already rummaged through. *Best to find out now and get it over with.*

He climbed deep inside the opening and confirmed it was wide enough that he could push through if he just stayed low. He'd drawn his stone dagger. "Well, little Peyak," he said into the darkness, "let us see what you've really found."

He felt the others hovering in the gap behind him as he twisted past the first turn. The space immediately ahead grew darker. The sun was now lost to his back and his eyes readjusted to the gloom ahead.

So very dark. Except for the curious red glow which grew brighter with each careful step.

He crouched lower though the next turn, lost halfway somewhere within the snake effigy's neck. Above, at least ten feet of dirt and grass. Ahead, only darkness and the promise of finding Peyak or at least a wider space to fully stand.

At any moment he expected to stumble into the bodies, rows of the deep-rooted dead now swaddled in decayed wraps. It was an actual burial mound for sure, he thought. No other building would feel this … *foul.*

He thought of Peyak and kept moving.

The red glow was now strong enough that he could even see his own shadow against the dirt wall. Moving right beside him in a distorted shape that chilled his own heart.

There was a final turn and then, at last, he reached the main chamber. What he saw next, was taken in several quick images which he put together later.

The cavern, the absolute center of the mound, stretched further than his eye could see. It was braced at its walls with thick timber frames. Several ropes dangled from the ceiling, hidden in the impenetrable shadows above. From each hung a small jar which glowed red in ghostly flames.

Someone had carved strange pictures and symbols across the dirt wall. Many looked as if they'd been scratched violently by hands and claws that weren't even human. He was thankful he could not read the language, but knew well enough what the images meant. This was truly a place of death.

He saw Peyak then.

Laying only a few steps away towards the center of the chamber. Lifeless and curled into a childlike ball.

Directly above Peyak, floated the head.

Kishethwa thought at first it might be Peyak himself, some trick of the light. Or, even some horrible accident. But Peyak's head was exactly where it should be, curled into his still body.

This was another head all together.

And, except for the arms, it was *only* the head.

There was no body or legs. None that he could see.

It simply floated in the darkness above Peyak, hovering in midair. A terrible white face, lacking any color as if it had never once seen the sun or was completely devoid of blood. Some red and black paint had been smeared across its forehead and chin. Its two arms, uneven stumps with claws from what Kishethwa could see, swayed just below. Long dark hair dangled behind the head. Its mouth parted dripping and dark.

Kishethwa stepped backwards, and it was now looking straight at him. The eyes were white and wide, like two tiny moons floating in the cavern's darkness, and almost looked as if they were smiling. When it blinked, he saw that the lids were painted bright red.

Kishethwa pulled back his hatchet when a second appeared. This head dropped from the blackness of the ceiling to float beside its brother.

"Peyak," Kishethwa cried out in a voice that somehow sounded only like a whisper, not a real scream.

A third appeared now.

It came from the darkness in back of the cavern like a misshapen owl, swooping straight towards him. He noticed its fangs first and then, as it passed over his friend's body, and kept coming for him at a speed he'd not imagined possible, he recognized the distinct *hungry* gaze.

Kishethwa started screaming.

Real screams.

He stood directly over the four men, watching them sleep like a new father looking over his own sons. He knew it was a slumber from which they would not awake until morning. Eventually, even the morning would not help them.

The others were already moving about outside the lodge. He could hear their hushed gibbering and the slapping of many feet on the dirt as countless lines of shadow worked at the mound again. His Keepers moved about the shadows slowly, gloating over them and snapping hungrily at random forms. Before morning, his magicks would hide most of their labors, until they returned again the next night.

So much work still to be done.

But soon, it would be complete. And then, he would travel out again. To grow his family.

Inside the lodge, he ran a long finger across the sleeping faces of his newest children, etched the ancient symbols with his dirty nail on their skin. At the last man, his skeletal fingers spread to cover his entire face. He'd come to know this one the best. He closed his eyes and savored the feeling of the man's heart pulsing against his skull.

When he was done, he stepped back and raised his arms over the four. Their bodies trembled, eyes opened wide again into the night.

They were ready.

He stepped back through the doorway and turned his thoughts again to other matters.

The fifth man, for instance. The one he'd kept.

There was indeed much work still to be done.

The others had not believed him when he finally awoke. They did not want to hear of "flying heads" and "monsters." Yet, neither did they know where Peyak was, missing now for two days.

They would not discuss the dreams, the nightmares he'd had while he slept. So much more horrible, more vivid, than before. Visions of lumbering shadows and skeletal faces, of the tall man wrapped in deep red, his eyes shining silver. Calling to him through a cold mist. Yet, Kishethwa could tell from their reactions they'd had similar visions.

To stir them, he recounted a dim memory of digging in the dirt with his bare hands beside countless others, and carrying the jars up a long ramp. Then, he showed them his blackened hands. Filthy. Dirt jammed deep beneath his cracked nails, from use.

Their own hands revealed the same, but they only turned away when he pressed the matter. That the large mound looked more complete than ever was disregarded. That several heaps of fresh dirt lay piled now against their own lodge was also ignored.

He'd left them that same morning, followed into the woods by Nikamu's angry taunts and cursing.

He knew what he'd seen.

Walking alone, chasing after the rising sun, the forest's tall lush trees surrounded him again and comforted with each step as he put more distance between himself and the dead city. It would many more suns before he reached his village, but there he would assemble more men and come back for the others.

It wasn't until hours later when he realized that the others would not be there in many more suns.

Away from the place at last, his head clearing for the first time in days, he now knew without doubt there was something truly evil in the dead city. More than just the crypts and bodies within. Something else. They'd walked into a trap, he grasped now. And, as he marched swiftly through the underbrush, he found himself thinking more and more of Peyak. And, also, the others.

What have I left them to?

That's when he'd turned back.

He'd run the whole way, but it was night by the time he reached the edge of the city again.

By then, it had changed.

The moonlight cast directly over the whole site as if it were resting only a few feet away, so Kishethwa could see everything.

Their very bones glistened in that ghastly light.

Corpses in various stages of death shambling between the mounds, their decayed garments and skin hanging loosely off rotted remains. Most were nothing more than skeletons on thin grey frames with yawning jawbones and deep black eye sockets. White shards of bone poked from out of shredded leggings, bowed ribs caked with dirt. The holes from which they'd dug and wriggled out earlier pocked the whole of the land. Others were more human, but with noses and lips decayed away, the skin taut and furrowed around the waiting skull just beneath.

He saw where one man had secured his own lower jawbone into his belt. A woman with a papoose on her back, the *child* inside nothing but a dirty skull that rolled inside the rotted swaddle, snapping at other corpses as they passed. He noticed another woman with worms where her eyes should have been. One hulking form carried a collar of skulls across its chest, each one tied to the next by their own hair, a long strand that still trembled with life. Kishethwa could hear their sharpened teeth chattering.

Each figure moved clumsily as if led by some giant unseen hand. Too many for him to count. A hundred alone moved together in a long line which led to the giant mound, each one staggering forward with its singular chore.

The mound was almost complete. Only a small portion was still uncovered as the unending line of undead continued to fill in the gap, one basket of dirt at a time. Just inside, bodies now moved within the buried lodge's three levels, filling the once-empty rooms. The vacant wood coffins now teemed with life. Bone fingers tapped against the casket's ledges, the unseen bodies just within.

There was also a new mound.

The abandoned lodge he'd slept in with the others was now half covered. Twenty or more sluggish forms moved about its walls, tapping the fresh dirt into place.

Nikamu and Linto were among them.

They were now, it seemed, prisoners of this horrifying undead tribe. Kishethwa crept closer for a better look, staying within the shadows and notching an arrow into his bow. He had no real idea yet how he might free them. There were so many of the things moving about.

His brothers worked on their knees, shaping the earth, beside a gaunt figure whose half-exposed skull was crusted in black dirt and maggots. On the other side was a dark shape with long white hair hanging over its face, the matted tresses squirming with unseen life.

Though his stomach turned at the sight, he was thankful he could not see its face.

But, he saw the faces of Nikamu and Linto.

They were both drained of color. Their faces had turned almost grey in the moon's light. Their eyes were deep set and blackened, looking almost like the skull sockets that worked only feet away. Their gaze was vacant and glazed. They looked as if they were already dead. Just like all the others.

Where was Ephit?

It's only a spell, he told himself. *Our priests can surely heal them.*

Kishethwa stood straight and drew his bow upon the unseen thing with the dangling white hair. He felt the arrow trembling between his pinched fingers.

Something stirred at his right, only a flicker of movement, and Kishethwa turned to it.

A floating head, the same monster he'd seen before, soared towards him from out of the night. Its white face was stretched into a fierce snarl, the elongated jaws pulled back to reveal dripping fangs. Dark stringy hair fluttered behind it like smoke on the trail of its flight. The two arms, which protruded straight from its neck, were thick and hairy like a bear's, and equally clawed. The thing hissed at him like a great snake. Memories of his previous encounter flooded his mind with horror, and it remained the most terrifying thing he'd ever seen.

Kishethwa shouted back at the thing and fired.

The arrow missed high and vanished into the night behind the still-approaching head. Kishethwa had already notched and fired another.

It struck this time, and the creature's head erupted in a grisly splatter of bone, dust and inky blood before spiraling awkwardly to the ground.

Spinning backwards, Kishethwa swung his bow into a skeletal figure that'd cheated behind him. The bow snapped in half as the thing tumbled backwards to the ground. Moving towards it to finish his duty, the warrior dropped his broken bow and drew the stone hatchet.

"Kishethwa."

He stopped and turned, though the voice had been inside his head as much anything he'd heard.

Standing among the others was a new figure. It was one he'd seen somewhere before.

It wore a long crimson shroud and carried a narrow scepter like a high priest. The skin was pale and stretched tight against his long sinewy build, the head hairless and topped with a crown adorned by four short antlers and a gleaming stone in the center of the forehead. Its nose was nothing more than two long slits, and the ears were pointed and huge like those of a great bat. Silver shimmered in the heavy-lidded eyes.

Different than all the rest. Where the others were dead things that were now partly alive, it seemed this thing was the exact opposite. Kishethwa found that thought even more horrible.

Kishethwa remembered now. It was the same man, the same thing from his dreams. It was the man in red who'd haunted his nightmares these past days and nights. The same man who'd saved him from the flying heads and carried him from the mound's cavern. Even now, two of the flying monstrosities hovered just behind it.

"Who are you?" Kishethwa shouted. "What have you done to them?"

The figure stepped closer and smiled when Kishethwa lifted his hatchet in warning. Kishethwa saw its fangs.

"You may call me Ciucoatl," it said.

"How did you know my name?" He stepped back.

"You injure my heart, Kishethwa. Do you not remember the hours we spoke as true brothers? Is so much lost when you wake?" He waved a hand as if he were caressing his face. "I know many things about you Kishethwa, son of Miskwiwi, father of Neeswi. I just didn't expect to see you again so soon."

Just hearing their names in that hideous voice almost drove him to his knees in despair. "Release my friends," he said, his voice shaking. Several of the undead had moved to stand just behind the red-cloaked figure. Nikamu and Linto stood with them. "Monster, what have you done to them?"

"I've only freed them."

"By taking their lives?"

"Life is only the breath of a wolf in the winter," the figure smiled. "It is like the little shadow which briefly runs across the grass and then loses itself again in the sunset. Death is the only empire which truly lasts."

"How can you do this."

"I have," it said. "That is how. Before, and again. I hope that when you —"

Kishethwa lunged with his axe. The thing's ashen face only stared coldly as he swung down at it. It hadn't moved at all.

Something slammed into Kishethwa and he crashed sideways into the ground. He rolled to his feet with the axe still in hand and realized immediately that one of the flying heads had smashed into him.

It still hovered between him and the thing in red.

He recognized its face then. Though it was drained of color, smeared in black paints and swollen from abuse.

It was Peyak.

The hunter's face floating freely in the air, eyes dull and mouth gnashing hungrily.

The axe fell from Kishethwa's fingers. His mind was flooded with such dreadful thoughts and feelings. How was such a thing possible? Had Ephit met the same horrible fate? What dark magicks and gods did this thing revere?

As if to answer, he heard the figure laugh.

It had moved back into the crowd of horrible shapes, who moved about him at every side, moving back to their chores as he waved his hands this way and that. Nikamu and Linto had already vanished back into that throng of decay. Peyak's head even winked at him, then followed closely after the others.

All the while, the horrific laughing continued.

Much later, having run blindly through the woods for two days and nights, Kishethwa thought he could still hear it.

Kishethwa finally reached his own village after many nights, though he wasn't exactly sure how many.

It had been a journey half-spent in shadow. What he saw in his nightmares and in the waking world were blending more each passing hour. The world seemed hazier and more grey. The sun hurt his eyes, made him nauseous. He told himself it was because he had not eaten in so long. He'd lost thirst and hunger a week ago.

Seven small huts made up his entire village. No one moved among them, not a single soul. Yet, two had already been entirely covered in dirt. One of those was Ephit's home. Kishethwa imagined the family inside together. Waiting for…

"You may call me Ciucoatl," it had said.

Kishethwa's own lodge was free of dirt and it proved empty except for the three new coffins someone had dragged into the center of the small dwelling.

He did not know where his wife and son were. He could only assume.

Probably with the others. Until it was night again.

Then, there would be more work to do.

He lay down in his coffin and waited.

NOTES: The "mound builders" is a catchall name for the many tribes who constructed various mounds for burial, residential, and ceremonial purposes in the years 600 B.C.E. to 1000 C.E. These structures were scattered about the eastern United States and were typically at-topped pyramids or platform mounds, at-topped or rounded cones, and elongated ridges. At first, the newly arrived Europeans assumed the mounds were built by non-Indians who had vanished years before (supposing that the current "natives" could not have constructed such structures, supported by the fact that the current tribes admitted the mounds had been there when they arrived!). Thomas Jefferson is noted as one of the very first Americans to conduct a methodical exploration of the mounds, one in a long line of scientists who ultimately proved the paleo-Indian connection. Southern Ohio, specifically, remains peppered with such mounds, many of which were ruined in the last two hundred years during development. Some, known as effigy mounds, take on unusual shapes, such as the outline of cosmologically significant animals [The most famous, Serpent Mound in southern Ohio, is five feet tall and over half a mile long]. Mound builders outside St. Louis built a mound eighty feet high in a city once populated with thirty thousand people. Mound City, north of Chillicothe, Ohio, was called "City of the Dead." Mound-building cultures (specifically during the years 500 – 1000 C.E.) were historically known by other tribes for worshipping Death, and burial sites include evidence of great treasures and human sacrifices. These specific mound builders vanished suddenly from North America in 500 C.E., and the cause is still much debated to this day. "Flying heads" and evil "vampire" magicians also appear throughout several Native American legends.

VINLAND
1009

The man was a giant.

An enormous monster who'd somehow stepped out of legends and campfire stories into the center of their village.

He stood an arm's-length taller than any man Kano had ever seen, was as heavy as two, and his arms and neck were full and taut with hard-lined muscles. His face was half-hidden in shaggy corn-colored hair, and the two horns atop his head, some kind of hat, had sharp points which glinted in the setting sun.

The axe he'd drawn glinted also.

Even more so. It was made of strange rock that glittered like the sun's reflection over moving water.

Kano held his breath as the giant wrenched the weapon back and took aim. The cape of startling white fur whipped behind the man's shoulders as he flung the axe with a bestial grunt. It rotated twice in the air, instantly covering the distance between, and then sunk with a deep crunch into its intended target.

The giant's brothers, a dozen men lined directly across from Kano, rumbled in approval. One of them, their chief, who looked like a great big bear with red fur, growled something proudly in their own language and the others laughed. Each was as repulsive looking as the last. Faces like wolves, some thankfully hidden behind strange stone masks that covered their eyes and noses. They'd arrived days before in long canoes that looked like massive snakes with high lifted necks and snarling jaws.

The men moved aside as the giant stepped back into their pack, and Kano noted the look of approval in their chief's eyes. It had been a good throw.

Now it was Nal's turn.

The hunter stepped quickly into the same spot where the other had just been and stared down towards their target. The tree was twenty paces away, with the hilt of the giant's axe already protruding from its center.

The whole village, even the women and children, had circled about and now watched as Nal inspected his own stone axe, turning it slowly in his grip. Nal looked up, caught his brother staring at him, and nodded with a subtle smile in his eyes before turning back to the tree.

Kano grinned back, unworried. His brother had always been the best hunter of all their people. Chief Etsä, standing a pace ahead of all the others, also looked certain of the outcome.

Nal lunged forward and threw his own axe.

It traveled in a high arc, the head behind and low for half the distance, before finally turning over and dropping with an audible *THUNK* into the tree just a hand above the other axe.

The village erupted in a blend of challenging hoots and joyful cries, and Kano joined them. As they cheered, the giant stepped back into the clearing towards Nal. With each heavy step, the strange gleaming shirt he wore under his cape clicked like a snake's rattle.

The huge man glared at Nal, who stared back from within the dark blue paint the priest had painted in a wide band around his eyes, then nodded. Nal returned the gesture, and the two walked slowly towards the tree to retrieve their weapons. Walking alongside each other, Kano mused, it looked as if Nal were now the little brother.

Chief Etsä and the strangers' chief moved into the clearing now and began waving and pointing again. Except for a few words, exaggerated hand gestures remained the only way the two groups could truly communicate. Still, in just a few days, Kano had learned some of the strangers' words. *Malke* was the white sweet liquid the strangers had, and the long shining weapons at their hips were *sverds* or *oxs*. Their terrifying canoes were called *drakkar*. Also, apparently, Kano and his people were *skraelings*, though, based on the delivery, this was clearly an insult of some kind.

They also called Kano's home *Vinland*. This word, however, was always said with genuine respect.

Kano watched as his brother and the other man pulled their axes free from the tree, and inspected the new gouges. Three times they'd tossed, and on each occasion, neither had missed his mark. The two exchanged weapons for a moment, each inspecting the other's. Nodding politely. Kano could also see they were attempting to speak.

Just behind him, the two chiefs had parted and now waited for their men to return. Both looked pleased.

Nal and the giant moved back slowly together, and bowed slightly before their respective chiefs.

"Bows," Chief Etsä said, putting his hand on Nal's shoulder. "They use bows!" he called out to his people, and the whole camp broke into excited chatter. Nano clapped his hands. Nal was even better with the bow.

"*Lúta!*" the other chief shouted out and his own men roared as one. It seemed from their fervor that the other man had some skill in archery as well.

The two men nodded again and moved to their respective side of the clearing, where bows had already been found for each. They'd formed a crowded circle around Nal, giving him just enough space to finish fixing the quill of arrows to his hip. Kano had pushed through the mob to reach his brother

"And what brings you, little squirrel?" his brother winked, looking up. "Come to help me find the truest arrows?"

"Makes no difference," Kano whispered to him. "You're always the best anyway. You'll defeat the giant easily."

"Heimdall," Nal replied, setting aside an arrow. "The giant, as you call him, is called Heimdall by his people."

"'Heimdall,'" Kano tried the word. "That's a strange name."

"I suppose so."

Kano thought, then grinned. "Then, you will defeat Heimdall easily," he said.

Nal laughed. "Very well," he said, and poked his brother hard in the chest with a finger. "For you."

Then, he grabbed his bow.

Nal won.

The giant, called Heimdall, had been very good. Even Kano would admit this. Nine of ten shots into the target.

Nal was better.

The same steady hand and eye that had once taken down five bucks in one chase and slain the raging wolf called Farbite, hit true again.

Chief Etsä awarded him an eagle's feather on the spot and Kano assumed that would be the end of things. That the strangers would get back into their odd boats and return to the sea.

They did not.

Instead, the two chiefs huddled and spoke again. Waving arms and speaking in voices that sometimes even frightened Kano a little. Then, as the sun dipped behind the western tree line, Kano and all the others watched as his brother and the giant squared off again in the center of the village.

This time, a test of strength.

To heave a log as far as they could. Why Chief Etsä had ever agreed to such a contest, Kano could not imagine. Its outcome was evident even to him. The stranger was simply too big. The man lifted the heavy log each time as easily as if he were picking up a small basket of berries. All three of his throws went further than Nal's. Much further, and the other strangers had laughed and cheered with each toss.

Kano decided he hated them. He wished they'd simply get back on their hideous ships and leave forever. Or, that his brother would be given another chance to prove he was better than the giant. A game more evenhanded between the two.

But there were no more games that day.

Instead, the chiefs spoke again before the strangers returned to their own camp south of the great marshes. It was not known if they would return again.

Then, Nal pulled him aside, and Kano knew.

Long before the new sun appeared over the wetland, Nal shook him awake and the brothers stepped into the cold darkness together. There, two of the strangers, the giant and another one as young as Kano, were waiting for them.

All through that night, Kano tossed about unable to sleep, wondering what this next day would bring. A few times, he'd stolen a look at his brother sleeping on the mat beside him, and saw that Nal wasn't sleeping either. Now, here they were at last.

Today's game was simple enough. Nal and the other were to hunt deer only until the sun was directly over the village again. Then, their prizes would be counted and weighed and a winner declared. Kano and the other boy had been approved to help scout and carry the catches.

Except for several men on watch, three more than usual, Kano noticed, the rest of the camp was sleeping as the four hunters stepped into the deeper woods.

It was the closest he'd yet gotten to one of the strangers. They were as huge as he remembered, even bigger so close, and lumbered through the woods like bears. They both wore long pants made of unfamiliar cloth, held up by a blood-red sash. Their shirts were sleeveless ponchos of the same material. The giant's cape of white fur had been replaced with a darker hide, and their wide leather belts carried only a single grey-colored dagger. Their longer blades had been left back at their camp, no doubt, as were the grey rings the giant had worn across his chest. On their feet, soft leather shoes not so different from Kano's own moccasins. Up close, their skin was not as sickly white as he'd first thought, and their eyes were the color of the sky.

The four stopped at the crest of a short hill, where Nal and the other looked across the darkened valley below. The tops of the trees only now glistening with the first touch of a red-tinged dawn. Kano's brother turned to the stranger and the two nodded again. The giant stepped away from them with his second close behind. In turn, Nal tapped Kano to follow him and moved quickly the other way.

Kano followed but looked back several times to watch the strangers vanish into the dense and shadowed treeline. He'd wanted to see how these strange men hunted. A week before, he and some of the other boys had snuck out and watched them fish. He'd been surprised to see they used one of the same tricks his own people did. Lights tied to the front of the boats to invite the fish to the surface, the men simply scooping them up by hand. Did they hunt as well?

He doubted it. He could still hear them moving heavily through the woods. Kano chuckled to himself and chased quickly after his brother.

The hunt, after all, had already begun.

They returned hours later, just as the sun crested the village and hung over its multihued treetops to drop shadows at their feet.

They'd killed four deer that morning.

Nal had moved quickly down known trails, an advantage Kano

admitted, and set up in several known trail crossings, food, bedding, and watering spots. At each, he'd passed on several smaller deer, holding out for the bigger kills, then shaped precise shots that'd taken them down. Huge bucks with ten-point antlers, one that weighed almost as much as three men. Nal had dragged that one back himself, and Kano helped gut and tie each for the trip back.

The giant Heimdall had killed seven, but they were much smaller and the arguments followed. Kano watched with the others while the two chiefs grumbled and pointed and thumped their chests over which of the two men had performed better. It seemed, no victor was ever to be declared.

That night, all of the deer meat was cooked over the fires and men from both clans sat together to feast on the morning's gifts, to visit, and to celebrate the two men. Around several fires, songs were song by men from both camps. Food shared. The village women brought out newly picked berries. The strangers had brought more *malke* and something called *mungát*, which tasted horrible but the hairy men liked very much.

Throughout, Nal and Heimdall stood beside each other, looking over the gathering. Pointing at the various smoking pits of deer, and briefly reenacting what had happened for each via gestures and imagined bows. Kano lingered just behind them and listened.

Ower, the village storyteller sang a war song and then told the story of Ghorke, a hero from days past who'd defended the people against an army of ghostly wolves. Ower and another man acted out all the parts and Kano studied the strangers while his fellow clansmen watched the performance and whispered to themselves, no doubt explaining, or arguing over, what they'd just seen.

When Ower was done, one of the heavier strangers with a long dark beard, stood and started to speak. Tapping his chest, he gave his name as Tyrker and the whole village grew quiet again to listen.

The man pointed east towards the ocean, and struggled, Kano realized, to tell them all of their travels across the water. In the dirt, he'd drawn their boats and huge waves. Huge mountains growing in the water, mountains that were cold, he acted out by shivering and curling his arms around his chest. He imitated the sounds of thunder and the moved his arms to become the lightning. A great storm that had struck their people. Many boats lost.

He spoke of someone called *Thor*.

Thor, he claimed, was a man, a great warrior with an axe called *Mjolnir* that was used to fight terrible monsters who lived beneath the ground and men who were as tall as the trees. From what Kano could tell, this warrior had some power over the lightning. Throughout, the others nodded approvingly, with firm expressions on their faces.

Finally, Tyrker told them of a land called *Valhalla*. Pointing through the blaze's smoke to the dark sky, the dark-haired giant stood and enacted a place in the sky where he would go someday. A place where all the women were beautiful and carried swords. Where there was always more food and *malke*, and *mungát*. The strangers laughed and cheered at that. A land in the sky where many great hunters would go, it seemed. Kano watched when Heimdall tapped Nal's chest so that he would look, then flexed his enormous arms and chest as if to further explain the story.

Powerful men. Heroes.

Nal had nodded politely, as if understanding. Though, Kano suspected his older brother was just as mystified by this place as he.

As the fires burned down, Kano thought over *Valhalla* and *Thor* and tried to make sense of it all. When the strangers left again into the darkness back towards their own camp, he could almost see this mysterious place between a small cluster of stars above.

By the time he'd fallen asleep, he would have sworn to Nal that he had.

Before the blood, there was just the footrace.

A test of speed. So, Kano did not at first understand why Nal again stood across from the giant. Kano could easily name two men who were faster. It soon became clear, however, that Nal had been chosen to represent them for each of the contests. As had the one called Heimdall.

When the race started, it also became clear this was to be no ordinary footrace. The stranger's very first step took him directly into Nal's path, where the giant lowered his shoulder and unleashed the full weight of his massive body. Kano's brother pitched sideways, both legs lifting from the ground as the larger man drove him over. As Nal smashed into the dirt, the giant simply stepped over him and kept running.

The gathered crowd grunted as one in disapproval and surprise. Kano, also, stepped forward, the complaint only half off his lips when Chief Etsä ordered them all to stay quiet. Nothing in their leader's face registered either rage or surprise at the giant's action. Instead, the chief simply waved them away as Nal scrambled back to his feet to give chase.

So these are the rules, Kano thought, and moved quickly with the others like a flock of birds after the two runners. Pushing ahead to get a better look. Nal had already gained back almost half the distance between himself and the giant, who'd now reached the creek. The other man was moving well, Kano allowed, surprised to see someone that large moving so swiftly. He was again reminded of the great bears in the western hills. Nal, the deer, sprinted just behind.

More than half the course led directly through the marshes where red berries floated in knotted clusters and the water was thigh deep in most spots. They'd put a small fire on a boulder at the north end of the marsh, its smoke lifting away on the cool autumn breeze. The flock of spectators, including several of the hairy-faced strangers, had moved west to a small knoll where they would be able to see most of the race. From there, they watched from a distance as Nal finally caught up. The giant turning to fend off Kano's brother, Nal knocking the arm aside and shoving back. The man staggered, lunged at his brother again, both men now crashing to the ground.

The run through the marsh proved slower but more of the same, each man taking the lead for awhile before the other caught up and the two resorted to shoving again. However, now that Kano and the others understood the rules, it had become truly exciting to watch. Each trip or stumble, each pull, sprint, and splash, brought another spirited reaction from the crowd. Suddenly, the giant touched the chosen mark, the flame-topped boulder, and turned back. Nal jumped aside when the man passed, ducking his intended shoulder, and made for the stone himself. He touched, spun round, and rushed after him.

Nal stayed on the giant's heel the remainder of the run, hanging just behind his left shoulder. Waiting, Kano knew. Then, just as the marsh ended, he'd made his move. He surged forward and, as the giant turned back to grab hold as he had many times before, Nal suddenly lurched back, got one hand on the man's back, and his left leg in front of the stranger.

The rest was easy.

The giant's motion, with Nal's hand, carried him forward over the leg and Heimdall spilled head first into the ground. Water splashed over his back and across Nal's body as he stepped over the tumbling shape of the the stranger and continued past.

Kano cheered with the others and leapt frantically down the knoll, running back towards the starting spot. The stranger had already fought back to his feet, but it was too late. Though he was only an arm length's away by the time Nal crossed the starting spot, Nal had clearly won.

Kano's brother stood gasping for air in the center of the village, hunched over with his hands behind his neck. The giant huffed just beside him, rubbing a cramp from his side. Both were soaked from the marsh's water, their faces red and running with fresh sweat. Nal lifted his head and the two competitors looked squarely at each other, while they collected their breath.

As Kano watched, the giant lifted his hand and put it against Nal's chest. Kano moved closer, fearful the man would push Nal or grab him as he'd been unable to just moments before. Instead, he'd simply tapped Nal's chest twice and nodded. Nal patted the man's arm back and then the two had separated.

Until now.

For now, they stood as one again in the center of a small ring made from the mob of people. This newest contest had begun just after sunset. Now, Kano noted that the moon rested high above their heads. Much time had passed indeed. Too much time.

It would not end. Neither man would quit.

Nal should quit, Kano thought, fighting back the tears of rage and hurt from his eyes. *He must.*

Both men were shirtless, caked in dirt from the ground and a few scratches. Their hair had fallen free and now lay matted across sticky faces and backs.

Nal's nose was broken. The dried blood still coated his upper lip and chin.

The two met again, arms entwined, shoving back the other, rotating away, grabbing hold of necks and legs. Nal had wrestled with his friends, but it had not been like this. These men were clearly not afraid of getting hurt, or of hurting each other. These men, his brother, moved as if there were nothing more important than driving the other man to the ground again.

Throughout the night, each had had their turn at that. Mostly, however, it had been the giant. He was just too big, too strong. At first, Nal had been quick enough, moving easily around the ring, waiting to grab the giant's legs. However, as the night wore on, the man's size had proven too much.

He seized Nal, wrapping him in both arms and slammed with him again to the ground. The giant then wrenched his arm up to pin Kano's brother. The forearm caught Nal in the throat and there was a dreadful choking sound as Nal struggled beneath. The massive arm suddenly drove up to his chin, pushing his head back. Nal kicked his legs, squirmed to free himself but could not.

The giant rolled off and pulled himself slowly to one knee. His breath sounded short and uneven on the cool night's air. Nal, meanwhile, remained on the ground, gasping. The giant raised to his feet, and slowly stepped away.

Nal turned to his side, spit on the ground, dragged himself up to his hands and knees. Slowly, he lifted once more to his feet. Across the ring, the giant stared back. Shook his head. Then nodded.

Nal held up his hand and called for more water.

Kano was ready. He raced from the crowd again to his brother with the half-full bladder. Up close, Nal looked even worse than Kano'd even feared. Beside the bloodied nose, his cheek was bruised and swollen. There were scratches across his forehead from where he'd been pushed into the dirt.

"How are you?" he asked carefully, not sure what else to say. He could tell each of his brother's breaths was painful.

"To tell the truth, little squirrel," Nal replied softly, taking the water. "I think I preferred the deer hunt." He took a swig of water and spit it out onto the ground. The froth on his lips was pink with blood.

"Why continue?" Kano blurted suddenly. "He's too big. This game is lost."

Nal took another sip, swallowed it, and passed the bladder back. The crowd watched the two, waiting. "Chief Etsä has granted a great honor to me, Kano," he said. "You would not disrespect that honor either."

"But you won already once today," Kano argued. "Now, he has won. Let it end there. Tomorrow there will surely be another game."

Nal laughed, but the sound was quiet and weary. "Look at their men," he said, glancing into the crowd. "Their chief. Look at their swords and shields."

Kano stole a glance as his brother waited.

"Do you truly believe they keep coming back to play games with us?"

Kano did not answer.

"This is much more than a game, little one. Decisions are being made here tonight. By both peoples."

Kano stepped back, only half understanding. But, it was enough. The look in his brother's eyes took care of the rest.

As Kano stepped back into the crowd, Nal smiled broadly and waved the giant forward.

The other paused, smiled back, then answered the challenge.

The cold wind rushed over him, pushing the long hair from his shoulders as they sailed blindly into the night. The wooden boat creaked and groaned beneath him, the ocean's water sloshing against its sides. Cold salty water sprayed against his face like tiny fingers of ice and he pulled closer the fur-lined cloak the giant had lent him.

Heimdall stood towards the back with his hands on an oar that steered the massive canoe from the back. He stared into the darkness ahead of them, his eyes as focused as any hawk Kano had ever seen. For the first time, too, he recognized something that looked like joy in the stranger's face.

Kano sat beside his brother, the only other passenger on the foreign ship. Both looked out together into the waiting darkness ahead. A single sheet of skin hung across a great pole to catch the wind, and flapped in the night's wind above them.

Nal had been at the stream behind their village, washing the blood from his face when the giant found them. He'd stepped out of the darkness towards them and Kano's first thought was to run for help, but his brother waved him to remain still. The stranger had stepped forward, kneeled to one leg and took a sip of water from the stream himself. He'd been waiting for Nal to finish. When he had, the man waved for Nal to follow. Nal turned back to Kano, and the man grunted something. Pointed directly at Kano and grunted the same word again.

He'd touched his chest and waved them both forward. Following the commotion from the camp behind them, their walk through the woods together had been deathly quiet. By the time they'd reached the coast, the low swish and roll of the softly breaking ocean waves was a welcome sound.

Now, Kano sailed over the same ocean. On one of the giant snake boats he'd spied before from so far away. He'd felt the carved snout, and felt its glinting fangs and deep eye socket. They'd pushed the boat out into the sea together and then Heimdall had done the rest.

Guiding them into the oblivion of absolute darkness. Only the stars glinting high overhead.

Terrifying.

Wonderful.

Kano ran his fingers along the tops of the hard shields, secured against the sides of the ship. Felt the dark water kicking up against the tips. At first, he'd feared they'd fallen for some trap, that he and his brother were being simply taken prisoner, enslaved to some foreign land. Nal assured him they were not. Soon, the look in the giant's eyes did as well.

The man pointed north into the darkness. "Newfound land," he told them. Kano and Nal sat quietly, not sure what he meant. He then pointed east towards where the morning sun returned each day. "Green Land," he said, tapped his chest. "Green Land." Pointed again, demonstrating something further. "Ice Land," he said.

Kano turned and peered into the darkness, trying to see what the man was pointing at.

"Green Land," Nal repeated the word out loud.

"Vin Land," the stranger said pointing west back to the unseen seaboard, back towards their own home. Kano could barely make out the black outline of the shoreline.

"Valhalla," Kano blurted out, and pointed up, grinning that he'd remembered the word. He felt Nal stiffen next to him and the warning look from his older brother.

The stranger laughed, however. Smiled broadly, as he glanced up to the stars and moon above. "Valhalla," he called into the wind. He looked down again towards Kano and nodded his head, pleased. Then he turned the oar and the boat shifted against the wind, turning once more into the darkness.

Kano leaned closer into his brother. "He may be our enemy in the morning," Kano said. "But it seems, at least for this night, he is a true and noble friend."

"Then," Nal smiled, more to himself than Kano, "Perhaps it is best if we never see the sun again."

The great cat had already killed three men.

It lived in the low rock-strewn hills just south of their village. Some said it was a witch who'd lived in those same hills for a thousand years who'd recently assumed the shape of a catlike monster. The kind of beasts *Thor*, no doubt killed, Kano mused. However, Nal told him it was only a very large cougar.

Kano had seen its tracks only once. Hunting with his father the previous winter. A huge paw, as big as a bear's, but with only four toes like the other mountain cats. And, while there were no sharp nails in the print, Kano knew they were still there. Nails that sprang out when the beast was ready to kill. Its marks were deeply made. The creature, whatever it was, was heavy.

Heimdall had returned them to the village just before sunrise. Nal and Heimdall then left to hunt the creature together. At a given point, they would separate and hunt alone. Thus far, the sum of the contests was considered even by most. Here, there would be only one victor. After that,

Kano would not even imagine. The games had stopped being fun the night before.

The two were to hunt alone. Not to return until one of the men had found and killed the great cat. Everyone else had been ordered to keep away.

Kano, naturally, had followed closely behind.

Keeping at a safe distance, where he would never be heard or seen, he'd shadowed them through the southern wood and into the lower hills, then watched as the two men separated and moved slowly in opposite directions up into the hills. Each with a bow and full quiver of arrows slung over their shoulders. The stranger also carried a huge axe, one that required both his hands to carry. When the two men split, Kano trailed Nal.

Nothing happened that first day. There was no sign either of the great cat or the giant called Heimdall. When his brother stopped that night, Kano found shelter beneath a full pine tree and slept alone. In the morning, Nal moved higher into the hills and Kano stayed with him.

When he found the tracks that morning, he thought he'd somehow only imagined them. "Blessed Spirit!" His whole body shook with excitement. They were the same as what he'd seen before.

Fresh tracks. Running north.

Kano stood to yell for his brother, to call him back and show what he'd found. But he didn't.

They weren't his tracks to find.

Helping his brother this way would be unfair, and he would not disgrace Nal or his people that way. Kano stepped over the prints and chased quickly and quietly after his brother. As he followed, the cold eastern wind whistled through the multihued trees. Another winter moving in.

Awhile later, Nal found fresh tracks himself. He'd moved quickly after them, with Kano giving chase just behind. With the sun now setting again in the west, casting an auburn glow over the tree tops, Kano knew they were close.

His brother had stopped, freed the bow from his back.

They *were* close, Kano thought, crouching behind one of the many rock outcroppings.

His brother tensed, looked down into the hills below.

Suddenly, a horrible roar escaped the same trees.

No animal. A man screaming.

Just below them somewhere.

Nal raced forward, and shielded the sun from his eyes to get a better look. Kano clung desperately to his hiding spot.

A piercing animal's snarl echoed from the hills below.

"Kano!" his brother shouted when it subsided.

More human screams followed. Deep, angry words Kano could not make out. He'd frozen, unable to move.

"Kano!" Nal screamed again, and looked back towards where he was hiding.

Kano stepped slowly from his spot.

"Come!" Nal shouted. "Quickly!"

Kano obeyed his brother and dashed the distance between. "How long have you known?" he asked.

"Silence, Kano. You must go back for help. Get the others."

"Why?"

"Go now! Bring them back here."

Kano looked down to what Nal had found.

The giant Hemidall was pinned against a rock wall, his axe laying on the ground at his feet. Shoulder glistening wet and red in the dying sun. Swinging his bow to keep the beast away as the great cat, larger than even Kano had imagined, scratched and snapped at him.

"Little squirrel," Nal said and grabbed his shoulder. "You must go now."

"Why? Just let the stranger die. After, kill the great cat yourself and —"

His brother's look of disappointment was worse than any scolding he had ever received.

"But what will you do?" Kano asked.

"Finish the game," Nal said. "I'll finish the game. Now run, little squirrel. Run!" He jumped down the embankment, notching an arrow as he did.

Kano ran, just as his brother asked.

The small canoe floated out to sea, the waves carrying it away into the darkness, the lone figure peaceful and still. Filled with personal treasures, including the skin of the great cat the two men had killed together.

Nal's body lay atop, resting in rich skins and covered in a beautiful white fur the strangers had gifted to cover the many ghastly bites and scratches.

Heimdall had carried Nal back himself.

Even after the others found them, found the dead cat. Even though his arm was slashed open and he could barely move, still Heimdall demanded to carry Nal himself.

Now this.

A funeral in the way of the strangers. The way of burial for their greatest hunters and warriors.

To honor Nal.

Their chief had personally requested of Chief Etsä and Kano's father that they might celebrate Nal so. Told all again how he'd saved Heimdall, and the price he'd paid for his bravery. An archer soared a fiery arrow over the waves between and flames soon engulfed the canoe.

Kano could see its glow vanishing into the sea's darkness. He thought again of the night the three had sailed into the same darkness together. *Who was with his brother now?*

Heimdall, the giant, stood just beside Kano throughout. He squeezed his shoulder once when it was all over.

In the morning, Heimdall, and the rest of the strangers were gone. They never returned again.

Later, Kano would often sit by the sea and think of his brother and the giant called Heimdall.

He liked to imagine that the two had somehow visited *Valhalla* together. Walked into its golden halls to join the other celebrated hunters of the world. Met the great chief *Thor*. Found new contests and adventures to test themselves for the rest of time.

Sometimes, when the lightning storms flashed over the dark eastern waters, he knew that they had.

NOTES: "Viking" is a catchall term (much like "Indian") for the various seaman from Sweden, Norway, and Denmark who sailed out into the world as looters, traders, and mercenaries from 793 to about 1066. During this time, Vikings quickly established settlements along the coasts and rivers of mainland Europe, Ireland, and likely reached as far south as North Africa and east to Russia and Constantinople. Thanks to the abundance and variety of foods in Nordic countries, these men were typically larger and stronger than most Europeans, and their customs held to the harsh requirements of war, ice, and the sea. Norwegian Vikings colonized Iceland about 870, and legendary Icelander Erik The Red colonized Greenland a hundred years later. Always seeking new lands to conquer, and weaned on a passion for adventure, Viking eyes soon turned further west. Erik's son, Leif Erikson, inherited his father's love of travel and set sail, landing in Newfoundland in 1001. Further south, in 1003, they discovered an even more beautiful land of green grasses which he and his travelers called Vinland (vin means meadow). Winter approaching, Erikson and his men built shelters along Follins Pond, a lake located on Cape Cod, Massachusetts. Several skirmishes and more friendly meetings soon occurred with the skraelings, those who already inhabited the land. In the spring, Erikson sailed home. His brother, Thorvald, made the second visit. Later, Erikson's own daughter and her husband, leading other settlers, took a turn, also putting down roots in the Cape Cod area. The settlement did not last. By 1066, the Viking era of vast and swift exploration and settlement was over. There remain Nordic maps as old as 1440 (which are remarkably accurate and considered copies from much older maps) that show the Hudson, the Chesapeake Bay, and the tip of Florida. The skraelings, *the mysterious inhabitants of this new land, quickly became forever part of Nordic history and myth.*

RAT DOG
1325

"One day, the spirits took man and all the animals, great and small, to the center of a large open field. They stood man opposite the beasts and cast the first light of the sky into the ground causing a huge rift to open. As the chasm widened more and more, the spirits explained that man was to be held apart from beast. Man would be given great powers and understanding, but he would forever walk alone among the creatures of earth. As dog stood with the other animals, he watched man standing alone and wondered who would help him on his long journey. Dog looked to the sky, and at the last moment that the great split was almost too vast to cross, he jumped. And stood with man."

— Native American myth

They found the abandoned village just after the storm, so each empty wigwam was crested in a peak of fresh snowfall that glistened and twinkled in the full moon's light like tiny stars across soft blankets of silver. It would have been pretty, the girl thought, if it hadn't been so damn cold.

And, if the wolves weren't so close.

She chased that thought from her mind and returned her full attention back to the fire. Or, their lack of.

Back and forth. Back and forth.

Her right forearm still burned in complaint, but she continued to ignore it, and pushed and tugged the small fire bow again. With each quick repetition, the bow's cord turned the wooden drill once more into its hearth board. The kit had been in her family for years, kept in a small bag her grandmother had beaded with stained melon seeds. It had only recently become hers.

She shuddered, blocking the fresh memories, and pushed down harder on the rock with her other hand, which was held against the top of the drill to increase the friction below. Her fingers, wrapped in strips of old hide, trembled while trying to hold tight to the tools. They were swollen and heavy, and felt as if someone had smashed each and every one with the butt end of a hatchet. Despite the agony, she held tight and kept sawing.

If they didn't have fire soon, they would die. Either from the cold or the things panting and scampering just outside. Had they escaped so much to come to this?

Back and forth. Back and forth.

The blackened hearth board pinned under her knee smoked some in response. "Please," she said aloud, finding strength to saw even faster. The voice had sounded unfamiliar and weak, as if a complete stranger had made it. Only a little smoke escaped from her mouth on the chilly air. It seemed her body had become frozen through, just like the streams and lakes. The winter wind outside rattled the wigwam's birch bark sides as if to remind her to keep going.

Back and forth.

The wood powder caught in the notch of the hearth board and flared suddenly like the sun, then turned orange with life. The small wisps of smoke increased and she hunched low to blow across the glowing embers, feeding them with her frosty breaths. Her jaw chattered so badly, the puff barely escaped her cracked lips.

She dared to stop bowing for just an instant and grabbed blindly for some bulrush kindling. Her petrified fingers couldn't close around the wood shavings, and she ended up just dragging them with her whole hand onto the board to lay beside the glowing embers.

The kindling caught.

"Yes!" she rasped and reached for bigger brushwood. "Look! Do you see what I did?" she asked.

The dog, who lay curled in a tight ball just beside her, lifted its ears at her question. Its golden-brown eyes, the left encircled in dark hair that always made it look as if it had one giant eye open, looked at her and then turned to watch the thin twist of smoke rising towards the small hole at the top.

The girl slid the hearth board away and fed the budding flame a few small twigs. Thank the gods, there'd been a small stash of firewood beneath the floor of the empty home. She collected the fire kit back into its bag and slipped it over her neck again. The frozen wood crackled with new life and she added more to the tiny blaze. The tent soon took on a distinctive glow which reminded her just enough of home.

Now there was an actual fire in the center of the pit and she warmed her trembling hands against it. They itched and burned now from the inside. She imagined the others, her brothers and the other men, coming back from a winter hunt. Their faces red while they warmed their hands by the fires. The women would bring them all something to eat and fire-warmed skins to cover them. But, they were all dead now.

She was the only one left.

She and Rat Dog.

She turned to look at the dog and saw only a jumble of tan and black with a long scraggly black tail wrapped around the nose and face. She'd laid two of the rotted bulrush mats beneath it for warmth, but its hair remained crusted with ice. Though two wide eyes blinked back just over its tail, in the flickering fire light, he looked little more than a discarded pile of bones.

It was from this same opinion that the others had named him. Its shadow, they claimed with laughter, looked just like the wood rats that raided the corn stores each fall. Always hunched low and scurrying faster than the other dogs. A shape that was skeletal and long with a scraggly tail and a jagged tuft of hair sprouting between its arched shoulders.

The "Rat Dog."

It had never become one of the tribe's guard or hunting dogs. For years, it'd simply hovered just outside the fringes of their camp, finding just enough scraps to get by. Sometimes, some of the other children would chase him for fun. The others …

She pulled the tattered hide robe closer around her body and breathed deeply, feeling the warmth of the fire against her numb face for the first time in days. Now that the cold might not kill them, the girl turned her attention to other troubles. She stared into the fire, her next thoughts lost in the dancing flames.

Just outside, one of the wolves again scratched to get in. For now, a failed attempt.

Earlier, she'd ripped up two of the several wood platforms which made up the wigwam's floor and used them to block the doorway. They were now braced on the back with two of the larger logs and trembled against the wolf's tests.

That's all the wolf was doing, she knew, with its halfhearted poking. Simply testing the barricade. Deciding how easy it would be to put its full weight against the barrier to knock it over. Or, how long it would take its jaws to snap through the interlocked wood strips and lashings. She, herself, had no real idea how long the hastily made barrier might really hold if they ever really tried to get in. It would certainly, she knew, last longer than the leather flap that'd been there before.

Beside her, the scrawny dog sighed deeply and closed its eyes again. The single dark circle around its one eye still stared back at her.

The girl smiled. It seemed, at least to the dog, that the wooden barrier would hold for awhile longer. She could no longer question his view on such things.

It was Rat Dog, after all, who'd somehow led them through the storm straight to the deserted camp. Who'd barked at the strangers as they chased after her into the woods, telling her exactly where they were as she made her escape. As if his single giant eye had led them. It was also he who'd chased away the wolves when the pack had first picked up her trail.

If only she'd had a whole strip of deer to reward him. Instead, she tried to share one of the salted fish strips she'd found hanging in the lodge. The dog had nosed the strip, then moved away, clearly declining its prize. "No wonder you're so skinny," she grumbled after it, taking the fish back for herself. The strips had proven stale and terrible, the worst thing she'd ever eaten, but she gnawed on it anyway to curb the ever-growing ache in her belly. Aside from the stale fish, she'd lived on nothing else but snow and some pine cone seeds for several days. It was no time to be particular.

She tapped at the fire with a branch to take her mind off food. Aware that the scratching sound outside her door had stopped. The flames, she imagined, floated just above the wood, like shafts of sunlight moving over the lake. She used the stick to make the individual flames dance and duck and recalled one of the dances the men had done at the last harvest gathering. One flame, which she imagined as her brother, moved onto the stick she was holding and then stood at the tip, blazing with life again.

A wolf outside gave a short howl. It had been one of the younger males, she decided. There were two of those. She'd heard such cries before, of course. Late at night, while laying on her mats beside her older sister with hides pulled up to their chins. They could often hear the wolves up in the hills, crying out to the moon, their wail carried across the whole world on the night's wind.

Her mother told her that some believed the wolves' howls were made by the voices of dead souls who still longed to return to earth. At the time, it had been the saddest sound the girl had ever heard. Now, the howls meant something else altogether.

Her father's people kept a winter camp just twenty miles down the river. There she might be safe. She could at least warn them of what had happened. That had been the last command of her father as he'd shoved the fire kit and a shawl into her arms and left to fight the others. Now that the storm had paused for a few hours, the only thing that stood between her and completing this duty were the wolves.

Sometimes, it almost seemed as if their howling was merely a challenge. Meant to tease her. Daring her to come outside and play in the snow for just a little while longer.

And, they were so very close.

The wolf. She imagined the great spirit of the tales sprinting between the mountains, his giant black paws barely touching the moonlit treetops.

The fire crackled, and the sound pulled her back to the wigwam. She dropped her stick into the fire then slowly nurtured the flames with more of the larger logs. The whole room reeked of pungent smoke now but she was glad of it. Where, before, the structure had struck her as cold and dead, it now smelled … *alive*.

Throughout, the dog slept in its tight ball. She'd come to envy his talent for sleeping through the howling wind and awful wolf calls. She, herself, had not stopped to sleep in two days. Not that she knew of, anyway. There were moments during her long trek that she now had no memory of.

Perhaps, she thought, that was for the best.

She reached for the post she'd found lashed over the doorway. Its tip would file away well enough against one of the large rocks which lined the fire pit. Soon, it would be a sharpened spear to replace her only other weapon, a branch she'd snapped off a tree two days before. She carefully worked the end against the top of the stone, her hands growing more flexible with each passing moment. She turned the developing spear again and filed along the other side for awhile.

While she worked, she pictured them. The wolves. The two younger males were medium grey and streaked heavily across their heads and backs in black. They'd spent the better part of the night scratching at the entrance and padding together around the four wigwams. The mother wolf was light grey and a head taller than a younger brown-haired female.

The last was the large male, pitch black from head to tail. When she'd last looked, he sat atop a short ridge just above the camp. A light snow had sprinkled its dark hair and built up along its haunches. Even from a distance, the girl thought, it looked as if he weighed as much as two grown men.

The five beasts had followed her from a distance for more than six miles before the two grey males charged straight at her. She'd lifted her sharp stick and shouted curses. No surprise that still they came.

The dog had appeared then.

From where, she didn't know. Later, she'd decide that he'd been following her for miles, or perhaps, that one of the gods had somehow dropped him gently down from the sky as a gift. Regardless, his shrill barks joined her own shouts and the wolves had dashed back deeper into the wood. She knew they preferred prey that could not fight back.

So, they simply followed her. Her and the dog. Even when the snowstorm had started, and through the flickering wall of never-ending snow flurries, she could still see them. The black one in the front, matching whatever pace she managed, with the others closely behind. Throughout, the pack had kept an even distance and followed.

They would wait.

In time, she would collapse in the snow. Too tired to take another step. *Why didn't I grab a pair of snowshoes?* Too cold to continue. In time, the dog would fall behind or get trapped in one of the many snow drifts they'd fought over. It was how wolves hunted.

Too bad for the wolves then, she smiled lightly, that she and the dog had found the camp. It was not her time. Not yet.

She turned the spear. "This," she warned the sleeping dog, "is how I shall hunt." Even as she'd spoken the words, they'd sounded foolish. Spear or not, she knew she was no match for five hungry wolves. Yet, she still continued to hone the point sharper while small puddles, where the ice had started to melt, spread under her boots. And, for the first time in two days, she could even feel her toes wiggling inside. At least, there was that.

She closed her eyes against the growing warmth of the fire. For a just a moment, it almost seemed as if she were sleeping …

The dog lifted its head suddenly with ears sprung high and straight, and she twisted around to follow his gaze, tightly gripping the makeshift spear in both hands.

The wall behind them rattled as if something had brushed against it. She, too, now heard the soft patter in the snow aside. One of the wolves rushing past. Rat Dog started to growl and she found it difficult to believe that such a low rattle was coming from that dog. Head lowered almost to the ground, his front teeth now bared.

The dog looked back to the barricade now. Then, to their right. Back to the entryway again. She saw that the fur on the back of his neck had lifted as he raised slowly up to all fours, and she followed his lead, moving into a crouch with the spear pointed at the barricade. Her knees ached with the movement. How long had she been sitting by the fire? It felt like years. Her shirt and leggings felt damp and raw and rubbed painfully against her chafed skin with each movement.

The wood blockade at the entrance shuddered with impact.

This was more than a test, she realized. This time, it was for real. The wolves could wait no longer.

The wolves were hungry.

Claws dug furiously at the door outside. Heavy dark wolf claws, sharp like obsidian daggers. She could hear the pieces splintering under the sudden and deliberate violence. The whole barricade shook under the weight of the thing digging at the other side. Her steps towards the entrance were slow and uneven. She felt as if her legs might just fall out from under her.

The whole wigwam had filled with the savage growls of the creature fighting to get inside and the dog barking roughly behind her. There was now a small split in the barricade, and a hideous snout pushed into the space and burst through the wood platform, shoving between the collapsing slots.

She stabbed out with her spear and it missed high. The barricade slew sideways, the braces she'd lodged in place slipping backwards. The girl threw her heel against the platform to hold it in place.

A second wolf appeared at her feet, shoulders and head pushing into the newly emerged gap. It snapped at her legs, and her pokes with the spear only seemed to enrage the beast more. Its head turned to face her directly and snarled with gaping jaws.

Forty-two teeth, she knew, and each and every one now glinted individually somehow in her mind. She counted a dozen at the front to cut into flesh. Four longer fangs, sharp and dripping with hunger, to pierce muscle and hold the prey. Still more lined the middle to slice and shear. Finally, framing the black shadow of its throat, she saw even more tiny daggers to grind and pulverize. It was a mouth designed for one purpose. To destroy and eat flesh.

She stabbed down and the spear struck. The beast yelped and withdrew from the opening. The first wolf, however, continued to struggle at the barricade where even more wood had already splintered away. The riddle of her refuge had now been solved.

The barrier would not hold.

In moments, the two wolves would be inside the hut. *To destroy and eat esh.* In the ever-widening opening, she could now see golden eyes shimmering with hunger in the firelight.

Fire!

What other choice was there now? The barricade was going down anyway …

The girl staggered back to the pit and grabbed hold of the first half-burnt log she could get her hand around.

The second wolf head reappeared in the gap. Its front paws were fully in the wigwam now.

Flames singed her skin, as she tossed the short log across the lodge where it landed just beneath the wood blockade. The wolf retreated again with a sharp growl. The Rat Dog cowered too, retreating for the first time to the opposite side of the wigwam.

She dropped her spear to grab two more burning logs and scrambled back to the door to lay them more carefully against the barrier. Flames rapidly curled up the blockade's side.

Her eyes stung as the lodge filled with smoke and the snarls on the opposite side grew more desperate.

The entryway caught fire.

She knew the entire hut would be in flames shortly. Or that the door would simply burn out. To gather a few more moments without being torn to pieces, that part had been well understood from the start. It was this next step that had been a little fuzzy ...

She coughed on the smoke that now completely filled the wigwam. The flames curled up the entire barricade now, spreading, licking the top of the entrance.

Her stinging eyes assessed the wigwam for the hundredth time. She could probably rip away some of the wood to break open a small outlet in the back. But, the wolves and all their eighty-some fangs would only be waiting for her on the other side as soon as she'd broken free. She looked where she'd torn up the flooring and the dark ground waiting beneath but knew it was far too late, the ground far too cold, to tunnel underneath. Finally, she looked up.

There, where the smoke clogged and gathered across in a spreading black veil across the ceiling, was the answer.

The smoke hole.

She could not even see it through the smoke anymore but knew it was there. Too small to push through, but she could tear away more of the ceiling and get up onto the roof of the wigwam. From there, she had no idea what she would do. She would be standing on the roof of a burning hut, surrounded by hungry wolves. Perhaps, then, she'd think of something.

Maybe a chance to warn her father's people as she'd been told to do. Maybe a chance to live ...

Remaining here, however, would only bring a fiery death. Or one in which the ravenous wolves burst through the burnt-out door at last.

Climb!

She picked up her spear and lifted to wedge it between two ceiling slots above. Then, it was up the short wall, clinging with her fingers and moccasined toes like some fantastic insect.

The branches and lashing grumbled and snapped beneath her weight. It hadn't been so cold, if the wood weren't frozen through, if she were anything more than a little girl, she imagined it just may have simply snapped and dropped her back to the ground.

The structure held, however, and she gradually pulled herself to the top. Jamming her toes in place and holding with her left hand, choking on smoke, she pulled apart the wood built around the hole atop.

Snow from the roof fell down the opening onto her face. Still, she tugged and ripped away more wood. Her fingers felt like stone.

The opening widened enough and she heaved and squirmed herself into it. Fresh cold air rushed across her face and mouth. Her head and shoulders broke free into the night, her hands grasping blindly about the snow-covered roof for some hold or leverage. Legs dangling in the center of the wigwam, she dug into the snow, ignoring the chill, and grabbed hold. Dragged herself completely through the hole at last.

She'd escaped and lay now atop the roof of the wigwam. The snow was cold and wet against her body and face. She reached back inside to retrieve the spear.

Then, through the smoke, she saw Rat Dog.

He waited just to the right of the fire pit, looking up at her. Ears sharp and high again, tail wagging as if the two were merely playing some kind of game.

"You …"

The dog barked at her.

What have I done?

"Come," she called out, and reached her free hand down to him. It barked again. Excited and pacing just beneath. Her hand dangling several feet from the floor, she knew she could not reach him. Nor drop down and lift him up.

Perhaps, she admitted, she'd known this even before she'd started climbing.

She rolled away from the opening and looked straight up at the swarm of gleaming stars above. Somewhere in the wood, one of the wolves howled into the night. She'd left him behind. Alone. Defenseless.

What have I done?

The girl rolled back and looked back down the smoke hole. As one, several wolves now answered the first call.

The dog blinked up at her. Barked. The entrance behind him had almost burned down now. Half of it was collapsed, the other half in short flames. If the wolves truly wanted to… If Rat Dog wanted to, he could brave the flames and probably burst safely through the entrance now.

"Run," she said. "Go on now."

It cocked its head as if trying to understand.

"You must go," she said. "Please."

The dog barked more furiously at her.

Her fingers curled painfully around the roof's snow and pushed it down at the dog. He recoiled a step. She squeezed more into a clump and tossed it more deliberately.

Rat Dog scooted away from the hole, skulked over with its tail between its legs.

"Go!" she now shouted. "Stupid dog! Go!"

She could hear the wolves again. Ever closer.

She broke away some bark from the roof. There was such pain with the motion, she wasn't sure of the cracking sound had been the wood or her own fingers. She threw the wood at the dog and struck him in the side. The smoke below gusted into her cold face.

"Stupid Rat Dog!" She threw more snow down at it, briefly recalled the other children doing the same. Once, long ago… *Rat Dog,*

Rat Dog, Stupid Rat Dog …

Tears crept down her face as the dog slunk for the door.

"There. Now run. Please…"

The door collapsed sideways in a burst of orange embers, flame and smoke. The very next moment, Rat Dog sped past it.

The girl gasped deeply, and rolled back over to face the stars. There, she quickly whispered a short prayer of thanks to her ancestors. Above the crackling fire below, she could hear the sound of large animals moving about the snow. She told herself that one of them was Rat Dog escaping into the woods and fought up to her hands to see.

Oh, no.

The spindly dog stood just a hundred paces from the lodge.

Around him, on all sides, prowled the wolves.

There were four of them, but the large black wolf was not among them. Or on his bluff.

Then where?

She assumed he was in the woods watching his family hunt. Or maybe even now watching her atop the roof. Waiting himself. For her to come down.

The wolves paced slowly, keeping an almost perfect circle around the dog. Rat Dog stood in the direct center, legs half lost in the snow, with his head down and back up, tail low.

As she watched, one of the young males lunged at the dog. Rat Dog charged back and both animals snarled and snapped jaws.

One, a voice she now recognized, yelped in agony.

She looked away. Began sliding down the back of the burning wigwam. With the wolves focused on the dog, it would be her only chance to escape. She landed with a soft thud in the snow, spear in hand. Behind her, the dark woods waited again. There, as long as the wolves did not pursue, she would follow the stream and reach her father's people by morning.

He, the scrawny thing the others had named for a rat, had somehow given her life once more.

More snarls and rumbles of beastly battle carried over the wigwam. She moved away from them and into the darkness.

But only for awhile. She had made her decision.

"Wolves," she shouted. Her voice was half lost against the blustering wind.

Rat Dog lay in the snow, struggling on its side away from the male wolf who stood over him. Both animals snapped and snarled furiously at the other. The snow was splashed with dark strains that were not shadow. She could see where the wolf had been bit.

And Rat Dog too.

"Wolves!" she shouted again.

This time, her voice carried well above the wind and all four beasts turned as one to stare at her.

"Get away from my dog."

The brown-haired female charged straight at her and she smashed her spear straight across its head.

The spear snapped in half. The wolf yelped and recoiled back towards the others, as the girl snatched the sharp end back from the snow and stumbled into the ring. The wolf there, the one that'd been attacking Rat Dog, jumped at her now. It snarled halfway, then tumbled over.

Rat Dog was latched to its chest. Biting at its neck.

The second male dashed at her now. Where she'd stumbled through the snow, tripping twice and moving slowly towards the ring as if walking in water, this wolf moved across the snow as if he'd been walking on hard dirt. His huge chest drove the snow aside with each step. Jaws snapping.

She stabbed at the beast. Her arm jerked back in agony as the wolf yowled and pushed past her. Pain ripped across her back, and she turned with the assault and swung out blindly. Something large slammed across her legs.

She lay a hand against his fur. "Hello, Rat Dog," she said, petting his side. He felt so cold.

The wolves had regrouped around them again.

"You are so very skinny," she told him, and stroked his side calmly.

The reflection from the fire behind the wolves cast their giant shadows across her and the dog. She could see where she'd hurt the one wolf. Stabbed it through the shoulder.

She stopped petting Rat Dog and now lifted her broken spear tip like a dagger. He'd somehow risen to its legs beside her. She could hear that his breath was labored and slow. The snow at her feet was red.

The two stood together when the wolves finally closed in.

Another shape moved into the clearing then. A shadow that stepped out of the night and joined the others.

The large male. Their chief.

He was the largest wolf she'd ever seen. The others paused their advance when he appeared, waiting again.

The wolf paced slowly towards them, his huge eyes glaring directly into hers. She knew the story of how one of the gods had once intended to turn all the animals into men but only one of the transformations had come about before he'd been stopped by the other gods. Only the wolf's eyes had been turned human.

She thought of this now as the great wolf stood among the others and stared at her. He was looking at her.

Really looking at her.

The way her father did when he was angry and thinking, and deciding some punishment, some scolding to give.

There was little doubt what punishment this sharp-fanged chief would give. Rat Dog growled at her side.

The two young males continued their advance to finish things at last. Then the black male rumbled deeply and they stopped. One, the one she'd cut, made as if to continue forward again.

The dark wolf's lips now curled back, showing the long fangs. Then it lifted its head, and howled.

The females joined in first. Then, the other male. The last had lowered his head and tail into the snow.

The black wolf looked at the two of them again. The girl and Rat Dog.

Then, he turned and trotted back slowly into the night. He vanished into the shadows as quickly as he had appeared.

The other wolves followed. All of them.

The girl stood alone with Rat Dog for some time in the snow. Afraid to move.

The two finished watching the wigwam burn while she listened to the wolves vanishing back into the woods from which they had first come. She could hear their fading howls lost into the night, and it was again the saddest sound she'd ever heard.

When morning came, the girl began walking again and the dog was close behind.

NOTES: *Evidence suggests dogs were first domesticated in East Asia, and that the very first people to enter North America brought their dogs with them. These dogs were considered part of the family and were given names based on their appearance, behaviors, or personality. Some excelled at hunting while others were excellent protectors. Before Europeans introduced the horse to North America, the dog was used as a method of transportation, pulling sleds, litters, and carrying heavy loads. When Native Americans left their homes to hunt, dogs would protect their wives, mothers, children, and even livestock. The dog's keen sense of smell was used for both hunting and to search and find missing persons. Many tribes believed that a dog with the markings of a circle around one eye had supernatural powers of sight and such dogs were considered quite special.*

THE THIRTY-FIRST TRIBE
1607

John Smith, the Englishman, was a moron.

There was, and it seemed increasingly so each passing day, no other way to explain it. *Any of it.* Though, Kekataugh and the other chiefs were still trying.

First, Smith and his people built their village on Shiwi's Toe, a godforsaken peninsula in the middle of the swampland halfway up the Powhatan River. A terrible place infested with countless mosquitoes and prone to flooding, so that it was very often an island. There was barely enough room for their small wooden "fort." The surrounding water was tidal, brackish, and undrinkable, and there wasn't enough game in the cursed place to support a small village for more than two weeks. Even the animals knew to keep away.

Not that more game would have mattered. Smith and the English preferred *trading* for their food. They rarely hunted or harvested it themselves. In a year, they'd planted almost no corn or beans despite having been shown how, but instead traded clothing and strong knives for it. And, ignoring the tremendous and obvious powers of their "muskets," these bizarre men also preferred to trade blankets and strange pots for their deer meat and fish. The blankets proved quite warm and sturdy and the pots never cracked in the fires, so Kekataugh wasn't complaining. Someday soon, they would even get the English to trade their magnificent guns for food. Soon. But, what was so puzzling was that the English did not seem to fear this dangerous dependence. Instead, they spent all their time looking for gold rocks and adding to the defenses of their fort.

And now this.

Smith was again demanding to speak directly with Wahunsenacawh. However, Smith was clearly the English tribe's war chief. A soldier. A foreigner. Still an enemy, officially. And certainly, despite the fact that they'd shockingly set their home in the middle of Powhatan territory, not part of the Powhatan confederation.

Not yet, anyway.

As such, the Englishman remained Opechancanough's responsibility. Not Wahunsenacawh's. War chiefs spoke to war chiefs and Wahunsenacawh spoke only to his own chiefs. It was as simple as that.

Kekataugh shook his head in frustration.

What was so difficult to understand?

"He will not speak with me anymore," Opechancanough continued to fume. "It is as before. 'Speak with Powhatan,' he says. 'Speak with Powhatan.'"

Powhatan was Wahunsenacawh's formal name passed down from their father and had become the collective name of all his people, a confederation of thirty distinctive tribes and some fifteen thousand people of which Wahunsenacawh was the ultimate ruler.

Opechancanough sneered. "The Englishman is like a child having a tantrum," he said.

Beside them, Wahunsenacawh chuckled darkly.

"Do you find this amusing?" Opechancanough snapped.

"Perhaps," the elder brother now glared in warning. "Did you respond to Smith as I ordered?"

Kekataugh hid his own smile. *Will that put our brother back into his place?*

Opechancanough glowered back, but indeed assumed a more respectful tone. "We explained to him, again, this can not be," he said. "But still he persists to speak to our 'emperor,' our 'king.' He says that is you."

"Then our words simply do not yet carry our true thoughts," Wahunsenacawh sighed. "You and I rule Tsenacommacah together, brother. Don't take Smith's misunderstanding for my own. We simply must learn more English to properly explain this to him."

"Or, he must learn more Algonquin," Opechancanough said.

Wahunsenacawh rubbed his head in thought. "Has Newport returned yet?"

"No, wise *Mamanatowick*."

Kakataugh shifted his glance to Opechancanough. His brother had used Wahunsenacawh's official title as the supreme chief of their confederacy. It had been a challenge.

"He has traveled once more back across the sea," Opechancanough continued. "And will surely return with more supplies and more white men when the winter has passed."

Newport was Captain Christopher Newport, the Englishman they'd determined as the colony's peace chief, the man Wahunsenacawh might eventually convince himself to speak to. Though, even that seemed absurdly far out of the norm. Wahunsenacawh ruled over domestic issues, matters involving his own people. Not those regarding foreigners.

Wahunsenacawh sighed loudly. "Suggestions?"

"Ignore the English," spoke up one of the other *weroances* gathered in the small lodge. "Half are already diseased and they can not even feed themselves. Let us stop trading them food, and they will not survive the winter."

"If not," another added, "Once they have finally convinced themselves there is no gold, they will depart as the Spanish before them."

"Kekataugh?" His brother turned directly to him. "You remain very quiet tonight. Like a turtle hiding in its shell."

"Move them, Powhatan," Kekataugh replied. "Beyond our territory, away from our beloved Tsenacommacah. Then, they are not on our land and become only another people on our borders."

"A fine idea, Kekataugh. You should have —"

"However…" he was forced to add. He could avoid the subject no longer.

"Go on."

Kekataugh recalled the image of "James City," its tall sharpened walls rooted in deep trenches and the high embankments found at each of the fort's three points where the cannons and English soldiers waited. It was a place built for war.

"Moving them may only delay matters," Kekataugh said. "The English have shown little regard yet for borders of any kind. They explore and move about as if all of Tsenacommacah and beyond is theirs. When they should be planting corn, they instead improve their fortifications."

"They fear the Spanish," Wahunsenacawh said. "Who are also *our* enemy."

"Perhaps, *Mamanatowick*," Kekataugh replied carefully. "But their cannons are not now pointed at King Philip of Spain. They are pointed only at Powhatan."

Wahunsenacawh nodded and turned to his other brother. "Opechancanough?"

"My counsel has not changed," Opechancanough replied slowly. "And it shall not, as I agree with Kekataugh's opinion of the English." His face glowed lean and dark in the small lodge's lone fire, and the eyes glistened like a hungry wolf in winter. Adding to the image, the encroaching winds even now howled and rattled just outside the lodge.

"You desire for us to attack them."

Now, it was Opechancanough's turn to smile. Again, Kekataugh, was reminded of a wolf.

"Attack them?" The war chief chuckled. "No, I never said 'attack.'" He looked about the others, slowing at Wahunsenacawh. "End them," he said. "Annihilate them. Drive the English back into the black sea from which they came and burn their city to the ground. Let the swamp reclaim the rest. And do so now, before it is too late."

I have heard this same speech before, Kekataugh thought. *Many years before. And now, those people are no more. Surely, there is another way. I know Wahunsenacawh is trying …*

"They are few," Wahunsenacawh said aloud. "Two hundred at most. There is always time for *that* choice."

"Not as much time as you may believe, dear brother. Newport will return again and again with others. Their monstrous boats hold hundreds, and they will continue to arrive like great waves until we are all drowned."

Wahunsenacawh waved the notion away. "They could have two thousand and we still have enough men to defeat them," he said.

Kekataugh knew his older brother was focusing only on the first half of Opechancanough's argument.

Waves and waves of boats probably sounded just fine to the great chief. Regardless of who was on them.

They needed the bodies.

Disease had recently claimed several thousand of their people, some deadly illness carried by the cursed Spaniards that had spread though the empire's southern villages. It would get worse before better. Then, there was the ongoing warfare with the Eries and Monacans. Horrible, costly hostilities that had stripped away a generation of their very best young men.

There are no empires of a hundred men, Opechancanough reminded them often, a speech their father had also been quite fond of. It took vast numbers of hunters and farmers, traders and warriors to sustain and protect their world. If they did not do something soon, what kind of world would the current Powhatan be leaving his sixty-odd sons? What kind of world would Kekataugh be leaving his own children?

The Englishmen, he knew his brother believed, might solve all of this.

They were dumb, but strong. Well-trained in military matters, their weapons unmatched in all the world. Their craftsmanship extraordinary. What a fine addition to the Powhatan confederacy they would one day make. What excellent allies.

Their thirty-first clan.

They would join as the others had before. Becoming a part of one great Powhatan nation. Then, together, they would all strike the Eries, then…

Kekataugh caught himself, lost in childish musings. He realized now how easily his older brother probably did the same.

Before any of that, though, they had to deal with Smith.

"My first desire," Wahunsenacawh said evenly as if reading his thoughts, "remains for us to have the English join our confederacy. If Opechancanough and Smith can not sort that matter out, we simply must find another way to make it happen. Do I speak with Newport when he returns? Do I agree to speak with Smith? This may simply be how the English do things?"

"Captain Newport will be gone at least until spring," Opechancanough said. "Our spies report that there are some in James City who believe he may never return at all."

"Then it must be Smith," Wahunsenacawh patting his knees in decision. "However, before I speak with him, we must adopt him in the old way. The Brothers' Call."

"Smith has killed our men," Opechancanough said.

"As we have killed some of his." Wahunsenacawh shrugged. "This is the way of strangers. Soon, he shall become one of us. Then, he may get his wish and speak to 'Powhatan,' and we shall be strangers no more."

"This is highly unusual, great *Mamanayowick*," one of the other chiefs warned.

Wahunsenacawh sighed. "I know, wise friend, I do. But not so different than other strangers we have invited into our confederacy, the other brothers we have made. And, these pale Englishman are different from the dark Spaniards who came before. They will stay. One dawn, one way or the other …" he paused, lost in thought. "Well, go now," he turned to Opechancanough. "Begin the honored ritual as soon as you can."

Opechancanough looked quickly about the rest of the lodge to see if anyone else would argue now that Wahunsenacawh had made his decision. His eyes lingered for an extra moment at Kekataugh, challenging him to speak out again.

Kekataugh merely stared back.

"At once, Powhatan." Opechancanough said, finally, and Kekataugh clearly heard the anger in his voice. Surely, the whole lodge did. "I shall, as always," he bowed slightly, to soften his voice or to add insult, "carry out the wishes of the *Mamanayowick*."

"Thank you, Opechancanough," Wahunsenacawh nodded back, ignoring the possibility that it was an insult. "Thank you, all," he said, and the bodies quickly filed out of the lodge into the frosty darkness outside.

"Kekataugh," the chief called after them.

He turned around, already half-bent to pass through the doorway, as Wahunsenacawh waved him back. Kekataugh studied his oldest brother carefully as he moved towards him.

Wahunsenacawh looked healthy, though rounded and softened some with the luxuries of power in the face and belly. A long deerskin coat adorned with shells hung over his shoulders, his deep chest covered in precious rocks and a golden cross given to him by Opechancanough from John Smith himself. The hair had greyed more in the last years, and his eyes grown a touch more weary. Likely more so to do with the hundred wives he'd selected over the years than anything. He looked, Kekataugh smiled at the thought, at long last like their father.

"Yes, Powhatan?" he said.

"I called you back as Wahunsenacawh, your brother, not as Powhatan, your ruler."

"Brother, then. How may I honor you?"

Wahunsenacawh smiled broadly, patted his shoulder. "I could always count on you, Kekataugh," he said. The smile suddenly vanished. "I want you to go with Opechancanough and the others. Stay with Smith through the ceremony."

"Do you think — "

"I need you to make sure nothing happens to the Englishman. Opechancanough has always had too much fire in his heart. He is a tremendous war chief, and I love him. But, it is not a war chief we need right now."

"Mother often said Opechancanough's real father was a badger."

"I don't doubt it. When Opechancanough has completed his part of the ceremony, I want you to take Smith yourself and show him all of Tsenacommacah. You, above all my brothers, love this land. I wish that he learn some of that affection through your eyes. Then, bring him here to me for the last rite. By then, he will surely understand. Perhaps, even Opechancanough will understand when he sees who I have chosen for the last."

"An important role, brother. May I ask to who you've granted this great honor?"

"John Smith shall soon become our newest brother," The chief smiled. "I was thinking, perhaps, it should be his youngest sister. Matoaka."

A "sister" who still plays as a little child, Kekataugh wanted to say. Doing handstands to make the English laugh and stealing small items from the fort for fun. Matoaka. My silly niece who is known only by her nickname of "playful one" has not yet matured enough for this great honor.

"I know what you're thinking, brother," Wahunsenacawh patted his shoulder. "But Matoaka behaves like a child only because I indulge her so. Letting her flit about all day long like a dark-eyed butterfly. I hope, one day she will play some small role in the story of our great empire."

"One day," Kekataugh nodded. "Perhaps."

"Regardless," his brother shrugged. "It is time for her to claim her true name Matoaka and leave the childish nickname behind like another discarded cocoon. No more do I want to hear the name Pocahontas."

The day was filled with *waiting*.

They'd first waited hours for Smith along the banks of the northern Chickahominy River, where he'd been spotted earlier in the week. The man often traveled in small parties far away from the protection of his James City fort. Rarely hunting, or gathering wood. But exploring. Making maps. Again, as if all of Tsenacommacah were already his to somehow record and organize. Kekataugh and the other men had followed the tracks of his small party easily in the light dusting of snow that'd fallen the night before, and then gotten ahead of the English up the river. The two Englishman were killed and Smith got off two shots from his guns before three men took hold of him. Luckily, no one else had been hurt. Smith's "capture" had gone smoothly enough.

Now Captain John Smith was lashed to a tree not fifty paces away. Waiting.

Waiting to be executed.

The cords wrapped tightly around his legs and chest. Another garroted around his forehead. Cold air puffing from out his hairy mouth with tiny bits of ice crusted in the coppery beard. He glared defiantly as Kekataugh kept aim with his bow.

Yet, there was just a trace of genuine panic in his eyes.

Did Smith not yet realize this was an act? Or was it something in Opechancanough's eyes that even Smith could see.

The possibility that it wasn't an act at all.

Kekataugh's bowstring trembled slightly, the arrow notched between his finger and thumb in the cold air. Tugging back at his arm, hinting to release. The arrow drawn full back and leveled at Smith's chest. The other two men at his side in the same draw.

Opechancanough stood just behind them, watching.

Waiting.

But waiting far too long, Kekataugh decided.

Waiting for something to go wrong, no doubt.

For someone's finger to grow cold in the winter wind. To slip. To send the honed arrow point straight into Smith's heart.

How simple that would be, Kekataugh thought. *Maybe Opechancanough was right. Maybe it would be best just to get rid of Smith here and now and then drive the English away and be done with the matter once and for all.* He glared back at the Englishman, sighting him just over the top feathered fletching. *No …*

Kekataugh glanced again towards his brother, hoping the look would nudge him to continue.

The scene was simple enough. Opechancanough was to stop them, find some reason to retract the execution. He'd certainly met with Smith enough times to think of something. Something personal, some symbolic gift or friendly exchange he could cite to repeal the punishment.

Still Opechancanough waited, simply staring coldly at the Englishman.

The other two warriors looked at Kekataugh now for some signal as to what they should do. *Had there been some kind of change in the plans? Were they actually to shoot now?* The one warrior at his right had drawn back a touch more, ready to do just that.

Enough!

Kekataugh lowered his own bow.

He heard Opechancanough huff in frustration just behind him. "Stop," he called out, his voice filled with scorn. "Lower … your bows."

He moved in directly beside Kekataugh and glared into his eyes for forcing him back into his role.

Glare all you want, Kekataugh thought. *For I have done as our brother asked.*

The other men had also now lowered their weapons.

"This man once gave me a gift," Opechancanough said, each word a biting jab. He lifted something for everyone to see. Something small and round that glittered in the sun.

"A 'compass,'" he said. "Which always points true."

Kekataugh glanced at one of the other scouts, saw the amusement in his eyes too. What a stupid gift! Why would anyone need a little box to remind you where north, south, east, and west were? Any child knew this. But, it was something. And the ritual was moving ahead again.

"He gave me this gift as a brother," Opechancanough continued, "And I accepted it from him as such. I can not …" He turned to Smith. "Allow any to kill my brother. I would …"

Kekataugh hid his smile. He knew the next words would not prove easy for his brother.

"I would rather," Opechancanough pushed himself ahead, "it was me … Tied to the tree before you than my brother." The last words came out in a single rushed breath but they'd been said.

Perhaps, Kekataugh thought, they should have been spoken in English.

For, as the men moved to untie him, Smith gaped at them all in disbelief as if an absolute miracle had happened.

Opechancanough stuffed the compass back away and marched into the forest where the others waited.

English or Algonquin. It mattered not now. Kekataugh sighed in relief.

The first part of the ritual was over.

For the next few days and nights, during the subsequent rites, Kekataugh only watched. But always close enough to keep an eye on Opechancanough.

Another escort of warriors, a group of three as the ritual required, had forced Smith through the southern woods to one of the tribe's larger hunting camps. There, for three nights, they all sat around the raging firelight, and Smith spoke of his old wars with the Spaniards. How he'd once fought for the king of a vast country called France and of his many travels across curious lands named Hungary and Africa. Lands of strange beasts and stranger men. While the other men listened with fascination, Kekataugh could tell his brother listened only for information. Opechancanough wanted to know more about Captain Smith, the warrior. As a future ally or enemy, Kekatuagh could not say. Throughout these days and nights, food was served to all and the other warriors dressed each night to complete one of the sacred dances of brotherhood.

On the third night, sitting around the fire again, Smith was accused of murder.

On cue, one of the older men leapt to his feet and angrily blamed Smith for killing his son. The warrior's face had been carefully painted hours before to portray the awful spirit of Vengeance as he waved his arms and stomped his feet in character. As Smith had indeed killed a few warriors over the months, it was possible, and the Englishman took the accusation as fact. He stood slowly when his accuser drew out the long ceremonial blade.

The other men crowded around them, forming the perfect circle, and Kekataugh pressed in closely behind them. It was another dangerous moment, he knew. If Opechancanough had somehow gotten to the warrior playing Vengeance, it would not take much. A slip of the wrist. A stumble. The man carried a dagger, while Smith had none.

Kekataugh found Opechancanough in the crowd, his brother's face half lost in the shadows cast by the others as they made room for the two men. His brother looked detached from the chaos before them, lost to his own thoughts. The terrifying hoots of thirty warriors now filled the star-scattered heavens. Vengeance shouted more threats and curses at Smith, who stood his ground, eyes wide again with alarm. He too, it seemed, now sensed the thin line they were suddenly upon.

"How much longer?" Kekataugh asked, moving beside him.

"This is out of my hands now, brother," Opechancanough said coldly.

The hunting camp was completely filled with Opechancanough's hand-chosen warriors. Those most loyal to the war chief. Men who'd likely been challenged by some of Smith's war stories. Men who'd bragged for months about someday attacking the English fort. Anything could happen…

"You understand that Powhatan, our chief and brother, expects to see Smith in Werowocomoco by the new moon," Kekataugh said quickly. "He has commanded it."

Opechancanough stared ahead, watching as Vengeance slashed his blade at Smith. "Powhatan," he said. "Expects many things that may never be. For he is a dreamer." He turned to Kekataugh. "And commanding from the world of dreams is a dangerous thing, brother. He is not the chief he was."

"No, he is not," Kekataugh agreed. "He has changed."

But for the better, Kekataugh told himself.

"Tell me, Kekataugh, do you believe, as he does, that the English will join our confederacy as the others have? Do you believe they can truly become Powhatan?"

Kekataugh thought of the other clans, many who'd been coerced into joining out of fear after one tribe was completely exterminated for refusing. *He has changed,* Kekataugh thought. *We have changed.*

"I don't know," he said slowly.

His brother laughed roughly, looked back into the fray. He made the signal then and it was over. The other warriors stepped in between Smith and Vengeance and declared their brotherhood with him.

The knife lowered, the staged accusation dropped.

"Take him then," Opechancanough said. "Show the Englishman his new empire." He moved away slowly, vanishing into the darkness.

Smith was now Kekataugh's.

The two traveled together for many days and nights, escorted by three warriors and stopping in a dozen different Powhatan villages. Smith was welcomed and fed at each. Gifts exchanged by both sides.

At each stop, Kekataugh drew Smith another map in the dirt, always revealing more of the land called Tsenacommacah.

He brought Smith to the great northern river and watched the cold morning mists curling along the deep embankments like armies of ghosts.

Then to the western foothills.

Throughout, he found the Englishman polite and quick. His command of the Algonquin language proved greater than Kekataugh had known. Kekataugh learned more of Smith's people. Their struggle across the sea and the problems in James City. His respect for Smith as a leader, holding such people together, had grown. Smith was a good man.

In the end, Kekataugh's maps included James City itself.

Another shining star in the firmament of Tsenacommacah.

Whether Smith truly understood the insinuation, the idea that, for the first time, the colony had formally been recognized by the Powhatan, Kekataugh did not know.

Finally, he brought him to the very boundaries of their empire and walked its outskirts for three more days. Scouts of their enemy, the Erie, no doubt watching carefully from afar.

The final night, he stood beside Smith and watched the sun setting over all of Tsenacommacah. He pointed to where the trees and rocks were tinged purple and crimson in the setting sun and several eagles soared between the shadows of dusk.

Smith nodded and smiled back.

We have changed, Kekataugh thought again.

Now, it was just up to a little girl to show them all how much.

Powhatan had been right about his daughter.

Matoaka was ready.

Kekataugh first led Smith before Powhatan in Werowocomoco, their capital city. There, his brother properly challenged Smith, cursed him in front of all the other chiefs. The two ceremonial stones were brought out and Smith laid across them with three warriors stepping in, clubs raised above his head.

Then, suddenly, Matoaka rushed from the crowd and threw herself over Smith's body to sacrifice herself in his place.

She played her part as well as any adult woman might have. Her lines said with such emotion and sincerity, Kekataugh had choked up with pride. A lovely scene.

How could he ever think of her again as "Pocahontas," the playful one?

When it was over, he congratulated the girl and moved on with the other men. In a lodge in the woods, some two hundred had already gathered to welcome Smith as their new brother, as Powhatan's son. The celebration would last another three days.

Kekataugh was painted completely black as the others, and stood apart in the darkness as the rest celebrated beside the fires.

His brother, the chief, found him there.

"Brother," Kekataugh clasped his arm, "Well met. Matoaka did very well tonight."

Wahunsenacawh smiled. "She did, didn't she? I can not think of her as a little girl anymore. Just tonight, she tells me of a young Patawomeck warrior who has caught her eye."

Kekataugh chuckled softly.

"Thank you, brother," Wahunsenacawh said, squeezing his arm for emphasis. "I am not sure we would be here tonight with Smith if Opechancanough had been left to his own. Though, I see you still do not believe adding this tribe to our empire is the best path?"

Kekataugh stared back, thinking. "I am trying," he said at last. "I am trying. Perhaps I can not dream as well as I should."

"It's easy," Wahunsenacawh replied. "Imagine a world in which our two people live peacefully beside each other. Working together. Where we are somehow united as one. That is what I do. If that makes me a dreamer, then... Well, come," he waved him back to the fires. "I'd like you to meet our new brother."

Kekataugh smiled. "I would like that."

"At least for tonight," Wahunsenacawh said. "We may all dream together."

NOTES: Only recently, based on other Powhatan traditions, have historians come to understand that the infamous abduction of Captain John Smith and ensuing actions of Pocahontas were most likely part of some elaborate ceremony adopting Smith and his people into the Powhatan confederacy. After the December ceremony, the Powhatan tribe lived in relative peace with the Jamestown colony for several years as the tribe provided more food in the first winter when the colony likely would have died out, and Captain Smith even arranged for several colonists to be adopted into nearby Powhatan villages to help solve food issues. By 1610, another four hundred Englishmen had arrived and disputes over land grew more common. The Powhatan could never understand why their own tribe was warring against them for territory, and why Jamestown (at first named James City) did not send regular tributes as the other thirty tribes did. Warriors were soon sent to punish the errant tribe, to remind them of their obligations to the rest of Tsenacommacah. When Wahunsenacawh died in 1618, Opechancanough assumed the role of paramount chief. In March 1622, Opechancanough's warriors killed more than three hundred colonists in the first strike of a war that was to last twenty-five years.

Opechancanough was captured and killed in 1649 and the Powhatan empire all but vanished.

Throughout the early years, Pocahontas's role as an envoy between the two cultures continued and developed, and several times, she played a principal role in negotiating various trade and military matters. Before her father died, Pocahontas (who was married to a Powhatan warrior at the time) was captured by the English, converted to the Anglican Church and was baptized as "the Lady Rebecca," and then married colonist leader John Rolfe in a diplomatic move arranged by her father and meant to end hostilities with the English. She traveled with Rolfe to England, where she became an instant celebrity in a public relations move to create interest in Jamestown and the New World. She died there in 1617 of disease. She and Rolfe had a son named Thomas, who returned to Virginia in the 1640s and became a successful tobacco farmer. The thirty-first tribe has thrived ever since.

WAR PAINT
1699

It had been a great honor to paint Chief Ozawakag's portrait.
The first time.

The eighth time, maybe not as much.

Tibikwábi kept his amusement at this truth well hidden while
the Frenchman, Alitouche, continued to work. He could see the quiet
desperation in his traveling mate's eyes, the frustration in his paint-stained
fingers as Alitouche dabbed with half-hearted energy at the latest canvas.
The Frenchman had hoped for a dozen paintings of the small village and
its people, not a four-day study of some chief's entire wardrobe.

Now, it seemed the only way to end matters without insulting the
tribe and risking their scalps was to either sneak out in the middle of the
night or simply wait for Ozawakag to run out of clothing.

Tibikwábi shook his head, and moved around to the other side of
the easel where he could better watch the Frenchman paint. It would
prove another long afternoon.

You'd think Alitouche would have learned after five weeks and a
dozen villages. Sauks, Ottawas, Shawnee.

All the buttons and needles and pots and shirts traded away already,
when all these people, especially the chiefs, really wanted from the white
stranger was a painted portrait they could keep and show others.

Or, *several* portraits.

Where other chiefs had merely grown disappointed and been
eventually appeased with more trinkets and etchings to keep for
themselves, Ozawakag had not graciously taken the hints that it was time

for Alitouche to move on. Instead, Ozawakag had gone into a half rage when Alitouche suggested, through Tibikwábi, that he'd like to paint something else. After shouting for awhile, the chief had even knocked the easel and paints to the ground, then stood over the Frenchman daring him to pick them up.

Tibikwábi had to give Alitouche this, however. The Frenchman understood exactly where he was. The apologies had been made very quickly, Tibikwábi speaking in Algonquin on behalf of the Frenchman, followed with a promise to do a few more painted portraits that the chief could keep himself. Ozawakag, himself, had then reset the easel and paints.

The chief now remained leaning against the rock with his chin thrust out proudly, face stern and hard, eyes peering thoughtfully over the forest. He'd put on a new jacket of multihued wolf hair, a silver-wrought dagger in a leather scabbard tied around his neck, hanging at the top of his chest. His grey hair was pulled back tightly and adorned in eagles' feathers. In his hands, he again held the British musket some trapper had once gifted him. For the first painting, it had been quite difficult to make him stand still, to accept that he needed to hold some sort of pose against the rock. Now, he stood as still as the rock itself, only occasionally casting satisfied glances at the other men standing around them and watching, and even then, only moving his eyeballs. As if he thought the finished picture would be better if he didn't once move.

Tibikwábi followed Alitouche's brush strokes, and watched carefully as the Frenchman mixed his colors, added shadow and depth to something that hadn't been there moments before. Its resemblance to Chief Ozawakag, as all the paintings before, was nothing short of breathtaking. As if suddenly looking at a perfect reflection against a still white lake. Or, even that Chief Ozawakag had somehow been shrunk and stepped onto the canvas. So perfect. You could almost reach into the painting and touch him. Truly magical. And, why many in the villages still refused to have their portraits drawn or painted, no matter how many blankets and steel daggers Alitouche offered.

Tibikwábi looked away over the rest of the gathering, and took in the men standing about with their war clubs and shining hatchets. A few carried old rifles. The paint across their own faces was the colors and lines of one thing.

War.

No wonder Chief Ozawakag was so easily agitated. His people now lived on the edge of what had become a budding and ever-widening war zone. Sioux to the west, French in the north, the English in the east. The entire area between them suddenly infested with a dozen tribes recently forced together into the same territory to align this way or that for space, hunting rights, and trading relations with the French or British.

To go into such a land, even as a neutral party, was still dangerous. Always. But, it was what Tibikwábi's own chief had requested of him. What the Frenchman had traded the rifles for. Now, Tibikwábi was responsible for the lives of five other men. Four of his own people, brother Huron, who'd been brought to bear the supplies, and Alitouche. Tibikwábi had almost convinced even himself that Huron neutrality in the matter, and friendship with many of the northwestern tribes, would see them all though the more dangerous areas the Frenchman wished to go.

"Into the wild," Alitouche had asked Tibikwábi's chief. "Take me where no white man has been before."

"Much war," the chief had warned.

Alitouche, Tibikwábi recalled well, had somehow seemed even more interested then.

To that end, their next stop was to be Fort Annecy, the last European outpost before the "wild" Alitouche wanted so much to see and paint. Beyond that, Tibikwábi was not entirely sure what they would find. More war, probably. That no white man had been there before? Tibikwábi was not sure there was such a place. The European trappers had been spotted further west and north than any man Tibikwábi knew. Always spreading out. Looking for new lands to hunt their beaver and building new forts to assist trade in the furs. Forts that now dotted the western lands. Wedged between the warring factions.

Perhaps, he thought, it would be best if they simply kept painting Chief Ozawakag until the promised four months were over and then he and the others could simply return home safely to their own families. He recognized the greater story lay west, but at what cost?

The Huron leaned back and thought on that while he watched Alitouche paint.

Later, when the sun dipped behind the western tree tops, the Frenchman nodded politely to Chief Ozawakag and stepped back from the painting. As before, the chief and the others quickly gathered around the picture and studied it, pointing and shaking their heads in solemn consideration. Ozawakag clearly remained somehow as excited about the process as he had the first time he'd seen it done. The others, a little less so each time. They too, it seemed, had seen enough.

Ozawakag patted Alitouche on the shoulder and smiled. Then he reached for the painting.

Alitouche placed his own hand over the top of the board to hold it still. "Please remind him," he said. "*Again* ... That the painting must dry over night and that he may have it in the morning."

Tibikwábi translated.

Ozawakag studied Alitouche, his smile already gone.

Alitouche stared back and Tibikwábi moved in closer to help avoid any misunderstanding. The other men, and their weapons, parted for his approach and Chief Ozawakag turned to look at him. He again eyed Tibikwábi from his boots to his hair, judging. His eyes had become dark and unreadable. Tibikwábi could have found more life out of the man's portrait.

"Tomorrow," the chief said at last in Algonquian. "Yes. Good. Tomorrow."

Ozawakag looked around the camp and suddenly reached out to grab hold of one of his men. The older man wore a deerskin jacket, beaded and laced, and Ozawakag now tugged meaningfully at the coat.

The man's eyes had grown wide with surprise, his mouth half open in unvoiced complaint as his chief wrestled the jacket from him.

"Tomorrow," Ozawakag said, turning back to Alitouche and fixing the jacket somewhat over his own shoulders as he tapped his own chest and the adorned coat. "Tomorrow," he smiled. Then he nodded and stalked away from the clearing, the others trailing closely behind.

"Tibikwábi," Alitouche collapsed back onto his stool and turned to him. "Am I understanding this right? He is now *borrowing* other men's clothes so that I may paint him in those?"

Tibikwábi nodded, unable now to hide his own smile. "You translate well."

"*Mon Dieu,*" Alitouche sighed. "I could paint this blasted man in my sleep."

"Not so loud," Tibikwábi warned. "He may ask it."

The Frenchman groaned, smiled, and slammed his paints box closed. "Can you sneak me out of here tonight? Safely?"

"Yes."

"Wonderful. At this point, I doubt I could bring myself to make even more one more sketch of Ozawakag," Alitouche began folding away his easel. "I think I'd rather paint the very Devil himself."

"Good," Tibikwábi nodded and picked up the Frenchman's box of paints. "Where we go," he said. "You might get the chance."

Fort Annecy, like many strongholds of its day or any other, was little more than a fortified trading post.

Here, men of many nations could trade their various wares — shirts, rifles, alcohol, hatchets — all the while continuing the flow of animal hides across the Atlantic. Black gold, the white fur trappers called it. Especially, the beaver pelts. Quite fashionable throughout Europe, and subsequently worth a fortune. The beaver pelts had become *the* currency and trade for the eastern tribes. Such commerce had become, Tibikwábi feared, the tribes' sole pursuit. Here, on the very boundary of the "wild" Alitouche wanted to see so badly.

Even now, several small tribes camped in hide tents just outside the fort. Some two hundred people. Mostly Ojibwa, a few Shawnee. Having already traded their season's catch to the fort inside, the men, women, and children now moved about together in the long shadow of the fort's walls seeking safety in numbers from the warring factions in the woods to the west. For, surrounding this practical business and trade, the fort's wood walls were still high and well manned with French rifles, its corners defended with numerous small cannons. Potential enemies, whether the British or some Indian nation, would pay dearly for any intrusion.

In the week they'd spent at the fort, Alitouche had added many paintings to his collection. Each morning, Tibikwábi would lead him outside the fort's gates to walk amongst the Indian camps. There, he would seek new images to capture.

For a single kettle, one Ojibwa father had permitted the Frenchman to paint a group portrait of his four children. In the painting, the smallest boy carried a small toy rifle one of the fort's soldier's had fashioned him.

Three steel knives afforded Alitouche the chance to paint two portraits of an Ojibwa woman holding her newborn baby. One cold morning, he'd simply painted an old dog curled and sleeping by a fire. Alitouche called the drawing a "still life" and Tibikwábi again marveled at how identical the final image was to the actual dog and flames.

Even now, Alitouche worked with "pastels," finishing the shading on several sketches he'd made earlier. There was the drawing of the bear cub they'd found trapped beneath a log on the riverbank. Tibikwábi smiled to think of the four men stumbling into the water to free the cub. Alitouche had almost washed away completely, but they found him sputtering and cursing downstream.

And then a portrait of Henri-Gustave Taschereau, a trapper out of Montreal they'd met who had a small lodge along Che'estaheh Creek, an Indian wife, and the strength to carry three ninety-pound bundles of fur at a time. The party had stayed with Taschereau for two days before moving on.

"You often put sun there," Tibikwábi said, pointing to indicate where the unseen light source must have been to produce such shadows on the woman's portrait. "To see her face?"

"Precisely," Tibikwábi turned, with an approving stare. "Don't want her lost in the shadows now, do we? Good eye, Tibikwábi." He tapped the picture, "Look here, where one might —"

"*Monsieur* Alitouche," a voice interrupted from the hallway behind them, and the two men turned to where Lieutenant Gaudet stood in the doorway. "How is our artist doing this evening?" he asked.

"Well, sir, I thank you," Alitouche looked up from his work. "Always kind of you to ask."

Gaudet was a small, dark, balding man and the commanding officer of the fort. The man who'd approved Alitouche's visit for a crate of rum and a promised portraiture, nodded, then glanced over Tibikwábi with a dismissive look as he approached the table. "What did you draw today?"

"Only a small cluster of tents, actually," Alitouche smiled. "Shawnee tents."

Lieutenant Gaudet lifted back one of the sheets. "May I?" he asked. Alitouche nodded. "My pleasure, Lieutenant."

The soldier quickly flipped through sheets, eyeing each one for only an instant. "Well," he said, "they look like Shawnee tents."

"*Merci*, sir."

Gaudet shook his head. "They really want to see this stuff back home, do they?"

"They go absolutely mad for it, Lieutenant," Alitouche leaned back. "My Parisian publisher plans to publish this book in Spain and Holland as well."

"With pictures of tents and men in deerskin jackets?" Gaudet smiled crudely. "But, you didn't come all this way just for that, did you, *Monsieur*? Bet some war shots would sell a fair share too, ain't that so?"

"All of Europe is fascinated with the New World and the peculiar natives who populate it." The painter ignored the barb. "They find these people quite interesting. In whatever human pursuit I happen to capture them."

"*Interesting*," Gaudet laughed, an angry sound. "Well then, they should visit us here some time. Find out how 'interesting' things really are."

"Yes, well," Alitouche shrugged. "Until that day, Lieutenant, these images will prove a practical substitute."

"I suppose." The soldier shuffled back through some of the sheets again. "Not quite sure what the fools find so bloody interesting though."

"It's simple really," Alitouche smiled. "They believe you're living in Eden."

"Eden?"

"The Garden of Eden. Or as close to as any man has known since Adam. Right here, today, is a new world as yet untouched, unspoiled, by the hands of man. That's what the people back home are fascinated by. Images from Eden. And, specifically," he tapped the portrait of the Ojibwa woman he'd been working on, "they wonder who are these unusual people that inhabit such a place? Are these 'Indians' truly the lost tribe of Israel? The survivors of fabled Atlantis, as many believe? Regardless," he said, studying his own work now, "they're clearly a people closer to nature, to the natural order of the world. To God's truest intentions. More than we, at any rate. Innocent of civilization's sins. 'Nature's gentlemen.' Magnificent in their simplicity. Like children. The 'noble savage' I've also heard them called."

"Well," Gaudet glanced at Tibikwábi again, then turned back to Alitouche. "Guess they got the savage part right anyway," he said. "These ain't nothing but bloodthirsty animals, Alitouche. All they know is war."

"Like the men of France and England, Lieutenant?" Alitouche asked, eyes wide in innocence.

Gaudet stiffened, eyes grown somehow darker. "I'll leave you 'gentlemen' to your affairs," he said.

When his steps vanished completely down the hall, Alitouche turned. "Sorry about that," he said, sorting his papers. "I'm sure he doesn't mean anything by it."

"Is that why you paint?" Tibikwábi asked, ignoring the unnecessary apology and falsehood. "To show others what you have seen?"

"In a way," Alitouche said. "You're a bit of an artist yourself, yes?" he asked. "The little symbols you make. I've seen you working on them here and there. Each one means something different, yes?"

"Yes. Put together and they tell a story of what has happened."

Alitouche nodded. "Yes, the neoclassicists are very into the symbolism too. Allegory. Allusions. Mythology. Telling stories. I'm more interested in capturing reality. So perfect that one could almost touch it. What the French call *trompe l'oeil*. The deception of the eye."

"Is that why you paint?"

"I suppose that's what it is. To capture something true to share with others. To make it as lifelike as possible. Which isn't easy." He flipped through some of his own drawings. "I studied the painting of still life, landscapes, and portraiture at the French Academy for years before I could get it right. Now, it is mostly just a matter of having the right paints on hand. That, and the drive to make the picture perfect. What is it? Why are you smiling?"

"Just different."

"How so?"

"My people. When we make art, it is never perfect."

"Well, you know, it takes years of study to — "

Tibikwábi laughed. "No. It not perfect because we make it so. Every piece, whether a blanket or shield, we deliberately make one thing wrong. One line crooked. One color out of place."

Alitouche frowned, intrigued. "Why?"

"Reminds us that we are men," Tibikwábi said. "Only the gods can make something perfect."

Alitouche considered the words, studied Tibikwábi for a moment before speaking again. "Why do you… 'make art'?" he asked.

"Big chief say, 'Go with Alitouche. Come back and tell us all what you do and see. Who you meet.' My images will do that. To show when we save bear cub, or when we meet the trapper Taschereau. They tell story."

The Frenchman nodded. "I must remember to learn these symbols before our time together is done. The folk back home would find these fascinating, I'm sure."

"Yes, *Monsieur.*"

"In the meantime, I best get back to work on these. Difficult to get the color just right, you know."

Tibikwábi nodded again and watched the man work.

It was another hour before they were again interrupted.

"Might want to grab that sketchpad of yours, Alitouche," Gaudet reappeared in the doorway, and called into the room. "Things are turning ugly in Eden."

Alitouche and Tibikwábi exchanged confused stares and moved after the retreating shape, though the Frenchman had indeed grabbed his sketchbook.

The commotion outside became apparent immediately. Its cause, took longer. All hands were on the top walls and at the cannons. Fur trappers scuttling to the safety of the inner shelters. The French soldiers lined against the ramparts, rifles aimed at the clamor washing over the high walls from the natives below.

Sporadic rifle fire from below.

And screams.

"What is this?" Alitouche asked. "Is the fort under attack?"

"Bunch of Iroquois in from the north," Gaudet replied pointing over the ramparts. "Must be two hundred warriors."

"*Les cieux et la terre!*" Alitouche gasped, his eyes widening with alarm. "Can the fort hold?"

"They're not attacking the fort," the lieutenant shook his head. "Not worth risking the beaver trade for that. We're their allies this year, remember?"

"They strike only their enemy," Tibikwábi said.

"The Ojibwa?" Alitouche rushed to the wall and peered down onto the scattered camps below. "The Shawnee?"

There, the massacre had already begun.

The Iroquois moved like smoke in and around the tents.

Clubs and steel hatchets. Cutting down the enemy.

Men and women. Those with weapons, and those begging for mercy. All ages. It mattered not.

Shawnee guns popping off in defense. Warriors trying to pull back together for a last stand. The resistance was too few, too late.

A hundred Ojibwa had gathered just outside Fort Annecy's gates, clustered no more than a hundred paces away and seeking refuge from the attack. Many of the Iroquois waited in the woods, waiting, it seemed, to see what the French soldiers would do.

"Open the gates!" Alitouche shouted, turning. "We can still save them. Quickly now!"

Gaudet simply stared over the battlefield below.

"Lieutenant," Alitouche grabbed his arm. "Surely, you — the Ojibwa and the Shawnee are our allies."

"As are the Iroquois, *Monsieur*," Gaudet turned to him. "As are the Iroquois."

A papoose yanked from the mother's back.

"Are you saying you'll do nothing then?"

"As we currently have alliances with all three tribes, we will remain neutral in this conflict. Those are the orders."

"Where is your honor, sir?"

Gaudet's face hardened even more, the eyes growing angry.

"Best get painting, Alitouche," he said, moving after some of his own men. "It won't be 'interesting' for long."

Alitouche started to argue, watched Gaudet's retreating back and then turned back to look over the massacre below. The Frenchman took hold of the splintered palisade to steady himself. Below, another tent burst into flames, the muffled cries from within thankfully carried away on the wind with the dark smoke.

"Please bring me my other pencils," Alitouche said suddenly, coldly, turning to Tibikwábi. "And more paper."

There was no emotion to be read on his face. It, itself, was like a blank canvas. Tibikwábi breathed deeply, considered the weariness in Alitouche's eyes, and then moved for the items. By the time he was back, Alitouche had already begun drawing.

One picture. Three. Then another.

Gaudet had been wrong about that. It wasn't over quickly. It went on for hours.

The Iroquois took their time.

Throughout, Alitouche continued to draw as quickly as he might. Not even thinking about what he was really seeing. Perhaps, Tibikwábi suspected, the Frenchman knew he would stop if he did. Instead, the white man simply captured the shapes, colors, and lines as he saw them. The last etchings were not even usable. It seemed that his hands had been shaking too badly.

As for the rest, when it was over, after the Iroquois vanished back into the woods, after the men from the fort slowly moved outside to burn the bodies, Alitouche had two dozen new pictures.

Alitouche now studied them at his desk, hands still trembling. It seemed to Tibikwábi, who stood just behind him, that the Frenchman's eyes were, for the first time, really taking in what it was he'd drawn. "The focal chapter of his future book," he predicted quietly as he worked, filling in his sketches with fresh paint. Though it did not sound as if he were particularly pleased by that realization. He told Tibikwábi he could imagine the title his editor would choose and even envision the words engraved over his rough sketches.

The Massacre at Fort Annecy.

"What do you think?" Alitouche's voice had been low and trembling. "Are they picture perfect?" he asked, though he would not look back.

"You will need more red paint," Tibikwábi said.

The ancient symbols covered both sides of the narrow gorge. They were of various shape, and colors, clumped closely together in some spots but also some higher and separate from the rest. A series of rotating hand prints. The profile of a hawk. Then several uneven squiggles dotted above and below. Most looked worn with age, the paints and dyes faded by the winds and rains and ten thousand new dawns. A few still shined more brightly on either side of the trail.

The graveyard lay just ahead.

The party had to march single file thru the slim pass towards it, with Tibikwábi leading in the front and Alitouche closely behind. The four other Huron followed with the supplies, items for trade, and two months' worth of the Frenchman's work. It was slow moving, but that didn't matter as the Frenchman kept stopping anyway to capture in his notebook whatever ancient symbol they were passing.

"That one is most like 'Morning Stars,'" Tibikwábi would translate for him. "That is 'butterfly.'" Their voices shattered the chasm's unnatural and eerie silence. Only the light high sound of some unseen wind twisting through the pass could they hear.

"This is clearly 'mountain', yes?" Alitouche asked, quickly scribbling the image into his own book. Working with Tibikwábi over the last few weeks, he'd come to learn many of the symbols in the Huron tribe. These, like many human symbols Alitouche explained, were not so dissimilar. Man's representation of his world somewhat universal, it seemed.

"Yes," Tibikwábi touched his hand against the faded shape. "Mountains. Many mountains. This mountain's rain clouds. Here," he pointed. "'Is Warding Off Evil Spirits.'" He studied the cluster of pictographs. "War, perhaps. Tells of a great battle with many men. The Wolf Army they were called. One great man led them."

"Who was he?"

Tibikwábi pointed to a square humanoid shape above the rest. "Yes. Tells he use a rattlesnake jaw to scare the evil away. Special jaw. Blessed by the gods. Many men die here."

"Who made these? Sioux?"

Tibikwábi turned and eyed the images on the wall behind them. "No," he said. "This near Sioux land, but this not Sioux place. Another people. Long before."

Alitouche nodded and made a note of it. "Why here?"

"Special place," Tibikwábi said, hurrying the Frenchman along. The sooner Alitouche saw his graveyard, the sooner they could all move on. A French trapper had told them of this place, as they were leaving Fort Annecy, and it had become their goal for a full week now. Tibikwábi knew they were close to Sioux territory now and not sure if his own people's ancient alliance with that nation would be recognized so far from home. "Very special here. The, ahhhh, what you call… 'Medicine man' come here. Many medicine man it looks. Many years. See things. Many things."

"Visions?"

Tibikwábi nodded. "What has happened. What will. Come here alone and spend days, weeks. Make tales forever. Sacred ground because it close to graves. Or, important to pass through. Part of journey."

Alitouche nodded politely, yet it was clear he still did not truly understand Tibikwábi's meaning. He looked over the pictographs again, and Tibikwábi could tell the Frenchman was even now chasing after their untold stories.

Something about small people. Little people the size of mice who lived in the hills. And another about a girl's journey to some kind of heaven and back. Alitouche's eyes raced over the seemingly endless stories.

"How many years?" he asked as if to himself. "How many men have climbed these heights to tell their tales?" More symbols. The woman, a queen it seemed, who was killed by a falling tree. A tale of eyeless ghosts …

"Alitouche."

Tibikwábi's voice must have shook him as much as someone grabbing him with both hands, for he actually jumped at the sound. The painter turned, seemed to realize for the first time he'd been lost somewhere. Somewhere, Tibikwábi suspected, beyond the chasm itself.

"We go now," Tibikwábi said, pointing past him and down the pass. "Must leave before it gets dark."

Alitouche took a deep breath, gathered himself back from wherever it was he'd been. "They're still not coming up?" he asked.

Tibikwábi looked back at the others, took in their faces, as they too eyed the symbols surrounding them. "No," he said, looking back to the Frenchman. "This special place. But not *our* place. They will wait here for us."

"Very well," Alitouche looked over the rest of the crew. "Us? I thought… You took me this far, Tibikwábi, and I know you did not want to do even that. You need not go a step further."

"I swore to my people, and to you, to be your guide, *Monsieur*. I will go on."

Alitouche smiled. "Thank you, Tibikwábi. We shall surely return by dusk."

"Yes," Tibikwábi, looked past him and up the narrow rise towards the burial ground, "I think that is good."

Alitouche held his next question, perhaps half-afraid of what Tibikwábi had truly meant, and grabbed hold of his paint box.

The path to the end proved steep and unsteady, and there was a small peak up top that dropped off some so that they could not see what was beyond. But Tibikwábi knew. He looked back once more to where the others had set down the provisions and found seats to wait for his eventual return. He and Alitouche took the final steps together to where the pathway opened up and led down.

The graveyard.

Small mounds scattered the landscape for a hundred paces in every direction. Rotted totems and posts, uneven and decayed, shepherded the graves. From each, hoary fetishes of bone and feather dangled as if frozen in time. Several posts were topped with skulls. The trees surrounding the dirt glade were slender, withered, and dark. Skeletal. The grass dotted and yellowed like a thousand rotted fingers reaching up from the earth.

Tibikwábi's body trembled some with the power of the place. He saw wolf skulls, shielding his eyes from the sun above and trying to focus on something that would settle his nerves. "We should go no closer," he warned.

He realized only then that he was alone, and turned. Alitouche had stopped several paces behind. Still frozen at the top of the bluff, staring out over the whole of the burial ground. His whole face was loose and sagging. Caught in wonder.

Tibikwábi looked over the grounds again. He'd seen such places before, but never one quite so ancient, so forgotten, so powerful. So terrifying and beautiful all at once. He could not even imagine what the Frenchman was feeling.

He urged Alitouche forward again, and the Frenchman looked back at him as if waking from a dream. He then came forward bit by bit with clumsy steps and slowly undid his easel. He set a fresh canvas in place. Fluttered the brush hairs between his fingers, began looking over the scene suddenly opened before him. "Here, for sure," he said, "is something no European has yet seen." He turned to Tibikwábi. "Certainly, not yet painted."

A single crow rested atop one of the tilted totems, its black eye glistening back at them as Alitouche turned and studied the bird. "Guardian of the dead," he said, "A perfect image to capture." He sketched the rough diagonals of the mountains behind. The sun against the bird's inky back as he used a pencil and made some faint lines on the board.

The wind whistled behind them, blowing up from the chasm, past the wall of symbols, and over the glade. Its icy touch grazed Tibikwábi's back as it passed. The crow lifted away suddenly, its caw echoing across the opening. The ancient bones rattled in the unseen wind.

Alitouche had drawn the first line, the lopsided post. Half-rotted away. The ancient mounds of a dozen forgotten warriors resting just beneath.

"Who were they?" he wondered aloud.

The silence around them suddenly so complete.

Menominee? Winnebago? Some more ancient people. Their voices, Tibikwábi now imagined. As if he could almost hear their dead speaking. The cold wind now creeping over his shoulders and running down his arms. He'd called the place *special* …

"*Maudire!*" Alitouche cursed.

The first painting was pulled aside, unfinished.

He started another.

One of the skeletal trees. A disjointed stone altar half built beneath. The sun's light cast a cruel red glow across the tops of the granite and Alitouche fumbled for the appropriate paints. He turned suddenly.

Tibikwábi had felt it too.

Someone watching. *No. Only your imagination.*

The thumping of his own heart filling the terrible silence. He stared ahead when Alitouche looked at him.

Alitouche looked over his subject again, made some more lines.

"No," he said, and pulled the next sheet away.

He sat at an empty easel, his hands folded against his chin in thought. Staring over the, now, seemingly endless graveyard.

"How?" he asked quietly.

"*Monsieur?*"

"How am I ..." He turned to Tibikwábi. His eyes were narrow in thought. "How in heaven's name am I to paint *this*? This place ... The thoughts in my head. My heart. I... How do I capture such a thing? There are no such colors in all the world."

Tibikwábi had no reply.

Alitouche nodded, searched back over the scattered mounds. "I should like to look at it for awhile longer if that's all right," he said. He'd folded his easel out of the way to see better. "Just for awhile."

They stood together that way for some time. Just looking.

When the totems' shadows grew long enough that they reached out towards the two men, Tibikwábi knew it was time to return to the others. Alitouche followed.

He'd painted nothing.

The two men left the graveyard together and moved slowly into the gorge, the setting sun casting red and orange against the painted walls as if small fires from long, long ago.

Down the pass, they found the others.

A dozen warriors, a clan Tibikwábi did not recognize, waited with them.

Their rifles and hatchets drawn. The faces streaked in the black-lined masks of war.

For just a moment, Tibikwábi imagined they were only ghosts, the Menominee wolf warriors of old, returned for one fleeting glimpse in the setting sun.

Then one of the "ghosts" aimed his rifle at them and shouted. And Tibikwábi knew they were real.

They'd been blindfolded and taken west, where they were imprisoned in the Sioux encampment for more than a week. Captives of a western tribe grown tired of increasing eastern infringements. A war camp, a hundred men and only a few women sent to guard its borders.

Alitouche was freed the first night.

After rummaging through his crates of art, and angrily demanding, through Tibikwábi, their tale and travels, the Sioux leader decided he was to go. The Sioux had no issue yet with the French, and wanted none either. One of the other Huron was selected to help him carry supplies and his paintings and find his way back to the fort. If he ever returned, they told him, the sentence would be quite different. This time, they said, he was no more than a child. He was innocent of his crime. The Huron, however, the Sioux chief explained with angry pointing and maps drawn in the dirt, knew better. Which left Tibikwábi and the other Huron in the hands of the Sioux, to be later adopted into the tribe or executed.

Alitouche, however, would not go. He traded away the rest of his goods for the freedom of the others. His pots and blankets and pins and buttons. All which the Sioux gladly accepted.

Two more men were released to join him.

For three days then, the Frenchman painted dozens of the men and willingly gifted the portraits to them as bounty for Tibikwábi and the other Huron. The Huron was freed.

Only Tibikwábi was to be kept prisoner now. The Sioux leader was almost smiling as he pronounced this final judgment.

Then, Alitouche understood. Tibikwábi saw the look in his eye when he had.

The last item left to barter.

The paintings. *His* paintings. The illustrations and canvases of a dozen eastern tribes.

Not a few pieces, but the whole lot.

Three months of work. Without it, Alitouche would return home with absolutely nothing. A failing that would likely end his career.

Later, at night, when it was quiet and he was left only to his own thoughts, perhaps, Tibikwábi thought, Alitouche would curse himself for taking even another minute to decide what he should do.

But he did take a minute, and, strangely, Tibikwábi found the delay almost agreeable. The final decision somehow more significant.

The exchange was made.

Now, Tibikwábi stood beside him again some five hundred miles away from the Sioux camp and back at his own village. Where their journey together had first begun. In the morning, the Frenchman would join a merchant convoy bound for Philadelphia. And then, the ship home to Paris.

Tibikwábi watched the Frenchman as Alitouche silently looked over the Huron encampment. Several fires warmed the camp in a golden glow that shimmered like the very sun itself.

"Quite beautiful," Alitouche turned. "Isn't it?"

Tibikwábi nodded. He felt the sudden urge to apologize again. He knew that it was for his life that Alitouche had given up everything. But in three weeks, the Frenchman would take no apologies.

"I make this," Tibikwábi said and held out his hand.

"What's that?" Alitouche moved closer and took the package. It was a bundle of hides as wide as his chest.

He looked at the top one. His eyes moved over the many symbols there. A dozen hides stacked together. Each one as covered as the next.

"The bear cubs," he read, then flipped to another. "Oh, yes," he smiled. "This was that great thunderstorm, yes? When Namakee ran about in the rain to make us laugh."

Tibikwábi nodded.

Alitouche's look grew distant. "The graveyard," he said, running his fingers over the painted lines. Then he laughed suddenly, "And, of course, our Sioux friends ... This is wonderful, Tibikwábi, truly. Your people will enjoy this for a hundred years."

"This yours," Tibikwábi said. "To take home."

"I couldn't. You — "

Something in Tibikwábi's look stopped him and Alitouche just dropped his head and smiled.

"Thank you," Alitouche said. He looked up at Tibikwábi. "Truly. Thank you for everything."

"You give to your publisher," Tibikwábi pressed. "Maybe he like." He knew it could never replace what Alitouche had lost to purchase his freedom.

"They'll love this," Alitouche said, holding the bundle to his chest. "They will. I shall put them right beside my paintings."

Tibikwábi's heart sunk in misery. "But..."

"New paintings," Alitouche said. "Ones I shall make on the boat ride home. Of our adventure here. Images of what I remember, what I saw. What I felt even, if such a thing is possible. I think now it is." He smiled. "That's what I'll show them." He looked back over the camp. "Even 'picture perfect' doesn't quite capture the real thing, does it?"

"No," Tibikwábi said. "But you will tell a good story."

"And if I have these," Alitouche asked, tapping the skins. "How will *you* tell your story."

"This mine," Tibikwábi grinned.

"What's that?"

Tibikwábi unrolled the canvas.

Alitouche stared at it for some time before speaking. "It's wonderful," he said. "You're a fine painter, Tibikwábi. Truly." He studied the painting again, then looked at him. "Again, *Monsieur*, I sincerely thank you."

Tibikwábi turned it to see himself.

Painted carefully over the canvas. A portrait of two men. Artists. A Huron and a Frenchman. Standing together.

Behind them, hints of the mountains of the west, the red sun of war, grey clouds and ravens, a river leading to the end of all time...

"What's that there? The break here in the river. Missing some paint."

"'Good eye,'" Tibikwábi said.

He studied the picture. "So it's not perfect."

"Yes. Man not perfect."

Alitouche smiled, put a hand on Tibikwábi's shoulder and looked over the whole of the Huron camp again. "But it's sure close," he said. "Isn't it?"

"Yes," Tibikwábi had to agree. "We're close."

NOTES: *Imagine the excitement and curiosity of finding humans alive on Mars today. This is how most Europeans saw the new world and the "strange" people who inhabited it. The appearance and lives of Native Americans quickly became a popular subject for artists and writers, and their publishers, in the "Old World." These men traveled about the various villages trading goods for the opportunity to collect a story or a few paintings to offer fellow Europeans a glimpse of the mysterious "savages" who lived across the sea. The idea of presenting the Indians as "noble savages" became a popular notion as, philosophically, European intellectuals on the verge of revolution grew more and more interested in the concept of god-made humanity freed from the man-made failings of civilization. To Europeans, Indians embodied the freedom and goodness God intended.*

The fur trade, supported almost exclusively by Indian hunters, had become a machine by 1700. So much so, that 75% of all pelts gathered in 1700 were actually burned to in ate prices in Europe. Companies were pulling in a 1000%

profit and nations such as England and France were soon depending on the trade to literally fund their wars. The most sought-after pelts were actually those that had already been worn and broken in by Indians. The combination of tent smoke, human sweat, and greasy fingers wiping off food always made the pelts soft and silky. Local tribes were recruited to provide the pelts in exchange for axes, guns, blankets, and brandy. The Indians hunted at night or in the early morning light with spears, snares, and pits.

SPIRIT OF THE LAKE
1758

Beneath a cloud-covered moon, the five canoes glided towards the unwary village like shadows drifting harmlessly across the lake's still black surface. Yet, each boat carried twenty Kanienkehaka warriors armed with spears and clubs. A hundred men sent to completely destroy the Erielhonan camp, to drive them once and for all from the lake's northern shores. More territory for their ever-growing empire.

"They call us the Mohawks," Tsokáwe had goaded his men earlier as they boarded the canoes. "The man-eaters."

Some of the warriors had chuckled, while others glared proudly at their war chief. Their enemies had given them the name as an insult, but the Kanienkehaka didn't mind. To suggest they actually ate their victims was offensive, but it also added to their already-fierce reputation. To that end, each of the men had also freshly shaved the sides of their heads, leaving only the center strip of hair, and painted their faces with red and black paint to look even more terrifying.

"Very well," Tsokáwe had lifted his massive war club. "Then if we are 'man-eaters,' let us feast well tonight." The men had cheered and hooted back as one in a cry that surely lifted all the way up to Grandmother Moon.

Now, Tsokáwe looked over the deep lake towards the Erielhonan camp and marked the faint telltale glow of several fires. It wouldn't be long now.

He wondered briefly how many of his men would be lost in the attack. How many new warriors they might seize. After the raid, many of the younger Erie men would be enslaved and later adopted into the Kanienkehaka tribe to help replenish its unceasing need for more warriors. The wars with the Huron and other tribes had been costly indeed. So many men lost already. *Perhaps we are "man-eaters" after all,* he grunted, pulling his jacket closer against the lake's cool air.

The boats advanced in the shape of an arrowhead, just as the geese do, his own canoe at the point with the others spaced and trailing closely behind. He turned back to inspect the others, and their painted faces made it look as if a hundred demons were staring straight back at him. Beneath the war paint, the men appeared just as anxious as he to get the night over with. It had been a long trip already, but the firelights dimly burning in the distance promised an end.

He heard something then, a splash of water somewhere in the darkness.

Muted voices suddenly broke out from one of the boats to his left, and he turned furiously at the sound. They'd traveled so long in almost perfect silence, it was absurd to destroy that now.

Two of the men had stopped rowing, and were pointing to the north. He followed their focus, but saw nothing along the dark lake. Tsokáwe held up a hand to stop the others and the five canoes immediately slowed into a silent glide. "What is it?" he hissed as the boats clustered together. "What did you see?"

"There was…" One of the pointing men shook his head.

"Speak!"

"There was something, something *strange* in the water." The man's eyes were wild, his face ashen in the half-light. Whispers broke out among the other canoes.

"*Tha'tesato tat!*" Tsokáwe commanded, and the men quieted immediately. "Strange how?"

"It was big," the other warrior said suddenly. "Moving just above the water. Something *alive*."

"Bigger than the canoes," the first answered Tsokáwe's next question before he could even ask it. "Two canoes."

Several of the men looked at each other and Tsokáwe warned them to stay quiet with his fiercest glare. *Bigger than two canoes? Each dugout was as long as six men.* His thoughts wrapped around the concept, even while he waved the men to start rowing again.

The group was well-trained, and each rower hit his mark at just the right moment using oars that'd been wrapped in old hides to dampen their sound. The boats were back to full speed in mere moments, their growing wakes vanishing quickly into the night. All the while, Tsokáwe watched the waterline to the north.

He'd heard stories, of course. Any of the People along the great lakes knew such tales. About things that still lived in the deep dark waters. Creeping and slithering along the lake's mucky floor, hiding in submerged caverns and lairs that existed long before man. A sudden chill slithered along his own back.

One of the men in Tsokáwe's canoe whispered quietly. An old prayer. Tsokáwe turned with the warrior's gaze and scanned the black water.

Onhka ki ken!

It, whatever it was, moved just beside him now.

Something very much alive. A dark shape that glided just beneath the water, dark enough that he could still see it racing along just outside the paddles within the canoe's wake.

Large. As wide as the boat, it seemed. Its black form ran as far as his eye could make out in the dark water. Tsokáwe wondered if it were only a cruel trick of the moon's shadows.

Then something lifted from the water.

As tall as any man and wider than the canoe. Tsokáwe could not tell what it was. The lake's water spilled off it, and its wake tipped the canoes.

Men started screaming then.

Tsokáwe noticed another shape lifting beside the second canoe. Then another. The same as the first. Other creatures! Whatever they were.

No, he realized with his next thought. *It was all just more of the same creature.*

The shapes suddenly vanished again.

Reappeared. Vanished. Dipped. Undulating in the water like living waves. In the broken moonlight, as the thing vanished again, Tsokáwe saw what looked like scales.

The canoes had long ago broken their arrow pattern. One now dropped far back from the others. It spun freely in the moonlight, already half-lost to the night. Its leader and crew all shouting commands and curses at one another.

Then the three massive shapes disappeared all at once and Tsokáwe's canoe rocked sideways, threatening to flip, as the men fought to hold the boat from tipping completely and icy cold water splashed over the side. Fingers gripped tightly to the boat, Tsokáwe realized he'd dropped his war club.

He looked back, and saw that the trailing canoe had started moving again, a few of the warriors managing to straighten it out again amid the commotion. *Yes,* he thought. *Now we will reorganize and get moving again.*

Something lifted from the water just behind them.

The enormous splash blotted out its true shape. It rose higher and higher with each moment until Tsokáwe thought its head would block the very moon. The men in the boat scrambled and fought to move away, and the canoe rocked as several men spilled into the frothing black water.

Then the shape dropped.

The boat and all its remaining warriors vanished in an explosion of water. Its huge wake rolled towards them out of the darkness. Whirling the boats, heaving them sideways.

Chabos swept the remaining canoes.

The men, battle-heartened Kanienkehaka warriors, the dreaded "man-eaters," were screaming and splashing about like Algonquin children. Though several arrows and spears were flung into the night at the giant shape, most men simply fought for the oars and shouted directions and curses. Amid all the tipping and shoving, several more warriors had already tumbled into the dark cold water.

A second canoe tipped over.

Scanning the shape, Tsokáwe saw what looked like a tail. A giant serpent's tail lifting from the water just past the capsized canoe. He heard his warriors calling out in the darkness. Lost somewhere in the water… With the thing.

Then silence.

"Row," he shouted hoarsely at his own men, pushing at the man just in front, and his own canoe slowly pulled ahead in the suddenly rolling water. One man, a warrior who'd stood to fling his spear, pitched over the side.

Something appeared beside them. One of the great shapes rising again from the water. Curved. Vanishing again. Running just beside the fleeing boat. Another spear jabbed out at the thing.

It shifted towards the boat, not away, and the swell knocked the canoe sideways, keeling it over sharply. Tsokáwe and the others leaned back against the turn, righting the boat. Then something slammed into the canoe. Something so large, the wood side actually split. A sharp cracking sound rang out just over their screams as the boat overturned and the men spilled into the water.

Blackness.

Tsokáwe fought back to the surface, choked out the icy water. His leggings and jacket were heavy with water, as he surveyed what remained of his war party.

Another canoe floated past.

Completely empty. Not a single man aboard anymore. As if something had leapt out of the night and just snatched them all away.

Tsokáwe told himself that the canoe had merely tipped and then turned back over, righting itself.

The last canoe of the mighty Kanienkehaka raced into the night, east, away from the Erielhonan camp. Shouts and curses trailed after its puny wake as Tsokáwe watched it vanish.

The shape suddenly lifted again in the space between them.

Massive and blacker than either the night or the water. Rising from the lake and racing directly towards him at a speed he'd not thought possible.

It moved at last into a patch of moonlight. Dripping in deep dark waters. Water from submerged caverns and lairs that existed long before man. He also saw the gleam of two enormous blood-red eyes.

And then, Tsokáwe realized exactly what he was looking at.

A man-eater.

The two boys, Tio and Tawit, waited just outside the chief's long house. They crouched comfortably in its shade with their backs against one of the long elm bark walls, half listening to the deep muffled voices on the other side, while the rest of their village went about its daily matters.

Mothers and daughters tended to the late summer beans and squash. Some cooked stews and cornbread in the village's two stone hearths, others stitched new leather shirts and leggings. Small girls cleaned wild berries or simply played with their cornhusk dolls. Several of the older men were working on a new dugout canoe, gutting the huge log with fire and short axes. Another group worked on one of the dozen longhouses in the village, as a leak in the roof had recently brought rain upon forty-some Kanienkehaka residents.

The last group was the boys. Except for Tio and Tawit, they'd all gathered around the small troop of warriors and listened while they reworked stories of the various battles and plans. Several tribal warriors had returned only the night before to collect recruits for another campaign.

One of them, the same man the two boys now waited for, had not been back to their village in seven years.

Karhakon.

He wasn't even a memory to the two boys, who'd only seen three summers when he'd left the village. But they knew the stories. They'd heard of his feats in the wars and how he'd once single-handedly saved Chief Maiis from Huron assassins.

They knew, too, that he'd been the village's greatest warrior. That no man had run faster or thrown a spear further and with more accuracy. Tio's grandmother told them once that Karhakon had won every game of skill as a child. That he'd even wrestled a bear once just for fun.

They'd seen him in the morning and though he was not as large as two men, as some had claimed, he was indeed everything they'd hoped to see. He stood taller than the rest, for one, and walked with a purpose and strength the boys had not yet met elsewhere in the village. His jaw and face were sharp and hard, arms taut and muscled. He carried an axe at his belt, dagger, and a long rifle from the English.

They followed until he vanished into the chief's house and then set watch. Maybe, eventually, they hoped to speak with him. He'd been with the chief for the better part of the morning.

When he finally emerged, the two boys leapt to their feet again. The warrior turned and tossed them a curious glance. His eyes were as sharp and hard as his face. Like a hawk. He nodded, then dismissed them. Kept moving quickly away from the chief's home.

Tio and Tawit chased after, making sure to keep a safe distance behind. If he knew they were there, or cared, he made no sign of it. He simply kept moving across the camp.

Two of the younger men had broken away from the other boys, Tio noticed, jogging over to intersect the older warrior's intended path.

"Karhakon!" the one called out, the young warrior's head newly shaven clean on both sides and the center strip adorned with two newly stained eagle feathers.

Karhakon bowed politely but kept moving.

"Karhakon," the one held a hand out to stop him. "We've been waiting to see you. Do you remember us?"

The older man studied their faces, thought. "You are Ohonte's son, yes? Onowa, is it?"

"Yes," the young warrior smiled, tapping his friend.

"You have his eyes. And you are Sawatis if I remember, yes?" Karhakon said to the other, who nodded. "I am sorry, men. It has been some time since I have been home. You have grown strong indeed."

The two laughed as if the compliment were funny. "Seven years," Onowa said. "You haven't been back in seven years."

"Seven years," Karhakon echoed. "Long."

"We are to join a Mohawk war party in Albany," Onowa said. Tio noticed that the young warrior had actually stood taller and puffed out his chest some when he'd said it too. "We will be two hundred warriors strong."

Karhakon only nodded.

"To kill Algonquin. And the beastly French."

The older warrior grunted something no one heard.

"What was that?" Sawatis asked, eyes narrowing.

"I pray you return home soon," Karhakon said, then lowered his head to move away.

"I heard you killed twenty men in a single fight up Lake George. Is that true?"

Karhakon stopped and stared hard at the younger man. Shook his head. "I don't…"

"I didn't think so," Sawatis grinned. "But tell us this. Heard you're meant to battle the *mishipishu?*"

"The 'water panther,'" the other warrior smiled, enjoying the joke.

"Some say it killed a band of warriors. That it crawled ashore and ate an entire village."

"Well, old women and children say it, anyway," his friend amended.

"And now you'll hunt this most mighty of beasts? Our most decorated warrior, the mighty Karhakon, against a children's story," Sawatis pushed. "Surely you know this."

Karhakon seemed to look past them to watch the rest of the camp. "It is our chief's wish," he said at last. "Long ago, I swore to him to protect our village."

"Against imagined enemies in a lake?" Sawatis scoffed.

Karhakon laughed then, and turned back toward the young, brazen warriors. The sound was somehow scary and Tio noticed that the other two had backed a step away. "Friend," Karhakon said quietly as he stepped towards them, a head taller for sure. "Imagined enemies are found in many places."

The two younger men had frozen, eyes cast downward, unable to meet his direct gaze. Karhakon loomed before them for a moment, waited. Inspected their weapons and bead work. Breathed deeply. Then, turned to leave. "I pray you return home soon," he said again. "*O'nen.*"

He marched across the camp, Tio and Tawit close behind.

To hunt the water panther.

The net was stuck again.

Sawen tugged at it, her arms already sore from the day's work. Water up to her waist, she looked up towards Teres who tended their catch. Four baskets of fish. Teres was lost in her own chores and Sawen knew, as usual, there'd be no help there.

Always on the last cast, she mused. *How the gods enjoy to tease.*

She stepped deeper into the lake's dark water.

Bending and stretching her arms far out, she jerked at the net again to free it. Most of the large net was spread wide and lost beneath the black water. Holding taut. Stuck on one of the submerged logs again. The lake's floor was packed with them.

The water lapped up against her chest now. She cursed angrily and pulled again. Harder than before.

The net yanked back suddenly. *Away from her.*

Almost as if something had tugged back.

She checked the wind along the lake. Only a low wrinkle rolled back towards her. The setting sun cast red and gold shadows over the the water's rippling surface.

The net wrenched back again. Stronger, this time. Enough to burn her deeply calloused fingers.

A great turtle, she thought. She'd seen one as large as a full-grown man before. If this was one, it would no doubt bite through the net and swim away. Then, she'd be up all night mending the tear.

She moved sideways, keeping pace with whatever was holding the net and latched the heavy cords over her shoulder, walking back slowly with stiffened legs. The net grew taught again.

Yanked suddenly.

Sawen spilled head first into the water. Felt her whole body being drawn out towards the lake.

She sprang to the surface. Gasped for air.

"Teres!" she shouted. The shout came out garbled and full of water.

She touched something. A giant log, perhaps.

No. It felt alive and slick. Something just beneath in the water. It shifted away from her. Slid away. She splashed face first into the water again.

She'd let go of the net, fought away from whatever it was. Her screams were wet and lost in her own frantic splashings.

She saw Teres on the shoreline, then. She, too, was shouting and waving her arms frantically.

Sawen felt another tug. This one, below the water.

Her leg. Snatched up by whatever…

It was the net. Her foot was tangled in it somewhere beneath the water. She shook her leg but it held tight. Her hands fumbled below to pull free.

Sawen now realized she could not touch the bottom.

It, whatever it was, had dragged her out even further. The water now ran over her shoulders. She turned, struggling to untangle her leg.

And that's when she saw it. Moving in the water. Lifting above her, half lost in both the net and shadows of dusk.

A flipper, she thought. Just like a turtle's.

A turtle larger than ten men.

It vanished beneath the water again, pulling down the net with it.

Pulling down Sawen too.

As the cold water covered her head, she told herself the gods were only teasing.

Karhakon stood in the shadows and surveyed the lake again. Its black and blue current rippled for as far as his eye could see, the other side lost to the horizon and clouds while a pair of hawks now swooped and played in the spaces between. The sound of a small current continued to lap quietly against the shoreline. There, at the water's edge, where he'd tied it to a fallen tree earlier in the morning, a basket of living fish jumped and splashed.

It had been several hours already and the bait had produced nothing. Not even a curious turtle or bobcat. In fact, except for the fish, Karhakon hadn't seen another animal at all.

Almost as if the place were truly cursed.

He'd learned that no one would clean or fish in the spot anymore.

That it had been shunned for many years.

He looked back to where the two boys hovered. Tio and Tawit. The two who'd followed him since his first day back.

How long had it been now? Two weeks? Four? Wandering about the woods to collect tall tales from others or canoeing almost aimlessly into the night to toss bloody bait into the lake. He'd collected most of the rumors from the tribes up north. A giant snake with a tail a hundred men long. Jagged back. This hunter vanished, that boat mysteriously overturned. The face of a cougar with huge whiskers and teeth. A swimming deer suddenly pulled beneath the black water in a single splash.

A nightmare.

Yet, he was the Mohawk warrior dispatched by his chief to drive off the nightmare.

No more foolish than any other mission, Karhakon supposed. *And, at least, this time, I am home. Back in the land where I was born, the land of my own people.*

He waved the boys forward.

"Nothing?" Tio, the smaller of the two boys, reached him first at a run.

The warrior shook his head.

"Will it ever take the bait?"

"I don't know," Karhakon sat down, keeping his eyes on the basket. "I suppose that depends on what *it* really is? One woman told me it's only a ghost. Others that it lives in the trees and comes down into the water each night."

"Do you really believe that?" Tawit asked.

"It's possible." He took a rock from the ground and turned it in his hand, thinking. "My father taught me it was the lake's guardian spirit. That it protected the water and its people."

"The *mishipishu.*" The boy looked out at the water and nodded.

"Yes."

"You are not afraid."

"No."

"Have you ever been, Karhakon?"

"Many times," he said and smiled. He then tossed the rock out into the lake and watched as the small splash rippled out like a growing spider web.

The three sat in silence for awhile while the basket of fish sputtered and bobbed lazily along the shoreline.

"What are they like?"

"Who?" Karhakon knew who he meant but waited. It had been one of the first things they'd wanted to know about once they'd worked up the nerve to speak to him. And, he remembered having the exact same questions twenty years before. "The English? They are men, like the French or the Erielhonan." He turned to look at the boy. "Like us."

"But we are stronger, yes? They fear the fierce Mohawk."

Karhakon shrugged. He thought of telling the two boys how the Mohawk massacred an entire village of Shawnee in a single morning. Or, perhaps, how he'd once joined some two thousand Mohawk and Iroquois braves in New York to meet their English allies. The pipes passed and the various war chiefs and tribes praised for days with many promises of great bravery and even greater victories made by all. And, when the day came to march to war, only three hundred braves appeared. He thought of telling them how the tall young English war chief called Washington did not trust his Iroquois brothers, thought them undependable. "They fear only the French," he replied. "The Mohawk to them are only more bodies that might one day join the French."

"As our brothers in the north did."

"Yes."

"Did you fight our brothers, too?"

"Yes."

The boy held his next question, realizing Karhakon had grown half lost in thought.

Karhakon stood slowly and brushed off his leggings. "We have destroyed many tribes," he said. "Our vast 'Iroquois Nation.'" He looked at the two boys. "For trade. And more power. And for the land itself. The French make false promises to the Huron and Ojibwas, Shawnee and the northern Iroquois. The British do the same. But, they are only men," he smiled. "Like us."

"Why must we fight then?" Tio asked carefully.

"The world has grown too small." He turned and looked out over the lake. "For all of us, it seems." He stepped towards the village and motioned for them to follow.

Had the boys looked back, they too might have noticed that the basket of fish was gone.

Karhakon drew the paddle slowly as his canoe drifted casually towards even darker patches of night. The seemingly infinite blackness stretched now in all directions, no land for miles on any bearing. The lake's surface gleamed an inky black below and, from the sides, the night circled and pressed like a living enemy. Above, even the stars were now lost to shadowed clouds. It was almost as if he and the canoe were simply floating in nothingness.

Only a lone torch, one he'd secured earlier to the bow of the canoe, provided some semblance of reality. Something his eyes and mind could cling to in the dreadful dark void that the lake had become. Its glow cast out in a circular flush of red-streaked gold that lit the front of the canoe but was quickly swallowed by the darkness much beyond.

Though he dragged two turkey carcasses from the back of the canoe again, trailing behind and below from rope, it was the light he most saw as the true bait.

Or, rather, himself. *Like a basket of fish.*

For several nights now, he'd paddled about the lake with his torchlight hoping to catch the creature's attention.

If there even was such a creature.

He'd spent the hours each night floating alone, thinking. About the last seven years. And, about what his father had told him about the water spirit. Wondering what would happen if his plan worked. He'd been much more concerned about less supernatural enemies. A wide patrol of Huron, perhaps, though none had ventured forth to challenge him.

Karhakon pulled in the paddle and placed it on the floor of the canoe. As the canoe continued to drift forward slowly, he stretched out the kink in his back, then reached into his pouch for his dinner.

The boys had packed him dried berries again. And several strips of salted fish. He looked back to where they waited and found only more blackness.

Tio and Tawit.

Karhakon smiled. He knew they would both wait until he returned many hours later. Then, the two would help him drag the canoe ashore, and walk with him all the way back to the village carrying the various ropes and weapons. His two "water-panther" hunters. Fine boys who would make fine Kanienkehaka warriors some day.

The smile faded, and Karhakon refolded his pouch. *Warriors.* He shook his head and grabbed for the paddle to drop it back into the dark lake.

His hand somehow latched around the spear instead.

He felt the handle, worn from many years of use. Feeling, not the first time, that he was only an invader.

The light wind had pulled the clouds away, and the moon's light flushed the lake's surface in blue. He cast his thoughts and gaze over the whole of the lake for the first time in hours. Still, he could not see its end.

Mishipishu. Water panther. A giant snake. It mattered not.

This lake was the creature's home.

Yet, he'd been sent to attack it as an enemy. To drive it away for the sake of his own people's needs. Just as he'd been sent many times before to drive out the Wampinoag, the Luluwalha, or the Huron. As the English and French had driven away the Mohawk. In the end, there was no difference. It was all simply a matter of territory.

The water panther and the Kanienkehaka had shared the space before. But, somewhere along the way, things had changed. It was no longer how the Kanienkehaka, the Mohawk, looked at land. Land was no longer to be shared, it was to be owned. Defended. Fought for.

The world had grown too small.

He pulled his hand back slowly, then reached again for the paddle. Dropped it back into the water and began pulling hard to circle the canoe. Back around towards the village.

The canoe shifted with his effort, quickly alternating the side of his strokes, and he soon had it moving at a fine speed again. He looked ahead as the water broke away from the bow, the lines of its wake racing away into the dark.

He'd lifted the paddle again and was just about to drop it to the other side when he heard the splash.

It had come from the darkness to his right. Maybe a hundred paces away.

It hadn't been a particularly loud splash. But something had surely broken free from the lake's depths and submerged again.

Something quite large.

Large enough that the ripple quickly escaped out of the darkness and struck the side of his boat.

The canoe tilted slightly with the sudden swell, but Karhakon pushed through it and continued on his original course. He eyed his long rifle, which lay ahead in the canoe some.

Another splash from the right and his head turned with the sound just as cold water spotted across his face and arm.

Whatever it was, it was closer.

He scanned the surface. In the newly freed moonlight, the water wrinkled in sharp distorted shades of blue and shadow. And, just beneath, a far darker shadows moved beneath his canoe.

Just beneath the surface, a mere arm's length away. It ran the whole length of the boat, at least as far as he could see in the dark, and was wider than the canoe.

It moved beneath the rippling shadows like a snake, winding back and forth in slow fluid movements that carried the dark shape past the canoe in mere seconds. Large bubbles gurgled up to the surface as it passed. Karhakon had carefully pulled in his oar.

It passed underneath, the length of three canoes before its massive outline, what must have been its main body, moved directly beneath the canoe and seemed to fill the entire lake.

The boat heaved on an unnatural swell that lifted straight up on a burst of froth. Karhakon had lifted to one knee with his long rifle in hand. Tracking the shape as it passed completely beneath the boat and kept moving forward into the night.

A single form lifted from the water, breaking the surface for a moment only.

The body continued another twenty counts, then tapered off again into a long thin snake shape. Its tail, he realized. The thing had vanished again in the night.

Karhakon was glad of it. His canoe had spun to a halt and he scuttled forward to douse the torch secured to the front of his canoe. He no longer wanted to be the bait. He did not reach the torch.

Just ahead of the canoe, a shape suddenly broke the surface. Lost somewhere between the torch light, shadows, and moon, it rose from the dark waters, dripping in water a million years old. He saw a rounded, gigantic horselike head. In the moonlight, yellow eyes flashed above a wide grinning snout.

His rifle fired in a flash of light. Powder singed his cheek, and the report echoed across the entire lake. Still the head rose.

Karhakon realized he hadn't even aimed.

Taller than two men, than three. Lifting higher and higher into the night.

He'd dropped his gun down with a thud to the canoe's bottom and reached next for the spear. A weapon he'd carried into many battles over the years. Familiar. Rising to both feet, he balanced in the center of the boat with it in both hands.

The moon rested behind the enormous shape. As tall as a tree now and lifting straight out of the water. In the moonlight, he could now see where several dark humps appeared in the lake just behind the first.

It moved forward, floating directly towards his lifeless canoe. It colossal face moved slowly into the torch light. Dipped lower to loom just above Karhakon and the canoe.

The water panther.

He saw the enormous whiskers, and the giant rows of teeth. The eyes which glowed both golden and like strange black jewels.

The torchlight smothered before its labored breaths. Warm and rank wind across Karhakon's face. The sound like a rumbling rain storm.

The *mishipishu*.

The canoe lifted against its approach and Karhakon fought to steady himself. His thoughts had turned again to his father and his tales of the water spirit.

He realized only then that he'd completely lowered his spear.

Karhakon stepped forward into the awaiting darkness.

An old man stood at the lake's edge and watched the sharp ripples along its darkening surface. It had been many years since he'd last seen these same waters.

In the morning, he would move once again with the others. North, this time. To join the British there and, perhaps, earn back some land as payment for fighting the Americans. There was so little room for the Kanienkehaka anymore.

He breathed in deeply, felt the lake's cool air against his wrinkled face. Smelled the dirt and spruce trees.

The memories came back quickly.

The time long ago when he and Tawit had hunted the water panther together. And followed the great warrior Karhakon.

He thought of that night they'd watched him canoe away and the long wait, for years, which followed.

Karhakon had not returned. And the *mishipishu* never troubled the village again.

The old man looked at the lake a final time and knew.

The world had grown smaller.

NOTES: The Great Lakes have long been said to host large serpentine beasts, cousins of the famous Loch Ness Monster. Local Indian tribes called the creature Mishipishu, the "water panther," and illustrated it in pictographs and etchings as an enormous serpent with a saw-toothed back and a catlike face. Pictures of the creature have been found near streams and lakes, and anthropologists today believe the carvings were used in warning to others. Today, these same beasts swim by the nickname "Pressie" in Lake Superior and "South Bay Bessie" in Lake Erie, and still have claimed sightings each year.

Many believe these creatures are prehistoric plesiosaurs, a general term for marine reptiles with long necks and ippers. Given the lakes' unlimited space (more than 94,000 square miles and up to 1,000 feet deep in some places) and an unending food supply, paleontologists believe some of these genuine dinosaurs could have survived as families hidden in deep glacier-carved caves. Another likely and popular candidate is the zeuglodon, a seventy-five-foot slender whale that lived in fresh water and, by all accounts, died out in North America with the T-Rex. While it may seem unlikely such a creature could survive, the coelacanth, another primitive fish thought to be extinct for 65 million years, reappeared in 1938 and the species is caught to this day. More mundane explanations include freakishly massive sturgeon, catfish, or eels. Lake sturgeon, one of the oldest species on earth, are known to reach twenty feet long and, instead of scales, sport rows of heavy bone and a gruesome head covered with skeletal plates. One North American sturgeon weighing nine-hundred pounds recently washed ashore.

The "Mohawk" primarily fought beside the British against the newborn United States during both the American Revolution and the War of 1812. After, most Kanienkehaka ed north into southeastern Canada, where the nation splintered into numerous settlements.

CHALK AND FIRE
1881

First, they cut his hair.

Someone called "Barber" slashed off the long braids that told everyone he'd recently become a man, and then hacked away, in mere moments, the rest of the length he'd grown for years to emulate his father and his favorite heroes from the old legends.

He was then given new clothes. The dark grey pants and shirt were stiff and uncomfortable, and they smelled funny, like oil. Underneath these, they forced him to wear another layer of clothing made from something called "wool flannel," which proved so itchy, he didn't know which was more torturous, moving around in it or standing still and then slowly feeling its prickles like thorns or spider feet against his skin. His own clothes, including a beautiful vest his grandmother had hand-stitched, were taken away.

Finally, he waited in line with several others and watched as each walked up one at a time to a huge board covered with strange symbols. They'd been told not to speak. Not that he could have anyway. Only a few of the others spoke any English and the rest spoke languages he did not understand. When it was his turn, he approached the board as the others had and then studied the letters, hoping to make some sense of them before choosing. He could not, and simply raised his finger to the one that somehow reminded him of home. A landscape of mountains and trees.

"Very good," said the white man standing just behind him, and then patted him on the back. "William."

He turned and watched the man write something in a book, his new name, and was then quickly led aside to make room for another boy behind him.

This had been his first day at school.

He sat at his desk in a small musty room with twenty other students while the teacher moved slowly down each row checking their work. Between copying sentences, he quietly wriggled his toes, trying to work out the persistent aches in his feet. Moccasins and bare feet were forbidden, and the pinching boots they were forced to wear still made his feet cramp. The fact that they were forced to march from room to room wasn't helping any, either. He'd been told he'd get used to it, but it had been two weeks and he was still waiting.

To take his mind of the feet, off the suspenders digging into his shoulders and neck, off wondering again why his father had ever agreed to send him to this terrible place, he looked about the room again and only half listened to the others reading. Blackboards covered every wall, each one covered in lesson plans and practice sentences in English, and he could smell the chalk dust resting in the boards' ledges. There was a picture of George Washington, who was, he'd been told, the father of his country. And another of President Garfield, who'd just been killed apparently by another white man. They'd been assured that some man named Arthur was now in charge of the country instead. He wondered if Arthur had a repulsive hairy face like Garfield, and absently touched a hand again to his own newly bare head.

"William, please read the next."

He quickly dropped his hand and grabbed the paper. "Rrrrome was not … bbb," he read slowly. Per his father's wishes, he'd learned to speak enough English from the soldiers on the reservation, but this reading thing was something else.

"Built."

"Built in a day."

"Very good, William. Can anyone tell me where Rome is?" She'd moved to the world map. "Rome was a great empire that — "

"*Key-seena.*"

The Arapaho girl beside him had whispered to her friend, and he recognized the Algonquian language, but did not know the words.

"Did you say something, Anna?" The teacher had turned.

The room instantly became even more silent than usual.

"She said it was cold, Miss Schmidt," her friend offered quickly. "It's cold."

"Anna, come to the front please."

The two girls exchanged defeated looks and then Anna stood to move slowly to the front of the class. William watched with the others, afraid to move.

"Only English is spoken here. You know that, Anna."

"Yes, ma'am." The girl had bowed her head.

"No one outside the reservations ever speaks Indian," the teacher looked about the class. "If you are to succeed, it will be with English. That is understood?"

"Yes, ma'am." He replied on cue with the rest of the class.

The teacher struck Anna.

The ruler smacked against her hand with a sharp noise that filled the whole room. The girl, herself, hadn't made a sound.

"For talking during our class," Miss Schmidt said. "Now please raise your head, Anna. For the other."

He'd seen it before. Anyone caught speaking their native tongue was punished in a variety of ways. Push-ups, extra chore time, a ruler to the mouth. One teacher even had something called a "rubber band" that offending students were made to hold in their teeth while he pulled back and snapped it back in their faces. The red welt of the ruler had already on Anna's hand.

She'd lifted her head slowly for her punishment. Her face looked like stone, and her eyes were somewhere else far away.

"Do not."

He discovered he'd stood from his chair. When or how, he did not know. He just knew why.

"Do not," he said again. "She only whisper." He could now feel the eyes of the whole room upon him.

The grey-haired woman started to argue, but something in his voice, in his look perhaps … Her eyes had grown unsure. "Sit, Anna. You've interrupted us enough this morning. See me directly after your chores today, William."

"Yes, Ma'am."

The next morning, after he'd taken Anna's punishment and some more for himself, they came for him.

A dark-skinned Apache boy he recognized from the halls sat down beside him at dinner and watched silently for awhile while he finished his daily bread and coffee.

"You're Dakotah," the boy said eventually.

"Yes."

"What's your name?"

"William."

The boy smiled. "Your *real* name."

He looked around. "*Mokpia Mani,*" he said quietly. He'd learned quickly there were some students who enjoyed tattling to satisfy their new elders.

The Apache squinted in thought. "Walking Cloud, yes?"

He nodded.

"Why did you help Yellow Bird yesterday?"

"Anna? I… I do not know." He touched the fresh cuts on his mouth.

The dark boy smiled again. "I'm Spotted Eagle. You can call me

James when the others are around. You're thinking about running away, aren't you?"

Walking Cloud froze. He had been thinking just that thing. All day. All week. Ever since he'd first arrived. Many students had vanished in the night. Some were captured by locals residents for reward money and brought back. Some weren't. "I do not…"

"They wanted to invite you first."

"They? Invite to what?"

"Tonight," Spotted Eagle said. "You'll meet them tonight."

They gathered in the woods, just past Letort Creek, a little before midnight.

As promised, Spotted Eagle had come for him in the dormitory two hours after all the lights went out. Amid the rows of cots, Walking Cloud lay awake with his eyes wide, afraid to move, to even breathe, waiting for all the others to fall asleep, and for the eleven p.m. inspection. Spotted Eagle had appeared from the darkness like a shadow, carrying extra army blankets, which they arranged to make it appear he was still in his bed. Then, he followed Spotted Eagle and two other boys. Spotted Eagle led them slowly down two hallways, then out a window in the back, which he propped open just an inch with a piece of tin.

The night air outside was crisp and inviting, and Walking Cloud took several deep breaths before following the others away from the building. They next passed the girls' dormitory, where three more joined their band. No one spoke. The lights of the teachers' quarters and main school glowed in the background as they moved low across the wide open field towards the creek. He knew that if he were caught sneaking about at night, he'd probably be put in solitary in one of the guard houses for a day or more. He felt the cool air on his face and decided then he didn't care. It'd be worth it.

Across the open field at last and over a makeshift bridge above the stream, he followed them deeper into the black woods. Looking back towards the school a final time, he noticed the field and path that led back to the cemetery. Two of the younger students had already been buried there since his arrival. Disease hid in every corner, every blanket.

"Come on," Spotted Eagle put a hand on his shoulder. "Not much further."

Another half mile back and he saw the faint glow of a fire. There were already five other students standing about the small pit, three girls and two boys. He'd expected to see Anna among them, but she was not. The one smaller boy he knew from carpentry class as Charles. The rest were strangers.

Spotted Eagle introduced him to everyone as Walking Cloud and he carefully filed away the other names. Raven, an Arapahoe girl. Standing Here, another Sioux. Boy in Rain, a tall Cheyenne who carried a wooden flute. Charles introduced himself as Quick Mouse, a Creek. Around the whole group he went and then followed Spotted Eagle's lead and sat with them around the fire.

He listened as the small gathering quietly talked about the week and people at school. They each joked about the terrible food and stinky blankets. Complained about the assignments and new chores in the fields. Discussed who had gotten sick and been taken to the infirmary. One boy imitated one of the teachers and got everyone laughing. Throughout, Boy in Rain performed softly on his flute.

After, the Cherokee girl then taught them all a song. Then, the Pawnee boy showed them a harvest dance his grandfather had taught him on the land. Walking Cloud and the others tried too. "Is it always like this?" he asked, catching his breath.

Spotted Eagle laughed. "Sometimes. Sometimes we learn and sing other songs. Older songs."

Walking Cloud had never seen so many tribes together before.

Every so often, one of the students would make an aside in his or her own language, but the group kept the conversation in their new language. "English is good for something, I suppose," Spotted Eagle winked at him.

Someone mentioned Captain Pratt, who ran the school, and the conversation turned to more insults and jokes. Pratt, who'd served in the Army's 10th Calvary in the western Indian Territory, hadn't forgotten his military roots one bit. Every day at the Carlisle school was about marching, drills, and discipline. To that end, Walking Cloud had taken off his boots like the others, and now wiggled his bare feet before the fire.

"You," one of the boys pointed at him. "How long before they stuck a toy gun in *your* hand?"

"First week."

The boy shook his head. "See? We all being trained for cannon fodder for their next civil war."

"Not us," Raven smiled. "We girls are learning to become obedient housemaids."

"Obedient *wives*," Quick Bear grinned and the girls giggled, blushing.

"Of course," Raven bowed. "And Christians, too."

"Maybe Pratt's right," Spotted Eagle said, and held up his hand to stay the grumbles and protests. "Maybe, we should learn their games."

"Oh, here he is again," one of the other boys waved him off. "Why they chose you, I'll never know."

"Our fathers thought this best to send us here. To learn the new ways. The American ways. To make us stronger. Many of the chiefs have already done this too. Has our new teacher taught us already to question our fathers so?"

"No, Spotted Eagle. But, do you feel 'stronger'?" The boy looked straight at Walking Cloud. "Do you?"

"The boots still hurt my feet," Walking Cloud replied quietly, not sure what else to say, and they all laughed.

"See? It is a school meant to further weaken. To 'diminish.' Wouldn't Miss Schmitt be pleased I used that word?" He made a face and the girls smiled. "Do you recall Pratt's other idea for the Bureau?"

Walking Cloud knew the "Bureau" well. The Bureau of Indian Affairs who'd ruled over every aspect of his tribe for some fifty years. Several around the fire groaned. They'd clearly heard the rant before. The boy shook his head and turned to Walking Cloud again. "Have you?"

"No."

"To send nine Indians, nine only, to every county in America. To spread us out everywhere."

"Why?" Walking Cloud asked, looking about the suddenly quiet fire.

The boy grinned, yet old angers ghosted behind his eyes. "To 'strengthen' us, I suppose. What do you think, Walking Cloud?"

"That will have to wait," Spotted Eagle said, looking up abruptly. "It's time."

"Don't be afraid," the girl next to him said.

Walking Cloud braced himself against the log he was sitting on. *What did that mean?* There was little as scary as someone telling you not to be afraid ... "Spotted Eagle," he leaned over. "What is happening?"

"You were invited," he said. "As we were once."

"Who?" He looked about the dark woods surrounding them. "Who invited me?"

"Have you ever heard of the *Jo-Ge-Oh?*"

"No." Walking Cloud scowled. "Who ... ?"

"A very old tribe," Spotted Eagle said. Walking Cloud noticed that the others had joined hands and were now sitting around the fire with their eyes closed. "Close your eyes now. Then you can open them. *Really* open them."

The girl on his right took his hand and Spotted Eagle offered him the other. "It is good," he said.

Walking Cloud took their hands and slowly shut his eyes.

He felt the fire against his face and toes. Listened to the cool wind moving in the trees around them. The crack of the fire.

Another sound carried on the wind. A faint murmur of whispering voices getting ever closer. It sounded like the others around the fire were whispering quickly to each other in a language he could not understand.

Were they only teasing? He fought with all his courage not to open his eyes yet.

Suddenly, the loud screech of an owl.

"Damn it!" Spotted Eagle cursed beside him. "Sorry."

Walking Cloud opened his eyes. Saw something …

Spotted Eagle yanked his hand and pulled him up. "Come on," he said. "Grab your boots. We go now."

"What was — "

"Later. That 'owl' was Spotted Tail. The guards are out and heading this way. We gotta get back now." Even as he spoke, the others had already completely covered the fire with dirt and were even now vanishing into the darkened woods.

Walking Cloud stumbled after them looking back towards where the fire had been just moments before. Looking for some sign of what he'd seen in the flickering light.

As he dashed through the woods with the others, he pictured again what he'd seen and tried to hold onto it as if it were a dream that might slip away which each passing step.

He'd seen a man. An Indian man in deerskin breaches and jacket, with long black hair in two feathered braids, with a dark stone tomahawk at his hip.

The man, however, had been no bigger than Walking Cloud's thumb.

And, he hadn't been alone.

The very next day, Mr. Feist, who taught the boys tinsmithing and blacksmithing, asked Walking Cloud to stay after class.

Walking Cloud was nervous but not too worried. Mr. Feist was one of the few teachers that he and the others actually liked. He was younger than the others, for one, probably only a few years older than Walking Cloud, and he often made jokes in class that made the time there seem to go faster. He was also part Indian, as much as maybe half. A Lenape, they thought. But Mr. Feist never spoke to them of that.

"Thought we should talk a minute," the teacher said once the room had cleared. He studied Walking Cloud for a moment. "Heard some students snuck out again late last night."

Walking Cloud expected as much and was prepared to deliver his best blank stare.

Mr. Feist just smiled. "Do you know why Captain Pratt started this school?"

Walking Cloud thought of something he'd heard just the night before, a phrase he'd been rolling around in his head ever since. That, and what he'd seen. "'To kill the Indian and save the man'?"

His teacher laughed. "Ah, yes. The boys love that unfortunate line. Have you figured it out yet, though?"

"Pratt believe," Walking Cloud started slowly, "that to be best, we no more be Indians."

"He believes the world has changed and that we all must change with it. Pratt believes, as I do, William, that the Indian is equal in capability and promise to the white man in all ways. That you can soon become lawyers and doctors."

"Just not *Indian* lawyers and doctors, yes?"

Mr. Feist smiled again. "Much of life is compromise, William," he said. "For each of us. Don't ever forget that. Don't get too lost in the woods."

"I do not —"

"We'll talk later," he stopped him. "Remember what I said." Feist excused him and turned to prepare for the next class.

Walking Cloud left the room slowly. Spotted Eagle waited for him just outside the building, and walked beside him. "How'd that go?" he asked.

"Good enough."

"Feist is a 'good-enough' guy. Tonight."

"Tonight what?"

Spotted Eagle looked back towards the woods.

"No," Walking Cloud shook his head. "We almost caught last night. Feist know. They be looking for us. I —"

"Me and the others are gonna take care of the teachers and security," he said and then smiled. "You're going alone."

"Out there? Myself?"

"Yup. That's how it'll have to be. Last night, no good."

"Spotted Eagle, I saw something last night. I do not know — "

"You afraid?"

"Yes," he replied honestly. He looked back out towards the woods beyond the stream. "But, but I will do it anyway."

Spotted Eagle laughed and threw an arm around his shoulder. "That's why they like you so much."

"Who? Who like me?"

"The *Jo-Ge-Oh*, of course," he grinned. "The little people."

The wood's infinite darkness crept in from every side, testing the small fire's glow. Walking Cloud welcomed it.

Despite the fear shaking in his belly and legs, he was still thrilled to be outside again. To smell the fresh air and leaves, to hear the wind in the branches and watch the moon's glow through the high endless treetops.

Until the night before, he'd never seen so many trees. It had been fifty years since his own people had last walked the eastern woods.

He thought of Spotted Eagle and the others still back at the school. They'd planned several commotions of some kind or another to keep the staff busy, to give Walking Cloud the time he needed. Time for what, he had no idea.

He looked about the small clearing nervously. It had already been an hour of sitting alone. Fidgeting while the cold night air worked its way into his stiffening bones. He thought of the *Jo-Ge-Oh*. Knew that Spotted Eagle was teasing. That they'd played a trick. Even now, some of the others, Boy in Rain maybe, or Quick Bear, were sneaking through the woods to jump out and scare him. To place little dolls out beside the fire pit to startle him.

Yet, Walking Cloud knew what he'd seen.

Maybe ...

The moon sat high above him now, and he lifted his head to it, closing his hands. He then slowly lifted his hands out as he'd seen the others do the night before.

Maybe ...

He again listened to the wind. Felt the warm fire against his skin. Sought peace in the total darkness which enfolded his visions and thoughts. How long he sat like that, with his eyes closed, floating in the fire's warmth, slowly breathing in the night, he did not know.

Then, he heard the whispers again. High and light in the wind.

I hope ...

"Mokpia Mani."

The voice was deep and spoken just a few feet away.

Walking Cloud felt himself falling.

When he looked up, he was no longer alone. Over the suddenly blinding light of the fire, the same man he'd seen the night before stood again before him. The Indian in the deerskin jacket.

But this was no sprite from the woods, not one of the little people from legends.

He stood taller than Walking Cloud, in fact, and even reached down to lift him from the ground. *The terrible coffee they make us drink is making me see things,* he thought.

"Kotu." The stranger introduced himself and his grip was strong and firm as he lifted the boy easily to his feet. "You are well?" he asked.

Walking Cloud felt hot suddenly, feverish. "I do not know." He shielded his eyes from the terrible blaze and looked around the clearing.

The woods had caught fire.

He stepped back from the inferno and immediately crashed into a tree.

No, he realized in the very next moment. Not a tree.

He looked about the clearing again, the pieces and images falling into place again. But so very different. Very.

"I am small," Walking Cloud grasped fully. "How did —"

The man waved him forward. "You come with us."

Several more men had appeared out of the giant blaze's flickering shadows. Each rode on the back of a terrible monster. Eyeless with gaping jaws and pointed snouts. Their skin was sickly grey and creased in fatty folds.

"I can not …" Walking Cloud felt along the back of the log, looking for an escape, trying to wrap his thoughts around what was happening. The others simply stared back at him, waiting.

"You safe," the man said. "We bring you back soon if you wish." He'd mounted one of the hideous creatures and dropped his hand to help Walking Cloud up. "We go, Mokpia Mani." Something in the man's eyes assured Walking Cloud he was telling the truth. No matter what else he would see and question this night, he believed that he was safe with this man. With Kotu.

He took the hand and felt himself lifted onto the back of the creature, where he wrapped his hands around Kotu's waist. "*Johta,*" he heard the man say to the others and immediately they were moving.

The fire vanished behind him in an instant as the strange creatures scurried faster across the ground than any horse he had ever been on. The forest soared by in a blur of moonlit shadows and unrecognizable black shapes. Walking Cloud clung tighter and braved to look past Kotu's shoulder.

The other riders vanished suddenly into the darkness and Walking Cloud clung even tighter. *Where had they gone?*

Suddenly, he saw it. There was a gaping hole in the earth just in front of them as he watched the stubby tail end of one of the beasts vanishing straight into the ground.

"Kotu!" he screamed.

"You safe," the man said again and leaned forward, urging their mount to move even faster.

The waiting hole swallowed them as quickly as it had appeared and Walking Cloud was suddenly consumed in total darkness as they dropped down into the very earth. Buried alive, never to see the sun again. He pressed his face against the man's jacket and closed his eyes against whatever new nightmare awaited him below.

Eyes held tightly shut, he felt his body lifted one direction, then the next. Up and down through endless turns and drops.

When the movement slowed, he risked a peek and spied the faint glow of silvery light passing by in a long-streaked blur. The tunnel's ceiling and walls were made of dirt and root. Up ahead, more light. Golden and inviting, and the creature ran directly towards it.

The whole passage flooded with light suddenly and they spilled out into a huge giant cave. The creature stopped running and Walking Cloud now looked around.

The cavern was filled with a whole village. Fifty Indians, two hundred maybe. Men, women, and children moving slowly about small wooden lodges and fires. The sound of voices and laughter. He could see the skins and meat hung to be dried, and several canoes beside a stream that ran through the center of the camp.

The other riders had already climbed from their monstrous steeds and Walking Cloud was lowered slowly to the ground. "Where are we? Are you …"

"The *Jo-Ge-Oh?*" Koto laughed, tapped his chest. "*Jo-Ge-Oh.*"

Walking Cloud's knees could barely hold him. He told himself it was only because of the jarring ride, and realized, looking at their gruesome steeds, that he'd just been on the back of a mole.

"What you want with me?"

The man shrugged. "We take you back if you wish. Come. Eat first. Rest." He waved him forward and Walking Cloud found the strength somewhere to move his legs after him and the others.

He became aware of eyes upon him again, just like in English class only the day before. He heard the whispers of those around him as he took a seat beside Koto at one of the fires. A dozen men and women were gathered together to feast. It reminded him of Spotted Eagle and the others. Of his own family back on the land.

A woman brought him delicious stew and cornbread. He wolfed down the meal, the best he'd had in weeks, and looked up to where the fires' smoke lifted through a hole high above. The moon's light spilled down, revealing a rotted out tree trunk above. Watching like this, the moon looked the same size as it always did.

After the meal, dancers, small children in colorful costumes, came out and entertained them all. Walking Cloud smiled, looked around the camp again. "This not the only camp, is it?"

"No," Koto smiled broadly. "Many camps. Many *Jo-Ge-Oh.* We always live here," Koto said beside him, and patted the ground. "From here to the great ocean. We once trade with Haudenosaunee many years. People of the longhouse, yes?"

"The Iroquois."

He nodded. "Tribes change. Much war. We start hiding more. To survive," he pulled a pipe and some tobacco from his pouch. "Some still see. If we let them," he winked. "Teach you friends *Jo-Ge-Oh* songs. Stories. Some nights. We hide the rest." Koto lit his pipe and passed it to him. "You no like school."

"No."

"You stay here. With us."

Walking Cloud's stomach lurched. He puffed slowly and carefully at the pipe. "I… No. Could I…"

"You could. Some do." He waved towards the rest of the tribe as if that explained something. Walking Cloud thought of the runaways who'd never been found. "Or we take you north. Away."

"Canada?"

He nodded, watched him with grave dark eyes over the pipe's smoke. "We take you."

"You would?"

"Yes." Koto nodded. "Or you go back to school."

"Then what?"

The man laughed again. "We see you again some night. You and friends."

"Why?"

"To remind you."

Remind …

To remain true to his own heritage? Or that he must hide just enough to survive? Walking Cloud looked about the great cavern. A space no bigger than large fire pit. Maybe it was a warning to never become a prisoner by masking who he truly was?

Which lesson did the *Jo-Ge-Oh* truly offer? Maybe all of them. Like so many lessons, there were different layers of things to learn. If he stayed or ran away to Canada, he knew he would never see his family again. Or, his new friends. He would never return to his own land.

"I'm going back to the school," he said suddenly.

Koto nodded once, looked slowly back at the fire.

Walking Cloud passed back the pipe, then watched the flames, feeling their glow against his skin again. Drummers and flutists played beautiful songs he'd never heard before. Songs filled with both spirit and mourning. The fire's warmth comforted like a blanket.

He sat with the others and listened until sleep overtook him at last. The last sound he heard was Koto humming quietly beside him.

When he woke, he was by the fire again. *His* fire.

It had burned out, smoke drifting away into the purple-streaked darkness of early dawn. He stood, looking down over it. A giant again. The log at his feet only a log again, which he stepped over easily.

He looked about the woods, but saw nothing. Maybe a sound on the wind. A melody humming like a morning bird's song he could almost recognize. He was alone.

Walking Cloud moved slowly back to the school, enjoying the feel of the grass and cold dew under his bare toes as he made his way across the field and the night's last shadows towards the dormitory. The others would be up in less than an hour.

He found the back window propped as Spotted Eagle had promised and quietly climbed through. When he dropped to the floor below, however, someone was standing there. Waiting.

"You're up early, William," the voice standing above him said. Walking Cloud looked up slowly. It was Mr. Feist.

"Yes, sir."

Walking Cloud briefly imagined solitary time locked in one of the guards' boxes, or endless marching, or some worse punishment. But, something in Feist's pleased look suggested otherwise. "You must have just slept though all the excitement here last night, yes?" he looked the other way while Walking Cloud stood and brushed the grass and dirt from his shirt and pants. "I was concerned about you. Thought you …"

"Might 'get lost in the woods'?"

"Yes. Something like that."

Walking Cloud thought for a moment. "Found, I think," he said. "Not lost."

Feist nodded. "I'm glad."

"My name is Walking Cloud," he added, and lifted out his hand to shake.

The teacher tilted his head in thought, took his hand. "My tribal name is Little Hunter," he said. "See you in class then, Walking Cloud?" Walking Cloud shook Little Hunter's hand and nodded.

"Best get some sleep then," the teacher said. "We've got a big project in class today."

And tonight maybe, Walking Cloud thought, imagining tiny fires that blazed like the sun and ancient warriors on the backs of moles. *Tonight.*

Lessons came in many sizes.

NOTES: The Carlisle Indian Industrial School was founded in 1879 in Carlisle, Pennsylvania, in vacant army barracks, to help assimilate Native Americans from the reservations into white American society. Students were given European names, clothing and education in a strict military-shaped environment that forbade tribal languages and customs. Half of each day was spent learning a technical trade of some kind and working to keep the school's cost down (as carpenters, blacksmiths, seamstresses, etc.). The rough discipline was typical of its time period for most American schools. The Carlisle school soon became the model for more than 300 Indian schools across the country in which, at one point, some 22,000 Indian students were enrolled—ten percent of the entire Native American population! Parents on reservations were pressured, often coerced, into sending their children to these schools.

Captain Pratt, founder of the school, had worked closely with Indians as a member of the 10th Calvary, and believed, quite ahead of his time, that Indians were equal to whites in all ways but just needed the same advantages of education and civilization. While in hindsight, his methods can be questioned, there should be no doubt that he, and other social workers who adopted this attitude, were beacons of future tolerance and equality for American Indians. It soon became believed by the government and social workers across the country that this would prove the most successful path. Yet, more than 10,000 students passed through Carlisle alone in its thirty-nine year history and only about 1,000 ever graduated. More died of disease, and it is estimated that as many as 2,000 simply ran away. The school was closed for good in 1918, and is today home of the U.S. Army War College.

The Jo-Ge-Oh are an Iroquois myth from the eastern woodlands. Most all tribes have tales involving a race of little people who live in hiding and often reveal themselves to teach songs, dance, or some more important lesson.

RELEASE ME
1934

Start with the woman or with the unhappy place she
was buried, it makes no difference. Without her, it was only another
spot of land, another forgotten town built along a foothill in western
Pennsylvania. Without the hill, she was only another ghost, a faded
memory from another time.

I came to truly know both in the fall of '34 when Ames Rowley
sent for me.

Though I had not heard from him in many years, the manner of his
wired message proved both urgent and curious, and I soon found myself
on a train heading east. After thirty years, it seemed this was to be my
return home.

Before I say any more of that matter, let me first give some account
of Rowley himself.

When we'd first met, he was merely a white man of evident
intelligence and enthusiasm who'd been educated in various private
schools throughout the northeast and was in his final year at Princeton
when he'd volunteered to join the "Great War." We met in the trenches
outside Vauquois amid half a million other Americans gathered to finally
push the Germans back out of France.

He'd learned I was a full-blood Lenape, and one night, amid
another barrage of German mortars and howitzer shells, he shared that
his own blood was part Indian, an eighth on his father's side. Over the
next several months, amid the ghoulish rot of those diseased and poisoned
trenches, he told me of his travels in Europe and of the people he'd met,

and I spoke of life in the Oklahoma reservations and how I'd enlisted with many brothers. We became friends.

The last detail of significance to note now would be that his full name was Ames Dorrance Rowley IV. The seemingly last of a long line of Rowleys who'd struggled in the eastern wilderness and eventually flourished in the midst of several successful ventures in both coal mining and lumbering. After the war, he'd inherited the full sum of the family fortune and its various enterprises, including the ancestral property. It was to this very land that I'd been so urgently called.

He'd sent a driver, an Irishman named Harman, to collect me at the train station in Harrisburg. I admit that the four-hour drive back through the primordial woods of western Pennsylvania proved as unsettling as I'd feared it might. Alone in the backseat, looking out through the window, I found it difficult to believe that my own people had ever lived, and even thrived, in such a ghastly place. The grisly trees stretched for miles on every side of the road, swallowing the whole of the uneven land in blackness and shadow. Craggy mountains and hills made the whole world seem chaotic and uneven. An ugly place. Yet, one that had apparently been my home for several years before we'd been moved west. I did not remember it.

We passed several decrepit homes tucked in clusters within the tree line. Dark humanoid shadows I could scarcely see hovered about the front porches. Workers for the one lumber mill that was still in operation. Many, the driver informed me in low apologetic grumbles, were merely Indian squatters who'd never left the land. I saw fewer such homes the closer we got to the mansion, and the lone street that ran through town was framed on each side by a handful of deserted buildings. Empty and dark. The windows boarded long ago against the Depression or brutal northern winds and rain.

We turned at last towards the manor itself. It occurred to me only then that, except for the driver, I had not truly seen a living soul in hours.

The hill stood alone, backed to the north by the Alleghany mountains, which loomed above like a black jagged wave. I could see the dark outline of the Rowley manor waiting atop, as the car circled slowly three times up to the top of the hill. Looking to the sides of the paved road, I couldn't help but think of war-torn Montfaucon and France.

Not since, in a place where bombs and poison had assaulted the earth for years, had I seen land so dead and barren. Only weeds and boulders sprouted in this dry dirt. The few trees that grew upon Rowley's Bluff were frail and twisted and, in the dark, they looked almost like skeletal fingers. Though it had rained earlier in the day, it seemed as if the ground remained only cracked earth.

We parked in front of the manor and I stood to truly look at it. It fit the land it had been built upon perfectly.

Even in moonlight, especially in the moonlight, it was ugly. The mansion was a gaudy, towering structure of rough stone jutting into the sky, its shadows playing off sharp angles of broken buttresses and lofty turrets. I remembered Rowley saying something about it being a French monastery for a short time. The time-eaten rock, patched unevenly with black ivy and dripstone concretion, buckled in several spots. The few windows were bare slits of dull light framed in thick lumber that pocked the sides of the mansion like narrow ebony scars. It seemed the Depression had found all corners of the country.

The driver took my bag, glared at me strangely, then led me into the dim house. There, I was led down long abandoned hallways to the study and, at last, Ames Rowley.

In France, Rowley had been a dark, handsome man with a strong chin and shoulders. Still in his late thirties, I'd expected to see the same this night.

However, the man sitting in the chair beside the wide fireplace was not the man I remembered. If I hadn't known that he'd died several years before, I would have sworn I was now meeting my friend's father.

Rowley looked at least sixty in the dim light, maybe older. His skin seemed as pocked and lined with dark wrinkles as the mansion's exterior. He turned slowly upon my entrance, his arms and neck stiff, as if moving was difficult. His eyes proved hollow and dark.

"Edward," he nodded. He sounded as tired and stiff as he looked. But, he'd smiled. "Thank you, dear Edward."

"I came as soon as I might," I said, reaching out to shake his hand. "Your letter was …"

His fingers were freezing. Stiff. Dead to the touch.

"Yes," he pulled them away from our shake and lifted those same rough fingers to his deeply rutted face. "Do you think me insane?"

"How may I help?" I asked and took the seat across from his own. This man had personally saved my life twice during the bloody storming of Montfaucon. What did it matter how his cable had made him sound? I would do whatever I could to help him. "These things that you see and hear?" I prodded.

Rowley lowered his head. "I have such strange thoughts, Edward. Such horrible dreams."

I thought of the things he'd said in his letter.

"The others keep away now. They think I'm …" He looked up. "But now you are here. You can help."

"Anything, Ames."

"Look first." He motioned to a table between us and I stood to get a better look. There, I found a large boulder that covered the whole width of the table. Wide and flat with symbols carved on its surface.

"'Beware,'" I read the Algonquian symbol easily. "It's a warning to keep away."

He nodded. "The locals told me as much. And a professor at Penn confirmed it."

"Where did you get this?"

"When I inherited the estate, I found several hidden in the basement. A geologist at the university estimated that the carvings are at least one thousand years old, that the rocks were unearthed perhaps a few hundred years ago. The one you stand before now was found just last month."

"Where?"

"At the bottom of this very hill," he said. "Buried a few feet beneath the earth. The men found it while planting a new electrical box to the house. My belief is that the others were found when the estate was first built."

"Beware?" I looked at the carving again. "Beware what?"

"Look closer," he said, and turned to the fire. In the flickering glow, his eyes shined just like black marble.

I leaned closer over the rock, and touched my fingers to the cold stone. I briefly imagined the hands that had crafted it. The hands, perhaps, of my own ancestor a thousand years before. I found new ridges, darker ones. Lost to the shadows and centuries beneath the earth. My fingers traced the shape, my mind filled with memories of my grandmother's blankets and the intricate designs that had so colored them.

"'The woman,'" I translated. "'Beware the woman.' The *great* woman."

"Before it was renamed Rowley's Bluff, this same land was once called *Tawwunasinall.*"

"I remember that name," I admitted, struck by how quickly I'd recalled the word and the instant emotion it evoked. I did not remember why, only that it was a "bad place."

"I thought you might," he smiled and for the first time, it was genuine. It was hopeful. "You're from here," he said excitedly.

"Thirty miles away," I corrected. "And a long time ago."

"You're Lenape," he said. "Your people once owned all this land."

"We lived here, yes," I did not care to discuss the uneasy distinction between the two. "But, how does that help?"

"You'll understand better what is happening here, I hope. You told me your grandfather was a respected medicine man. Surely ..."

"*Tawwunasinall,*" I dared to say the word out loud, to calm him, to assure him. "'Her burial place.'"

"Yes."

"The woman in your dreams?"

"My dreams," he laughed, but there was nothing pleasant about the sound. He stood suddenly, lifting awkwardly from the chair. "We will speak more of that in the morning. It will make more sense to you then."

"To me?"

"Thank you again, Edward," he said, and touched his hand to my shoulder. "You have no idea how much this means. I will send Harman for you to show you to your room. Good night, then." He shuffled slowly from the room, each step labored and forced.

I waited alone in the study for some time. Glanced over the books and paintings within the study, the Indian-crafted axes and masks. I turned to watch the fire and thought some of the man I'd met in France.

It was then that I first heard the voice.

It had been a faint sound and I turned, thinking that Harman had come at last to collect me or, rather, that Rowley had returned.

But, there was no one there.

Relasss.

I heard it again. Clearer now. But still, barely a whisper. Somewhere in the halls behind me. Or above me, perhaps. I wasn't sure where the voice had come from.

Relasss maaaaa.

I sprang from my chair. "Yes?" I called. "Who's there?"

Harman appeared in the doorway then and I nearly fell over from surprise. "Was that you?" I asked. "Did you just call me?"

He shook his head no and watched me curiously as I held up a hand for him to wait so I could listen again for the voice I'd just heard.

It was gone.

As I followed Harman from the room, I thought on what I'd heard. I could not make out the words at all. They could have been Lenape, English, or French for all I knew. But, I knew the voice was soft and melodic.

I knew it had been the voice of a woman.

Sleep did not come easy that night. My room was on the third floor of the western wing and I found it unusually cold and infuriatingly noisy. While the furniture and decorations were certainly affluent and modern, the mansion itself showed its age in the constant creeks and groans that echoed in the rafters and floorboards. It sounded as if the house were constantly shifting itself, still finding a spot to rest. As I lay in my bed with the blankets pulled close against the chill, I could also hear the constant scratchings of mice or rats moving through the ancient walls which surrounded me on all sides.

Amid this commotion, I'd convinced myself that I'd only imagined the woman's voice. After all, Harman had informed me that there were no longer any women on staff at the mansion and that he, a male cook, and Rowley were the only ones remaining. It was clear that Rowley's letter and an active imagination had gotten the better of me. Perhaps, I told myself, returning 'home' was more traumatic than I'd first thought.

To make matters worse, a thunder storm had begun, adding to my discomfort as its own sounds rumbled through the huge house and lightning flashed into my room to cast unfamiliar shadows against the ceiling and walls. I lay in the darkness with my eyes closed and remembered the night they'd come for us. When the soldiers loaded us on to trains bound for Oklahoma. I'd been no more than five at the time, and remember clinging for my father as I was lifted up onto the train.

Unable to sleep, I moved to my window and looked out into the night to watch the storm. In the next flash of light, I saw the surrounding woods. It was almost as if the trees dared to sneak just up to the boundaries of the hill and then stopped. As if they'd heeded the mysterious rocks' clear warning to keep away.

I fought to remember the trees and cottages of my old village miles away. And the lake we'd once swam and fished in. But, these memories did not come so easily as I had never been back to the land. Turning from the storm, I forced myself back to bed.

When sleep did finally come, it proved restless and filled with strange dreams. Flashes of a village. A fire. Lenape moving about the darkness together. Whether these were childhood memories or fantasies of another time because I'd returned to my ancestral land, I had no idea.

In the last dream, I lay on a short hill overlooking a Lenape village, where I watched the children playing and the woman working along the stream. I felt the sun warm on my face and smelled the cool fresh air coming off the mountains behind us.

A woman appeared to my right and I watched as she approached me slowly. She wore deerskin fringed with dark grey fur. It was her beauty I noticed most, however. Her sharp features and auburn skin. The long black hair that swayed behind her back, adorned with wooden beads and feathers.

She moved directly towards me, at a speed that was almost too fast, unnatural as if time had skipped, and sat down beside me.

Before I could speak, she laid her soft finger to my lips and looked at me. Her eyes were wide and golden brown, dark and mesmerizing.

She was, quite simply, the most beautiful woman I had ever seen.

She put her hand against my chest and leaned forward as if to kiss my cheek. She smelled of honeysuckle and lilac. Her lips proved soft and warm against me when she spoke.

A whisper into my ear.

"Release me," she said.

The lips had suddenly grown cold. Hard.

"Release me," she said again and I knew then that it was a voice I had heard once before.

I turned to her and lurched back.

Her face had turned completely grey and cracked like a splintered marble statue. The striking eyes were now only black empty sockets. The eyes of a rotted skull. Her hand, still on my chest, was heavy and solid. It ended in long rough claws.

I pulled away from her, screaming for my very life.

And woke at last.

In the darkness, I fumbled for reality again. Only half recognized the strange room I had awakened in. When I heard the rumble of thunder outside, I understood I was simply back in a guest bedroom in Rowley's mansion.

Yet, only then did I notice the weight still against my chest. The unmistakable feel of a hand and arm still laying against me. Someone in the room with me. So very heavy and … *real*.

I screamed again, this time while totally awake, and fell from the bed.

Whatever it had been against me retreated when I'd jumped, for I distinctly then felt the hideous weight slip away from me. I stood beside that bed in the dark, trembling. Reaching out blindly for the electric light to throw on.

The lightning flashed then, filling the entire room in blinding blue radiance. I turned.

There, against the far wall, in the lightning's light, I saw the shadow. It was moving away from the bed, back into the far corners of the room.

The flash ended and I was cast into the dark again.

I found the switch at last, and filled the room with light. The shadow, and whatever had made it, were gone.

Sleep did not come again that night.

For the unexplained shadow I'd just seen had been hunched over and crooked. Jagged and misshapen.

Its shape had not been human.

The next few days were spent beside Ames Rowley, huddled over old letters, diaries, and maps. His mind seemed unclear, getting worse by the hour, his words mere mumbles at times as he tried to share with me all he'd found. It was during this time that I learned more of the Rowley clan and the history of the land itself.

It was the Dorrance line of the family, for instance, who'd first traveled across the dark sea from Inisheer Island, in Galway, to the New World. Morgan Dorrance had been a trapper for the Hudson Bay Company, a true pioneer who'd ultimately settled in the area. In Dorrance's own words, I read of "Tawonsonal," the land where he'd been warned by the "local savages" never to hunt. That "even the animals kept away" from that place. Surely, he spoke of *Tawwunasinall*.

The family records revealed the eventual arrival of Arthur Rowley, who'd purchased much of the surrounding lands from Dutch land prospectors. Of his marriage to Teresa Dorrance and the early construction of the Rowley mansion in 1704. We read of the growing lumber mills and the Indian workers there. The difficulty in constructing the mansion as the same lumber workers refused to help build it. And, of the birth of his son Stanhope Dorrance Rowley. The line moved along, the mansion nearing completion throughout each generation. During the French and Indian Wars, it seems, French priests had taken control of the house for some time before leaving it barren again. Charles Dorrance Rowley finished the estate in 1810, and his wife soon gave birth to Ames Dorrance Rowley. The First.

From letters and diaries, we confirmed that it was this Rowley who'd taken a local Lenape woman as his wife and had a son. There was a single photograph of the two together but her face was lost in the shadows and primitive film. I couldn't help but wonder if it was a face I would recognize.

Letters between Charles, who disapproved, and the young Ames proved angry and threatening and later correspondence made no mention of the Lenape wife at all. Only of the "half-blood son," who'd been sent away to Boston. Rowley found the disappearance of the wife particularly suspicious. The same writings revealed that the Rowley family was an unfortunate line. Even more than typical of that age, several wives had died during childbirth. Ames Rowley II had been institutionalized for insanity. His diary spoke of flying heads blazing in flames and stone giants. He spoke also of a beautiful woman in his dreams. One that terrified him more than death itself. In one diary alone, he'd scrawled the words "RELEASE ME" more than a hundred times.

I had not yet told Rowley of my own dreams, or of the melodic voice I still heard at night floating along the ominous darkened halls.

From more recent letters, it was clear that the Rowley family had slowly shut itself off from the rest of society. That the boy, Ames Dorrance Rowley IV, would be sent away to schools in the East to escape that same fate. However …

"After the war," Rowley explained, "Father had grown, well, quite ill. My uncle, who'd meant to take the business and land, had died a few years before. It was a son's duty to return."

He showed me then on the map where the last rock had been found, a hundred steps from the base of the Rowley hill. With the rocks he'd found hidden in his own house, there'd been seven unearthed altogether. He proposed he search for others moving in a perfect circle about the hill.

It was to this specific task that I now set myself, standing at the base of the hill with a shovel in my hand. While Ames stayed up at the house, his body too weak for such work, I moved out from where the last stone had been found, and had been digging for several hours in various spots. I'd taken to only sleeping in short naps during the day, the nights spent reading with the lights on, and it felt good to be outdoors. Here, I hoped not to hear her whispers.

Despite the rain storm nights before, the ground was as dry and cracked as I'd first thought. Each jab of the shovel produced a small burst of dust that was carried away on the low eastern winds. I hated the hill already, couldn't stand the strange creeping feeling it left along my back and shoulders. I found myself often looking out to the surrounding forest instead. The place that had once been my home. Before the soldiers and trains, before Oklahoma and its fences. Before the trenches in Europe.

I was so lost in memory that I had not noticed Harman, the driver, approaching. Looking back up at the house, he told me that he wanted to show me something and I followed him without argument. Had I known where he was leading me, perhaps I would have done otherwise.

We eventually arrived at the family cemetery, a narrow plot of land on the back side of the hill, that faced the mountains. There, the grave markings and tombstones of seven generations were gathered under the brooding Alleghenies. On the dirty stones, framed by various angels and crosses, I saw and recognized many of the names I'd come to know over the last few days.

Harman waved me forward to the small mausoleum in the center of the plot. Here, etched above the hoary crypt's entry read the name ROWLEY. "This way," he said.

He unlocked the gate and crouched under the low entry into the waiting darkness within. I watched from outside as he turned on the electric flashlight within, and in the glow, I saw the clear outline of a stone coffin. I looked behind me, then ducked to join him in the stale dusty tomb. "I wanted you to see this," he said.

"You said as much before," I looked about the burial chamber. Filled with half a dozen marble dozen coffins laced in old spider webs. Was this to be the end of the mystery? Was this her burial ground? Was the "great woman" simply the ancient Lenape ancestor in Rowley's line. I noticed then that there was no grave for such a woman. All the others were white family members I'd come to know. "Why are we here?"

"Give me a hand," he said and grabbed hold of one of the stone lids.

"What are you doing?" I cried. "Does Ames know —"

"You need to see," he fixed me with a wild look and I suddenly found myself helping to push the lid away. It slid sideways with a grating noise that, in the cramped room, sounded more like a moan. "This is Rowley the third," he explained. "The father."

"It's an outrage," I protested. "You can't just — "

Even as I spoke, he shone the flashlight into the casket.

I gasped. Looked at Harman, then back at the casket. My heart thumping crazily, my head spinning.

"They're all like that," he said.

"What do you mean?" My voice was barely a whisper.

"The others. Open any casket," his eyes were wide, the light of the flashlight trembling in his hand. "Morgan, the brother. Or Ames, the second. The sister, Emily Foster Rowley. Take your pick."

"They all …" I'd stepped closer to it, looking in again. "All of them?"

Rowley's father had been buried some ten years before. The body I looked at now was neither a skeleton as I'd expected, nor even a half-rotted corpse protected by the elements in the dry mausoleum. Though the cloths had decayed, the man was fully formed and looked probably much the same as the very day he had died.

He was also completely made of stone.

Rowley and I sat alone in his library searching through various records and diaries, as well as books on Indian lore he'd collected. I flipped through the pages of Esbenshade's *Dark Wisdom of the Red Man* and then worked more slowly through *The Collected Ghosts and Myths of the Delaware*, written in French by Royce Hotze in 1680, in which I found harrowing tales of men who could turn into wolves, stone giants, and ghosts who lived backwards. I perused the diary of Emily Foster, the young bride who'd married the insane Rowley and then died mysteriously before her thirtieth birthday amid rumors that she was unable to step into the daylight. Looking throughout all for clues to the nature of this manifestation, this grisly curse that clearly still haunted my friend's property.

I researched Frankenberg's *Anomalous Anatomy*, having read before of rare conditions when buried bodies had turned into wood or stone as the ground's natural nutrients infested. But, these bodies had been in a crypt well above the putrefaction of the ground. I assumed Rowley's current condition were somehow connected to a genetic family condition that had plagued generations of his kin.

Throughout these endless days and nights of research, there had been more dreams during my fitful and sporadic sleep. Terrible dreams.

They often started the same, the same Lenape village, but had grown more detailed and more dreadful each time. I could tell now that I was in the past. Much earlier than my own childhood, I came to realize that these were the people who'd first crossed the wide expanses of the continent. Those who'd flourished ten thousand years before "civilized" men such as myself. Around us, for I was surely among them, the trees covered the whole of the land already but it was almost as if I could feel the retreating icebergs still hovering close by.

In some of these nightmares, I realized I'd become part of a mob, a pack of Lenape on some angry and terrifying mission. I felt myself snatched up into the air in another dream, the force of an unseen spirit, a giant hand, lifting into the dark sky before I woke up screaming.

In another, I'd been next to the strange beautiful woman again. Her curious golden brown eyes now filled my dreams. And when she whispered to me, when she said those words I'd come to know so well, I suddenly felt a heavy weight over my whole body. I looked up as the rough and heavy darkness scattered across my face. I had been buried.

My screams became choked as the dirt fell down on top of me. My body and arms stiff against the terrible weight. Still the dirt rained down. Burying me alive as I scratched vainly to escape. Burying us both together.

There were other books in the library, far darker texts that the mad Rowley Ames II had apparently procured over the years. Hidden among the darkest corners I found the dusty *Marvells of Science*, the *Daemonolatreia* by Remington, and also the ghastly *Necronomicon*, a Latin translation of which I thankfully could not read. The terrifying pictures were enough. I'd heard of the cursed book but had never seen one, and it was clear from the worn pages that it had been looked over by more than one generation of Rowley. I placed it back and shuddered at the thought of what I might have read.

It was at that exact moment that I heard the voice.

"Release me."

Not so much spoken as a sound that reverberated through the entire estate.

I could see from his look that Rowley had heard it too. He stared me square in the eye and it was the first time the two of us had openly acknowledged that we'd both heard this voice ourselves.

"Release me."

The sound again. Louder and more demanding.

"She's below us," I realized.

"The basement," he agreed.

"Her burial place."

I helped him to his feet, found an electric torch and then followed to the door which led to the lower levels.

It was just the two of us now. Both Harman and the cook had resigned and left the estate for good the day before. We were alone.

With her.

Electric lights flared and covered us to the first level and we stood there together. Breathing slowly and listening.

"Release me."

"Still lower," he said, his eyes wide with excitement.

"She is below us even now?"

He led me to another door and a set of stairs. "Don't you understand?" His voice was crazed but I followed him anyway.

He threw the door open. Below, the darkness stunk of mildew and rot. But even more worrying, before I'd cast the torchlight down, there was already a strange glow coming up the steps towards us.

Rowley steadied himself at the top of the stairs, then stumbled forward. Each rotted step bringing agony to his stiff bones. I followed closely behind, terrified of what horror we would find waiting for us at the bottom of those terrifying steps.

The glow emitting from below was bluish and grew more faded as our eyes grew accustomed to the darkness.

"Now," Rowley shrieked and I turned on the electric torch.

The room was flooded with light.

It was a large area that must have extended under fully half of the mansion. My light only drove away the darkness from half of the whole area. The floor was dirt, and under the light, it appeared dark and damp. Several broken shelves and rotted crates of storage were lined against the stone-blocked walls. The walls were peppered with grey moss and glistened with warm moisture.

A clump of full mushrooms had grown in the dirt floor. Thousands of them in several long clusters that spread from the center of the room. I covered my nose and mouth against their moldy stench.

The toadstools were an unnatural phosphorous green and I surmised easily that it was from these same mushrooms that the strange glow had originated.

"Turn off your light," Rowley said next to me.

I looked at him confused. Afraid to give up my light to such a dank and dark place. Yet, I followed his trembling hand which pointed to the center of the room and did as he had asked.

The room went dark and in the eerie glow of the toadstools, I saw for the first time what he had seen.

That the mushrooms had grown in the center of this subterranean vault in an obvious shape.

The shape of a woman.

We dug straight through the night.

Half a dozen oil lanterns had been spread about the cellar floor, which cast the entire room in a wash of flickering light. There were already several piles where we'd started other holes beneath the mushrooms.

"Deeper," Rowley shouted. His voice was odd, almost unrecognizable. He moved with a speed and urgency I had not seen since I'd arrived. In the unnatural light, his eyes shimmered with something I could only describe now as pure madness. He cried out, "We must dig deeper!"

The woman was buried here, that much was clear.

Who she was exactly, whether Rowley's own great-great-grandmother a hundred years before or another woman as yet discovered from another time all together, we had no idea. But we were now both convinced that a beautiful Lenape woman, one who'd once been considered 'great,' had been buried atop this very hill years ago. Buried just beneath the estate all these many years.

That the local tribes had warned others from the burial ground and that the hill, and those who foolishly dared to live upon it, had been since cursed.

Beware the Woman. The rock warnings had read. *The Great Woman.*

"If she were only freed," Rowley had sputtered, his eyes wild. *Released.* The curse on his land and family would be lifted.

So, we'd dug. All though that night and into the next day, we'd dug. We did not eat or drink and continued into the next night. Looking for her.

The room had grown hot and blurry. I needed to sleep, it had been so long. I needed water. Or, perhaps, just to escape that awful room and the implications of what we were doing. I knew from my dreams that she, whoever she was, had likely been buried alive.

Rowley had yelled. The sound was hazy. His voice parched and high. He'd found something. "Here," he cried. "Here!"

I stumbled towards him where he'd dug a hole almost five feet deep. In the ground, at the bottom of that hole, was something large and grey.

He touched it with the tip of his shovel. There was a clink sound. It was rock. A coffin, perhaps.

We worked together and carefully pried around it and found only more stone. Then, the edges. It was rounded, it seemed. A stone sphere of some sort. About the size of a full grown man. Or woman, I thought. We climbed into the hole and moved the dirt away with our bare hands now.

As we worked, I felt something move beneath me. The ground had shifted. We looked at each other briefly but kept digging with our hands.

RELEASE ME.

The ground shook again and the voice was so loud that we first huddled against the ground away from the booming sound. Rowley climbed from the hole and I followed just behind.

In the glittering lantern light, I thought I'd seen something in that hole. While no sane man would have admitted to such a thing, I could tell that Rowley had seen the same.

He lifted up the shovel and drove it with all his might into the stone disk.

It moved.

There was something black and wet on the shovel now. The same oozed from the grey rock beneath.

It opened!

The rock parted. Became something else.

Rowley fell backwards from the hole as I staggered towards the steps. One of the lanterns spilled over and the room went half dark.

Beware the woman. I'd reached the steps at last. *The great woman.*

No, a mistake, I know understood. The wrong translation, the words so similar.

And I knew what I had seen. An eye!

A massive eye staring up at me from the earth.

Great as in "Large." Not her position, but her size.

The Big Woman. The Giant.

The whole basement began to shake. Dirt spilling from almost every corner now.

A stone hand lifted from the back corner. Each of five fingers bursting from the ground like an enormous spider. Each finger larger than I was. The hand of a giant.

I saw its wrist lifting now from the ground. Moldy granite lifting ever higher into the room. Smashing supports and beams.

Rowley was screaming, and the sound he made was not human.

I leaped across the darkness to drag him away but the giant hand slammed me aside from a world of utter madness to one of complete darkness.

How I escaped, I will never know. That I could not save Rowley in the process is something I will have to live with. Other truths may not be so easy to accept.

I settled back in Pennsylvania and now the trees gently embrace me each night, no more the frightening specters of my past. I hope this helps.

The Rowley estate was completely destroyed that night. The body of Ames Rowley was never found. The entire hill had collapsed in upon itself, a gaping hole filling the space that had once been Rowley Bluff. As if some enormous thing that'd been buried beneath the hill had broken free at last.

Tawwunasinall.

I am told that it was an explosion of some kind. Gases hidden beneath the earth that had made the family sick all those years and killed the grass and trees. Gases that had finally exploded and destroyed the hill.

But I know otherwise. For, I saw the giant eye that blinked back at me from the hole that night.

Golden brown. Beautiful.

Captured by my own ancestors and hidden away. Buried.

Released after all those years.

Beware.

NOTES: Tales of stone giants and the various ways in which tribal heroes escaped, fought, or tricked such giants were popular among many Native Americans tribes. In most such tales, the giants were survivors of a more brutal race and time before man.

More than 12,000 American Indians served in the United States military during World War I, and historically, Native Americans have the highest record of service per capita when compared to other ethnic groups. The Lenni Lenape (or Delaware) were original people of the mid-Atlantic area: New Jersey, Delaware, and parts of New York and Pennsylvania, who were eventually relocated to Oklahoma, where the modern Delaware tribes are now located. Several small Lenni Lenape communities remain in New Jersey and Pennsylvania today.

THE KING
1988

Fat or skinny, it don't matter. It's the sideburns that'll make or break an Elvis.

Just about anyone can toss on the sunglasses and sequins, dye the hair black, and curl the upper lip. Not a problem. You see little kids and grandmas do it all the time. Swivel a hip, grab a leg, give 'em one good karate stance. And then another, if someone cheers the first. And, who can't imitate the voice? A little patter in between the songs. "Mama used to, ah, sing me this here, ah, lullaby."

But it's the sideburns that folk will sometimes forget to glue on, or grow out. To display 'em, long and thick and boldly reaching down both sides of the face, with the artless confidence that *is* Rock and Roll. The audience might not even know they're missing, but they'll know *something's* missing.

This Elvis had the sideburns, and six nights a month, three shows a night, he strutted 'em out onto the stage at the Deerhall Resort and Casino for a crowd of three thousand.

Background music. Something to look at.

Blue Suede Shoes. All Shook Up. Heartbreak Hotel.

He did 'em all. With two thousand slot machines rattling and dinging in the background. Fifty roulette wheels clacking. Jackpot bells ringing. Laughter. Collective roars at the craps tables.

Love Me Tender. Jailhouse Rock. Suspicious Minds.

Weekend comedians and crooners sometimes singing along. Ice-cubes rattling and coins trickling into plastic cups. Waitress shouting back orders to the bar just beneath the stage. No more than twenty people really watching at any one time.

Teddy "Elvis" Dees and the Hound Dogs.

Two thousand dollars a night, with half going to "Elvis" and the rest split evenly between the three Hound Dogs.

Steve was one of the "Hound Dogs." The guitarist.

This is his story.

About how he made a promise, and kept it.

And saved a nation.

"Hello, sir. Is Mrs. Rook available?"

"Who's this?

"My name is Steve Bessette. I was —"

"Who?"

"Steve Bessette. My grandfather was William Bessette."

"Don't know him."

"Chief Running Wolf?"

"Nope. What's this about? You collecting money for something?"

"No, sir. Ha. Sorry, no. I was hoping to talk with Evelyn Rook. If this is a bad time… Mrs., ah, Sharpshire at the Rosewood Nursing Home gave me the number. In regards to Mrs. Rook's mother and — "

"Hold on." He heard the phone being handed off to a new voice.

"Mrs. Rook?"

"Yes?"

"My name is Steve Bessette. I'm, ah, calling on behalf of the Tansisu tribe. My grandfather was —"

"Yes, yes. And?"

"Your mother, Susan Turtledove, was a member of the tribe?"

"A long time ago. Sure, I guess. She passed three years ago."

"I understand. We're just… Our records show she was a quarter Tansisu?"

"One-eighth. Guess that makes me a sixteenth or something, right?"

"Oh, I see. Right. Well, we… We've taken the first steps to restoring the tribe, finding descendents of the original members."

"What for?"

Steve played a vintage cherry red '63 Gibson ES-335 guitar, with stock humbucking pickups, rosewood fingerboard, old-cut Mickey Mouse ears, violin-style f-holes, and a Bigsby vibrato that still got the job done.

Some nights, it was still fun.

Most nights, it was still work.

Every so often, someone would come up during a break to say "sounds good" or some such thing. Maybe offer to buy the band a round of drinks. A lot of time no one said anything at all. They were only background music, after all. An Elvis tribute band. Something fun to listen to above all the other racket. Something to look at, maybe, when a customer stopped at the bar on a short break from the one-armed bandit.

He half watched the crowd from the risen stage just above the bar wearing black shirt and pants, with the guitar strapped around his back and a staged smile. A microphone of his own waited for the occasional "doo-wop" during "Teddy Bear" or "Don't Be Cruel." The real singing he left to the pro at his right. The guy in giant white sunglasses, a black silk shirt half unbuttoned, and one hip thrust half way to Lake Ontario.

"Where you from?" Elvis asked into the crowd. "Syracuse, you say. Grew up near Syracuse, it's probably my favorite place."

Steve ran through the chord progression again on his guitar, even dropped in a little fill that might have made Eddie Cochran grin, and waited for the knockout.

"What about you ma'am," Elvis turned to another smiling customer. "Where you from, sugah? Trenton, New Jersey? Grew up near Trenton, you know. It's probably my favorite place."

Still got Steve laughing every time. Maybe he was just tired. Elvis gave him a sideways look, letting him know to go into the next song. *Burning Love.*

Get the place jumping to end the set.

One more after that, then he'd drag his amp and guitar bag again through security and the long back halls to his car. Get home around two a.m., stinking of smoke, often too tired to sleep. Set aside a bit of cash so Mona and Drew could do something fun the next day. Maybe make up some for another missed night.

The rest of the money was for something else entirely.

Or, so he'd thought at the time.

The promise.

Ten years before, to his grandfather.

A deathbed promise.

The kind most people only see in movies. But they happen every single day, and Steve had walked right into his.

William "Running Wolf" Bessette, his mother's father, had been half Indian and one of the last known members of the Tansisu tribe, a small New York band that, like so many before, had slowly and simply died out over the last four hundred years. He'd even been their chief once. Long ago, when there were still a small handful of families left. Maybe forty tribesman. That kind of ended in the mid 1960s.

Second verse, same as the first.

Steve still remembered going to small gatherings hosted on the small Seneca reservation. Seeing the last of the Tansisu. The songs and dances his grandfather had already taught them being performed by others. Some costumes and skits. He vaguely remembered the ceremony where he received his own Indian name.

200

Little Wolf.

But, a lot goes on in twenty years these days. People die, move away. Blood thins. Most of the tribe had moved to Canada the century before, absorbed into bigger tribes. More recently married into the rest of America to vanish forever. He honestly couldn't recall the last time his grandfather or anyone else had been to such a gathering.

Guitar solo.

The old man laying in the hospital bed that day had not been the man he remembered. Not the guy who'd taken him hiking, told great stories beside bonfires, and played a mean game of poker. This guy was far too skeletal and frail, with tubes running out his nose and arms. And, holding his hand was like holding a witch's hand… creased with veins, hard and cold.

Steve still held tightly.

"Find the rest," was the lion's share of the last thing his grandfather ever said to him. A single lock of grey hair had been braided with wooden beads and a small feather. "Keep the tribe alive."

"As long as I'm alive," Steve heard his own voice only later, "I will."

Since, he'd tracked down twelve descendents and bought sixteen acres of land in western Connecticut with money saved from his second job. He'd mailed off some five hundred letters, made six hundred phone calls, and driven 100,000 miles. He'd argued with both the U.S. government and the Oneida tribe. He'd clumsily worn the hats of a lawyer, public relations rep, detective, lumberjack, and historian.

I will …

Steve brought it round to the B-flat again.

Break.

"Thank you, thank you very much…"

The land was sixteen acres of uneven hills with dense trees, mostly elm, and a small lake. A pair of barret hawks, dubbed "Wesley" and "Buttercup" circled overhead each day. The deer came out every twilight.

Towards the front of the property, at the end of a long dirt driveway, he'd half built a respectably sized lodge with an unfinished kitchen area and a small meeting hall with several picnic tables. Still needed drywalling and painting on the inside, but the back wall already featured a wide windowed display case a friend had built to house the tribe's "museum." A couple of photographs, beaded vest, worn flint and steel kit, and an eagle feather given by the Iroquois as a sign of peace in 1867. All of these things had been his grandfather's. The last great heirloom of the family, of the tribe, he supposed, was the wampum belt his mother still kept. Too valuable to trust out here.

Recently, he'd added a tall flag pole out front which flew the flags of the United States, New York State, and the Tansisu tribe. The last was handstitched by Mona, his wife, and fashioned after an old banner given to him by one of the descendents he'd managed to track down in Massachusetts.

Steve watched the three flags for a moment, felt the morning sun on his face, as he tried to wake a bit more after another long night of gigging with Elvis.

His son, Drew, sighed impatiently just behind him.

Steve turned and smiled. "You ready, pal?"

Drew eyed the waiting backhoe and nodded. His only job was simply to "keep Dad company." It was a job he was good at. Steve brought him and Mona as often as they could tolerate. It was always nicer when they were there.

The plan today was to finally finish the hole for the new sewage tank, maybe dig some trenches for the impending water lines. For five weeks, it always seemed to rain the night before he planned to come out and get that job done with the borrowed backhoe. Today was the day.

"It ain't gonna dig itself," Drew smiled.

They worked through to lunch. No surprises waiting in the ground, no buried boulders or clay as the hoe's diesel engine growled and smoked and its jaws clutched and moved. While Steve was a "Hound Dog" at night, it was his day gig as a master electrician that came in so handy on projects like this. Moving about construction sites all day, running miles of wire and checking code, he'd been able to pick up something of the rest through osmosis. Framing, drywall, plumbing, stonework. Just enough about each to be one step above dangerous. Plus, half the supplies he'd used 'til now were those steadily donated by contractor pals and materials collected from the "garbage" tossed out on various sites. Half-empty bags of concrete, drywall sheets, designer bricks and tile, roofing shingles, nails, you name it.

But all those supplies and modern adornments were secondary to the land.

The Land.

The tribe's only unifying link with the past and possible future.

Claimed and taken by others some two hundred years ago.

Without it, how else would the tribe ever come home?

Each time the hoe scooped more of the black earth from the ground, he couldn't help but wonder if some Tansisu had crossed over the same bit of land some three hundred years ago, two thousand years ago. Maybe camouflaged beneath a full deer hide, hunched low against the underbrush with bow in hand towards the lake down the hill.

His grandfather's people had migrated through much of New York State over the last hundred centuries. There was even some indication that they lived along the Atlantic before moving up the Housatonic River in the early 1600s. There'd once been half a dozen villages along Lake Candlewood alone.

Steve'd done his homework while he saved to afford some acreage. He'd bought just three acres at first, from his own savings. When some more of the property went for sale, he'd taken the loan, made the purchase, and quickly learned thirty Elvis songs.

Two years later, the tribe had its land again.

It just didn't have any of its people.

"The research requirements are ludicrous," Steve collected the cards to shuffle. "Don't these guys understand there aren't written records for this kinda stuff?"

"Of course they do," his wife smiled. "The BIA's been playing this game a lot longer than you have, babe."

The Bureau of Indian Affairs. The all-powerful overseer of all things Native American since 1824. "Bureaucratic monstrosity" was being too kind.

Steve dealt out another hand. "Most tribes now have to hire pros to investigate this mess. New York acreage is nothing compared to these guys. Drew, your bet. Pair to open."

"Check."

"Five," Mona said, and tossed a chip into the pot. "What did Health and Human Services say?"

"I was on the phone two hours with them. They do have some grants available it looks like. So, maybe…"

"Well it's something."

"Assuming I can work my way through the fifty-page application. After that, who knows. Another eight years. Some tribes spent as much as $500,000 putting a claim together."

"I got forty bucks I can lend you," Drew said.

"Thanks, pal. I'll let you know."

Mona folded her cards. "Is acquiring Uncle Sam's legal status really that important?"

Steve shrugged. "Means things like startup funds. Health coverage. Educational assistance. The kinds of incentives that could help some of these phone calls go a little smoother. I'm getting nowhere. Those benefits could make the difference in all of this."

"Is that why you got involved?"

"Of course not."

"Then give the others a shot," Mona said. "They'll come around."

"Do you believe this woman, pal? She's got no idea." He tossed his hands in amazement. "It's all just one headache after another. And you, you're just sitting there smiling."

"Did your grandpa worry about this stuff too?" Drew asked.

"This?" *No*, Steve thought. *Chief Running Wolf only worried about things like state-decreed assimilation and epidemics of typhus and smallpox.*

He'd worried about keeping the tribe alive.

"Kinda," Steve said.

"So, Chief, you ever get that sewage tank put in?"

Steve cringed. He hated when Curtis called him "Chief" because he always did it with that stinking sarcastic smile.

Curtis "Painted Arrow" Sawyer, the Hound Dog drummer, was a full-blooded Pequot Indian who often joked that Steve would lose his own fractional Indian heritage if he cut himself shaving.

Yet, he'd still introduced Steve to the Pequot Council, who'd helped talk him through some historical permit and name-rights issues. The Pequots, who'd once fished along the same streams and lakes as the Tansisu, were the tribe who owned the Deerhall Casino. Technically, Curtis — who still lived on the reservation with his wife and three teenaged daughters — was the boss. In just two years, thanks to new federal laws, many of the Indian reservations had been given the go-ahead to put up casinos and done so to great success. Steve often jokingly imagined a Tansisu casino in his little lodge, maybe four slot machines and a poker table to get things started. Not that the government would approve, of course. He had enough trouble, some fifty letters and two years, even getting the tribe's name back on several historical-society websites and the state registry of official tribes.

"Two months ago," Steve finished tuning his guitar and set it aside. Five minutes to show time. "Come out again some time and you can test the new facilities."

Curtis winked from just beneath his *Zildjian* cymbals. "Sure thing, Chief. You ready for next week?"

The Buckerspoint parade. The annual gathering of high school bands, Boy Scout troops, and politicians waving from convertibles. The Pequot tribe would be marching in traditional costumes again, and had formally invited the Tansisu to join if they wished.

Steve'd put the call out to those he'd found.

"Yeah," Steve said, already dreading the results. "We'll be there."

"Elvis" finally appeared up the back steps, saluted the band from the shadows. He wore his red shirt tonight and the sequin jacket with the biggest collars.

"You know," he growled in his best Elvis voice. "If life was at all fair, Elvis would still be alive and all us impersonators would be dead."

Curtis gave the expected "sting" on the drums — *Ba-Dum CHSHH!* Steve just shook his head.

"Let's get arockin' boys," Elvis smiled.

"Dad?"

"Yeah."

"Am I an Indian?"

"Part, sure."

"Will I get an Indian name like you and grandma. Standing Wolf or something cool like that."

"Do you want one?"

"I don't know. I guess. How does that happen?"

"The tribe picks one for you when you're ready."

"But you *are* the tribe."

"There are others."

"You think so?"

"I have to."

"For your grandpa?"

"And for you, now."

"Me? How's that?"

"You ask if you're Indian. You're about one-sixteenth. The rest is everything from English and Welsh to Italian and French."

"An American mutt."

"Best kind. But here's the thing, Drew. If you ever want to visit England, maybe find out a little bit more about who your family was, the people you came from, all you gotta do is get on a plane. France, Italy, Wales. You name it. You can go and visit any of 'em. Walk the same roads and hills maybe. Talk to people from the same heritage. Can't really do that with the Tansisu."

"But you can now," Drew smiled.

"You can now."

The day of the parade, Steve marched just behind three long rows of Pequot Indians in traditional regalia. The long beautiful dresses shined with a hundred different colors. The men wore rooster-tail headdresses and Gustoweah caps of coyote fur and duck feather. Handsome loop necklaces and chest plates of puka shells, bone, and horn.

Steve had braided his own long hair into several beaded strands, and wore a leather beaded shirt similar to one he'd found in old photographs of his grandfather. Both sides of the street were crowded with spectators. Folk up from New York City mostly for a weekend of gambling at the casino and the annual parade and festival.

Mona walked beside him on one side, holding his hand the whole way. Drew, though somewhat visibly embarrassed, walked on the other side carrying the tribal Tansisu banner.

There'd been no one else.

"Hey, Chief. The Big Guy wants to see you."

"Walkinghorse? He say why?"

'Big Guy' was Lawrence Walkinghorse, the Pequot Indian who managed the resort and casino. Steve had spoken to him only once in the three years he'd been playing there. A meaningless "good evening" passed in the hall one night.

Curtis shrugged. "Maybe he just don't like the way you play. Come on."

The main office upstairs was furnished in elegant wood and leather, the walls tastefully covered in original paintings of Native Americans and various framed artifacts. The secretary was a pretty girl with long dark hair he half recognized from the parade.

While waiting, Steve studied each painting, and one reminded him immediately of the night he'd received his own Indian name. He stood staring at it, trying again to remember the name of the other boy he'd been standing beside so many years ago. "Lone Hunter" was the name the other boy had been given. But, Steve hadn't yet recollected his real name and there'd been no records.

Lawrence Walkinghorse finally came out of his private office. He wore a smart business suit, and kept his hair in feathered braids. "Hello, Steve."

"Sir."

"Thanks, Curtis," Walkinghorse said. "I'll get him back down in a minute."

The drummer waved. "Good luck, Chief," he winked, smiling at Steve as he walked out.

"Come on back," Walkinghorse led Steve to his office, and indicated a chair for him to take. Steve sat and waited while Walkinghorse took the chair opposite and then stared at him a bit before speaking again. "How are things going?" he asked.

"Fine. Just fine, thanks."

"The tribe, I mean. The Tansisu."

"Yeah, no, good. These things take time, so…"

"You know," Walkinghorse said. "The BIA will never give you legal status."

"Probably not, no."

"Maybe New York will someday."

"Maybe New York."

"Anyone approach you yet?"

"About what?"

He smiled. "Starting a casino, of course."

"Who?"

"Businessmen. Outside money looking for a joint venture, perhaps."

"No. Why would—"

"You can't afford to be this naïve, Mr. Bessette. They will. And soon. Some see these ventures as a source of income for the Native communities. Schools, infrastructure, public services. Others see it as a source of income for themselves."

"That's not why I'm doing this."

"We know." He touched his chin in thought. "I knew your grandfather," he said. "Knew of him, anyway. He was a true ally of the Pequot, I'm told. Helped our people on various tricky matters over the years."

"I hadn't heard that."

"The two tribes were once close."

"I did know that."

"How many now?"

"We are twenty. Twenty-four maybe. We're still waiting on some paperwork to confirm."

"Not much of a turnout at the parade last summer."

"No," Steve smiled, "Guess not. Again, these things take time. Right? Jimmy Horus!"

"What's that?"

"Horus. Sorry. An old name just came to mind."

Walkinghorse stared in reply, clearly sizing Steve up. "Here's the thing," he leaned forward. "Sometimes cultural pride isn't enough. Sometimes, an incentive helps."

"Sure, I understand. I just —"

"In honor of our old bonds, and faith in a successful future, the Pequot tribe will bestow a $30,000 scholarship each year towards Tansisu education."

"Sir?"

"Disperse as you see fit. Our lawyers will draft something for you to look at."

"Me?"

Walkinghorse shrugged. "Who else?"

"Ma, I just don't think this is gonna happen."

"You're doing fine. Father would be proud."

"Our beloved Chief Running Wolf is the last, I think. It's been almost ten years and there were seven people at the picnic last month. Seven. And only three had Tansisu blood. You, me, and Drew."

"It's a start."

"We need active members to stay alive. Even with the Pequot's scholarship, they're just not coming."

"Give it time."

"Not much of that going around, ma. It's already taking all the free time I got, and then some more. Can't keep forcing my problems on Mona and Drew. Can't keep playing at chief here."

"My parents planned to move to New York shortly before I was born," she said. "Father'd fallen into some kind of printing business with a couple of fellas he met in college. But, the tribe called. Only about two hundred members left then. Thought he was the best man for the job. The tribe elders asked him to be chief. To give up his own desires for the sake of the tribe."

"Ha. Poor guy. He ever tell you why *he* said yes?"

"Sure," she said. "He told me it was because that's what chiefs do."

Saturday night. A full house again.

Steve could hear 'em just behind the curtain amid all the other commotion while he tuned his guitar. Elvis stood in the shadows, hands clasped in thought. Curtis and Tony set up quietly without much chitchat. Steve checked his watch. A couple minutes to showtime.

It occurred to him again that tonight would have been his grandfather's ninety-fifth birthday. Ten years now …

What might the next ten bring?

In the morning, he might just get on the letters again, do some more research on the internet for the latest batch of forms. Maybe.

"How 'bout one for Chief Running Wolf?" Curtis asked.

"Hey now!" Steve turned and smiled. Impressed Curtis had remembered. "Sure thing. Thanks, man."

Curtis just winked back.

The curtain opened slowly, revealing the crowd.

Steve made to start playing, then he noticed Drew.

In the crowd, next to Mona. And his mother.

"What the —"

His son was holding up the Tansisu banner. And wearing a red t-shirt. From the stage, Steve could just make out the words:

Tansisu: The Return.

The crowd around them, maybe twenty-five people, were all dressed in the same.

He realized only then that no one else had started playing music yet either. Elvis had not yet stepped onto the stage.

"What is this?" he asked turning. "What's going on?"

"We made some calls, I guess," Curtis said. "In honor of Running Wolf's birthday."

"How did — "

"Mona gave us your list. Couple of airplane tickets and a call to the limo company took care of the rest. Teddy picked up the bulk of the travel tab, I should add."

Elvis bowed. "Least we could do, man."

"Some guy named Jimmy Horus came by train."

"Jimmy."

"Yeah, brought his three kids too. The whole group's staying in rooms here tonight, compliments of the Big Guy. Tomorrow, Mona and a nice lady named Mrs. Rook got a real feast planned out at the Land. You're all taking one of the resort buses together."

The crowd behind him applauded now. Cheers spreading out from the cluster of red shirts.

212

Curtis had walked up behind him and slowly freed the guitar of his back.

"Ready to say hello, Chief?"

For the first time, the drummer had not been smirking when he'd said it. He'd just been smiling.

Steve looked over the faces in the crowd.

The largest gathering of Tansisu Indians in thirty-some years.

"Yeah," he said. "I think I am."

Elvis moved forward and grabbed the mic.

"Evenin', ladies and gentleman," he said. "Before we, ah, get started here tonight, there's someone I'd like to, ah, introduce…"

Chief Little Wolf.

NOTES: The renowned pairing of casinos and Native Americans began in 1988 when Congress passed legislation permitting federally recognized Native American tribes to operate casinos and bingo parlors on Indian reservations or tribal land. Today, there are more than 350 such gaming establishments in the United States, generating annual total revenues of an estimated $14 billion—More than the gaming revenues of Las Vegas and Atlantic City combined! With so much money, the program has brought both critics and some suspect business dealings, but for many tribes, it has also brought much-needed economic development to help provide public services for their members. Foxwoods Resort Casino, in Ledyard, Connecticut, is the largest casino in the world, and operated by the Mashantucket Pequot Nation, a tribe of some three hundred who are currently developing a $700 million expansion to be completed in summer 2008.

There are more than 560 federally recognized tribes in the United States today and a number of additional tribes that are recognized only by individual states. A complex legal process must be undertaken to receive such status as remnants of old nations systematically broken apart over the past three hundred years work to reestablish themselves. More than a hundred additional tribes, most being the smaller eastern woodlands tribes first lost, are currently in the challenging process of attaining this official recognition.

LIKE AN INDIAN
2006

David Hill wanted to dress up like an Indian for Halloween. Or James Bond.

The final decision, it seemed, had already been made for him by Principal Kramer or the PTA or some such thing. Official costume rules for the Brainerd Jr. High School Fall Ball.

"Can you believe it?"

The rest of the boys at the table collectively half shrugged and half ignored him, and kept eating.

"No witches, nothing violent. Nothing religious. And no Indians."

"Native Americans," someone corrected him.

"I thought it was American Indians."

"Whatever. Mr. Kramer said someone might find it 'offensive.'"

"True that."

"Alex," he turned to the boy directly at his right. The one who'd most remained perfectly quiet throughout the bulk of his five-minute rant. "Let's hear it directly from, like, the only Indian in a hundred miles. Do you find it offensive?"

"I find *you* offensive," Alex looked at David from under his dark bangs. "Does that count?"

"Ouch. I thought you'd back me on this. Maybe talk to Kramer. Tell him it's no big deal."

"Don't get me involved, dude." Alex stood to leave. He wore his standard black t-shirt, LED ZEPPLIN today, and camouflage pants. Only his golden-brown skin revealed a particular heritage of some sort. "You wanna dress like Pocahontas, that's your problem. I'll see you ladies later. I'm buying a slushy."

"What kind are you anyway?" Kriebel asked.

Alex stopped and rolled his eyes.

"He's half Sioux," David answered for him. "Top half, I think."

"Hysterical," said Alex. "How 'bout the half that's gonna beat you senseless after school?"

"His mom's full-blooded Lakota," David went on. "Grew up on a reservation. And his grandma's, like, the coolest old person ever."

"She is," another kid agreed.

"I'll tell her you said so," Alex pointed a finger at David. "Just be Bond, man. Weren't we were all going as a group or something anyway? The Bengals. Or Austin Powers characters or something…"

"I thought it'd be cooler to be an Indian."

"Why?"

"Because they're, well, cool."

"I guess," Alex said.

Margie Stormweather's face was aged with every single year of the seventy-two she'd already spent walking this earth. All wrinkly with dark stains around her eyes and cheeks. At times, Alex suspected she was really a hundred.

A year before, just after grandfather had died, she'd finally accepted her only daughter's wishes and moved in with them. She liked to watch dumb game shows and worked in the garden beside his mother when it was warm out. Taught him old songs. Scolded him when he got too loud. Fell asleep on the couch after lunch. Told great stories when it got dark.

Same as any other grandma, Alex figured.

Still, he always thought of her as his "Sioux" grandmother. The heritage was just too much a part of who she was as a person to ever really separate the two.

She was Margie Stormweather to some, but "Rain Flower" to most who knew her. Her songs were always in a language he only knew a few words of. The stories were always of the "Great Spirit" and nature. And while others, even on the reservation, now wore regular jeans and cowboys hats, his grandmother still only wore traditional deerskin ponchos and skirts. Beaded headbands. Moccasins. People stared when the whole family went to *Fridays* or the Mall. It was, regardless of his mom's suggestion that he "get over it," embarrassing.

Worse than that, though, was how *she* stared at *him*. Ever since she'd moved into the house. Always watching.

Like she was sizing him up.

Alex suspected that had everything to do with the fact that he didn't have his name yet.

His *Sioux* name.

For three years running, he'd declined to partake in the naming ceremony during the tribal powwows. While there were now even some ten-years-olds who had their names, who'd gone through the ritual, he had not. Not yet met with the medicine man, or stayed in the woods for a night alone with only his new name to think of.

Perhaps her concern, the reason she eyed him so suspiciously, was the possibility that he never would. And, with a powwow waiting the following weekend, Alex wasn't sure himself.

He came in through the garage door with David in tow, the two having just spent the last couple hours completely shredding the skateboard park. Pressure Flips. Nose Grinds. Alex even pulled off, to the hoots of the other skate rats, his first-ever Nose Kasper. His heart was still thumpin' from that one.

"What have you two hooligans been up to?" his mother asked.

"Nothing."

"Sounds wonderful. Hi, David."

"Hey, Mrs. Steins. *Hau Kola*," he added to Alex's grandmother, also sitting at the table.

She smiled broadly and nodded. "*Hau Kola,* David."

Alex shot David a quick warning look while moving toward the basement door. "We're gonna play some *Madden* before dinner."

"David, are you joining us for dinner?"

"Oh, no, Mrs. Steins. That's real nice but —"

"You stay," Margie Stormweather said. "Good boy, this one." She reached out to pat his arm as he passed.

David laughed. "OK, sure. Dinner sounds good."

"So," Alex's father asked, passing a half-empty basket of garlic bread. "Did we reach a final verdict on next weekend?"

Mrs. Steins shrugged. "Alex?"

Alex shrugged back.

"Is that a yes or…"

"I don't know," he said, and spent the next few moments staring at his plate. "A bunch of guys are planning a massive paintball battle for next weekend. Like forty guys or something."

"Lion's Den Park," David added between bites.

"Yeah. So I thought… I don't know."

"Well, your grandmother and I are going," his mother said. "And, Whistling Star told me that Blake and Jenny will be there."

"And I'd like to go also," his father added. "But, if you plan on staying home, let's settle on that now. Because," he winked, "I'll be staying with you, junior."

"Rats," Alex turned to David. "We better cancel that huge party then."

"I don't understand what the big deal is," his mother shook her head, ignoring his joke. "You use to look forward to the powwows."

"Can we, like, talk about this later?"

"I'm sure David doesn't mind," his mother said.

"No, I'm good," David smiled. "Go right ahead."

Alex groaned. "Why not take *him* then. He apparently *wants* to be an Indian."

Now it was David's turn to shoot a warning look, his face already growing flushed with embarrassment.

"Maybe I just need a break," Alex said. "I'm fourteen-years-old. Maybe all the costumes and drum beating are getting a little old. Like Santa Claus or Halloween. Maybe I don't want to go into the woods and have some medicine man put a 'Sorting Hat' on my head to figure out what my 'real name' is."

"You bring your friend." His grandmother said. "The two boys together will come."

Alex stared coldly straight ahead.

"You," Margie Stormweather pointed an accusing finger at Alex. "You are like the Wolf Hunter Boy."

"What's that?" David asked.

"I'll tell you both," she said. "First, we eat."

Margie Stormweather, Rain Flower, sat on a chair in the family room when she finally told the story. The rest of the family, including David who'd quickly taken the sofa seat directly across from her, had gathered around to listen as if she were reading a bedtime story to little children. David glanced over to where Alex was more noticeably sprawled in one of the two beanbag chairs across the room, a *Thrasher* magazine in his hands.

"Many moons ago," she began. "The people lived along the edge of great mountains. And many dark nights, beneath the howling winds, the wolves crept down from their hidden lairs and made war on man.

"These were not ordinary wolves, not those you find today. These were giants bred in the deepest reaches of those dark mountains, weaned from birth on the dark powers of the goddess Inahe, goddess of the mountain. Beasts of claw and fang that were unafraid of man or his fires. Beasts with the power of speech and magic. Eyes that shined like the stars.

"The strongest and bravest men of the village, called the Wolf Hunters, sometimes pursued their enemy high into the shadowed mountains. Many never returned from these hunts. Chief Turning Moon, however, wore a full necklace of heavy wolf claws around his neck. He was the greatest of all the Hunters. One day, his son, Asheä, came to him.

"'I am now a man,' he declared to his father. 'I will become a Wolf Hunter.'

"'No,' his father said. "'You are not yet ready.'

"'But I am of age,' Asheä argued.

"'Yes.'

"'And I am the most skilled in the whole village with the bow. The fastest runner. The best climber.'

"'Yes.'

"'We need great warriors to hunt the wolves.'

"'Yes.'

"'So many 'yesses', then why do you say 'no' to your son?

"'You are not yet ready,' Chief Turning Moon replied again. 'You do not yet truly fear Inahe, the great spirit who rules these mountains. You do not yet respect her power. Without that, all of your skills and strength will mean little. The wolves live high in the mountains, gathered in deep dark places.'

"'Every child knows this, father.'

"'Inahe rules these mountains.'

"'Every child knows that too. We were taught all this before we learned to walk.'

"The Chief smiled. 'See? You still see her as a child sees her. A man understands that it is not a learned tale. That you may be the strongest and the best, but surviving a hunt is always achieved by that which is beyond even you. You must truly understand that when you are in the Great Mountains, she is watching and you are always in her hands.'

"'I understand, father,' Asheä said.

"The great Chief studied the boy, then sighed. 'We shall see,' he said. 'Tomorrow, you will hunt with me. I will show you there is more to this than shooting the bow and being brave. I will teach you to climb. And to use the ropes. To recognize the winds that sweep men off the high mountain walls. To follow tracks down long tunnels where there is never light. Then, you will, I hope, truly learn Inahe.'"

David listened as Stormweather slowly recounted the hunt of the Chief and his son. She told of their dangerous ascent up the great mountains as the two jumped between high peaks, and braved jagged climbs against whipping winds. The dark caves became endless tunnels filled with hidden pits and ghostly spirits sent to deceive the two men. Terrifying chambers filled with hairy mounds of creeping bats. At last, in a voice that was somehow both rough and soft at the same time, she told of their battle with Prince Sungsiki, one of the young lords of the wolf pack. The two men slew the beast together and made back for home carrying their prize.

"'This prize shall be made as a sacrificial offering,' Chief Turning Moon smiled, as they worked their way back down the mountain. 'In honor of your first kill as a Wolf Hunter. In praise of Inahe. We shall give this to the medicine man.'

"'But I am very hungry now,' the boy groaned. 'We have been in these mountains for days. May we just have a little of the meat now?'

"'No,' the Chief told him. 'It would be disrespectful to the great Inahe and to the wolf prince we have slain.'"

David turned to Alex and saw that he'd propped up some and was now listening almost as intently as the others. He smiled at him but Alex ignored him.

Stormweather nodded at him when he looked back at her, and continued. She told how Asheä eventually decided there would be no real harm and indeed snuck some of the meat before the sacrificial ceremony was held. That same night, he awoke to a shimmering phantom in the shape of a wolf, glowing with power. He knew at once it was the very embodiment of Inahe. To punish Asheä and his tribe for his insult, she had turned Chief Turning Moon into a bat and left him with the other cursed spirits in a far, dark cave. Only if Asheä could prove himself to her, would he ever see his father again.

David listened as the young prince made his way back up the mountain to find his father. Fighting winds that had grown ever more terrible and strong. Rock grown more jagged and cold. Tunnels that had become longer and darker.

"When he recognized his father clinging among the other bats, he fell to his knees and prayed to Inahe for forgiveness. Only then, did she appear to him again. Beautiful and terrible, she was. 'Forgive me,' Asheä cried. 'I realize now my father's words. Truly, you are the ruler of these mountains, and I thank you for your help in seeing my father again. What, Great Spirit of the Mountain, may I do to apologize so that my father may be freed.'

"Inahe thought, ran a paw beneath the whiskers of her wolf chin. 'Your father, I shall free, young chief,' she said. 'But you must now take his place. At the first flower each spring until the end of your days, you shall come to me here and live as a bat with the others.

"'Yes, great spirit,' Asheä bowed.

"'But, when the first leaf falls, you may return to your people again to be Chief until winter's end. Then, when you hear the mountain's winds, you will also hear me there. Reminding you of who you truly are and your duty to me.' And so it has been ever since," Alex's grandmother said. "When you listen to the howl of the winter wind, you can still hear her calling to him."

"Cool," David said.

Alex, who his grandmother now nodded at, said nothing at all.

The powwow, like life, was framed upon a giant circle. Alex's mom had explained this to David when they first arrived. At the exact center of the sacred circle were the drummers, the heartbeat of the gathering. The next ring was the dance area, where, throughout the day, various assortments of costumed dancers had moved into the ring to celebrate their gathering, celebrate life, and celebrate the Great Spirit. Around the dance ring was a larger circle of spectators, of various ages and shapes gathered in folding chairs or on blankets. Behind them, around the outer edges of the arena, were the food and craft vendors. And finally, a ring where all the families had set up tents and teepees for the weekend. Beyond that, were the woods and the rest of the world.

Alex and David surveyed the vendor tables together, each boy sipping a *Coke* while sharing a plate of sugar-powdered frybread. They'd already eaten through several hot dogs, cobs of corn, and a huge package of spicy deer jerky. Around them, the crowd burbled with excitement and happy chatter and laughter. While many wore traditional clothing with beads and quill work, conch belts, and knee-high leggings, some were in American-military dress, and the rest wore just regular jeans and jackets. David noticed that Alex had opted again for his usual camouflage pants and a black AC/DC t-shirt underneath a light denim jacket.

"Dude, this would be so sweet for a Halloween costume," David pointed to a beaded wristband on the table. "The stupid costume rules stink."

"Yeah, well cry to Kramer about that."

"He ain't budging."

"Surprise. He's usually so understanding," Alex made a face. "Why do you want to be an Indian anyway?"

"I don't know. Your grandma is like —"

"Cool," Alex laughed. "Yeah, I got that."

"Look around, man. You've just got such a neat heritage. I don't even know what the heck I am, my family tree's so watered down. I'm just a boring American. But, you've got all of this great stuff." David lifted his hands to present a field of evidence, and Alex skimmed the booths behind them.

Even as they spoke, he could hear several drummers practicing in the tents behind. Someone was singing a Sioux fall song he recognized over the P.A. system in the main arena, the sound echoing though the large camp. A mother was helping her young daughter secure her beautiful dance outfit.

"You're a real Sioux," David continued. "And, you're, like, I don't know, my best friend and stuff. I thought it'd be…"

"Cool?"

"Dude, whatever."

Alex ran his hand across a stunning stone dagger that almost looked like jewelry. He found himself imagining a young boy no older than himself using such a prize on a grand adventure. Maybe hunting deer or even a wooly mammoth once long ago. "You could dress like a Viking," he said. "Those guys got around. They gotta be in your blood somewhere. I'll bet Mandy Emenecker would love to see you dressed as a Viking."

"You think?" David grinned. "Mandy Emenecker, huh."

Alex shrugged. "Okay, cut the dirty talk. My father approaches. 'Sup, Dad?"

"Just making sure you two haven't left the state. You see Paul yet?"

"Yeah." Several times already, someone had stopped Alex to say hello.

His father nodded. "They're putting together the list now." Alex turned back to the table, ran his hand along some CDs, and drank his soda. "What do you think?"

"I don't know."

"Is this for the naming ceremony?" David asked.

"Yup." Alex's father smiled. "What's the concern, Alex?"

"Nothing. Just… nothing." He moved from the table and David and Alex's father followed. "Why is this so important? To mom. Grandma. I'm half German, too. And Catholic."

"Think that'll change?" his father asked. "Getting your Indian name won't change that. Give me some of that frybread." He took a bite. "You'll still have both heritages. We'll still celebrate Christmas, if that's your worry." He put a hand out to slow him. "Listen to me. Your mom and I knew what we were doing. We always thought the blend of cultures would turn out great." He put a hand on Alex's shoulder. "And you have."

"So, then why do I gotta do this?"

"Because even if it's not important to you yet, it is to your mom and grandmother. Good ol' Rain Flower isn't going to be here forever. I think she just wants to make sure her heritage is going to continue after she's gone. You didn't know your grandfather."

"Grey Bear."

"He honestly believed that America would one day revert back to the way it had been before Plymouth Rock, and that whites were only a temporary setback. Like a bad storm or outbreak of sickness that would eventually end. A minor bump in a history that was some thirty thousand years old."

"Hard core."

"Yeah, well. That's not your grandmother."

Alex looked out across the spectators, trying to find her.

"She sees you, young man, and proudly sees the future. I just think she'd like it if that future were to proudly see the past a little bit too. Got it?"

"Yeah."

"Come on," he waved them forward. "They're going to be doing an Honor Song for the Walker boy."

"Little Thunder?"

"He's back from two years in Afghanistan. Your mother said he might even receive an eagle feather today."

The three moved around the ring until they were with Alex's mother and grandmother again. The powwow had grown startlingly quiet. The five watched as James "Little Thunder" Walker was introduced in his army ranger uniform. A drum that had been in the Walker family for four generations was used for the Honor Song. Then several tribal elders moved forward, told how he'd saved four men in Afghanistan and served his country with honor, then bestowed upon him an eagle feather. Alex's grandmother and mother, David noticed, had both cried a little bit. "This is really something, isn't it?" he whispered to Alex.

"Yeah," Alex replied. "It is."

After, the dancers returned. Young women in beaded moccasins, knee-high leggings, and dresses decorated with ribbon work and shells. Their hair ties and choker necklaces shined with colorful stones. They danced as one, bending their knees with a graceful up and down movement, turning slightly each time with the beating drums. Every so often, they raised beautiful fans. Much more calm than the mens' dances.

"The women are more earth grounded," Grandmother Stormweather explained beside David. "So they do not hop about as much. They turn to look for their warriors and hunters to come home."

David smiled back and shook his head. He caught Alex looking at her too. They both turned back to watch the rest of the dance. When they were done, the announcer declared it was time for the intertribal dance.

"What's that?" David asked.

"Means you can go be an Indian now," Alex held out his hand as many of the spectators moved out into the dance area. "Everyone can dance to this one."

"Serious?"

"Yeah."

"Do you want to, David?"

"Geeze, I don't know, Mrs. Steins."

"Come," said Margie Stormweather, standing from her chair slowly. "We will all dance."

She'd taken the hand of each boy and started towards the circle. Alex shot David a look behind his grandmother's shoulders. There was nothing to be done about it. She'd made up their minds for them.

In the arena, David watched the other dancers around them and listened to the drummers. The ball of one foot tapped on one beat and then placed down flatly on the next. Then again, with the other foot. That was it. Four hundred people, of all ages, shades, and sizes, all doing the same dance. David joined them.

Mrs. and Mr. Steins danced just beside him. David turned the other way and watched Alex and his grandmother dancing too. Alex was suddenly smiling as much as he did when he'd first pulled off his Nose Kasper.

David waved and Alex winked back.

They all danced together for many minutes, and David realized there was something almost magical about so many people sharing in the same thing.

When the dance was over, the family moved back towards their chairs. Alex, however, had started the other direction.

"Alex," David ran to catch up. "Where you goin', dude?"

"I'm gonna go learn my name," he said.

The medicine man, Sound of Drum, looked exactly the same as Alex remembered him, though it had been two years since he'd last seen him. Behind the fire's glistening light, the man was tall and gaunt with dark skin and long black hair that hung in two feathered braids over his shoulders. His eyes were white as snow in the half darkness. His face was shadowed in red and black paint.

White pines and jagged autumn sugar maples loomed in the shadows just outside the campfire. He breathed their scent in and remembered the nights at summer camp listening to the man's tales with fifty other children. For several years, he'd spent a week each summer at the reservation, living in teepees; a week of games, crafts, and learning his heritage. That had been a long time ago, he thought. He hoped the medicine man would not remember him. Like how he'd climbed atop one of the wood lodges and broken through. Or, when he'd punched Ron Hassrick in the nose. He surely didn't want any of those memories making their way into his new name.

He looked about the rest of the campfire. Six other kids were gathered in the chilly darkness, instructed not to speak, only to listen as Sound of Drum offered a ritual to Mother Earth and the Four Winds. Then he sat before his drum at the fire's edge and played for them.

Alex was the oldest. The others, a mix of boys and girls, looked twelve, maybe thirteen. They all had followed the medicine man far out into the woods. Away from the powwow. In the morning, they would return to the powwow with their new names. They would exchange gifts with each other to celebrate.

He thought of his parents and grandmother back at the camp. Wondered how David was holding up. He hid a smile. David deserved whatever harassment he was getting.

"The Great Spirit knows your name," Sound of Drum said quietly. "Tonight, he will share it with you. You," he pointed at Alex.

Alex stood and stepped forward.

"I remember you well, young man."

Alex wondered if the other kids could see his legs shaking. He looked the medicine man straight in the eyes, and thought brave thoughts.

"As does the Great Spirit," Sound of Drum smiled. He took another puff of his pipe, let the smoke drift between them, moved it with an eagle feather in his other hand so that Alex could barely see him. It was almost if looking at a dream. Alex tried not to cough.

Sound of Drum laid the pipe aside.

"This is a brave one," he said. "He has no fear for his body." The man had also dipped his fingers into a clay jar and marked Alex's temples with red paint. "He is fast and strong."

He gave Alex an eagle feather to hold between his hands and then closed his eyes and listened to the wind.

Alex did the same, and could not help but to think of Grandmother Stormweather's story of the Wolf Hunter. Would he hear Asheä's name tonight on the approaching winter winds? Or his own?

He heard his own.

The gym was dimly lit and crowded with small ever-shifting clusters of boys of girls in costume. The DJ was playing some lame dance song from the 1980s.

Alex huddled in his usual group, tonight surrounded by half-formed versions of Dr. Evil, Neo, Donald Trump, and Chad Johnson. He wore a top hat, sunglasses and black jeans.

"Anyone find David yet?"

"Yeah," Alex said. "I found him."

David stepped from the crowd into their circle.

"'Sup, ladies? Nice Slash."

"Look at this guy."

"Lame."

David wore camouflage pants and a black PINK FLOYD t-shirt. He'd also pushed his hair into his eyes as best be could.

"You're supposed to be Alex, right?"

"Ya think?"

"I thought you wanted to dress like an Indian."

"He did," Alex said.

The other guys just stared, confused.

The two friends spoke beneath the rest of the dance's noise.

"Cool?" David asked.

"Yeah," Alex smiled. "Cool."

NOTES: Modern powwows are held by American Indians gathering to dance, sing, eat, and socialize while celebrating the culture's heritage. Powwows vary in length from six hours to three days, and major gatherings can last as long as a week and have 20,000 visitors. American Indians and non-Native Americans alike assemble together at these festivals. "Powwow" comes from the Narragansett (northeastern tribe) word powwaw, which means "spiritual leader," and has since been used to describe any gathering of Native Americans of any tribe.

Indian names are earned and bestowed in special ceremonies, and each tribe has its own traditions surrounding the means and rules of this special rite. Twelve is a common age for this custom, though the names may also come much later. Indian names are usually unique to each individual, and related to some accomplishment, rite of passage, physical trait, dream, or life event. The name, however, may also be passed down from another family member. The name may even change over time, as "Little Bear" may one day become "Grandfather With many Horses." It is believed such names bestow certain powers and responsibilities.

DREAM CATCHERS
1510

The storyteller arrived just ahead of the storm.
He did not speak that night, however. He first wanted to rest after his long journey, he said. Besides, the eventual winds and thunder raged well until the next morning, and his words would have been wasted beneath that storm's fury.

That same terrible thunderstorm moved on the next morning as quickly as it had appeared, and on that second night, everyone gathered to hear him. The chief, himself, sat perched at the front of the tribal longhouse, surrounded on either side by several of the other men, including Ohneka's father.

The boy watched from afar as the five spoke quietly to each other, waiting — just as anxiously it seemed — for the storyteller to begin. The rest of the tribe lined several long rows down both sides of the enormous lodge. Two small fires burned in pits on opposite sides of the longhouse, casting spirited shadows against the birch-bark walls. The large crowd murmured with excitement and curiosity, as it had been several harvests since a traveling *Hageota* had last visited their village.

Ohneka could barely recall the last time. He was now twelve and vaguely remembered several boundless nights spent years before in the same longhouse, the tribe holed up together against one winter storm or another. Then, an Onandowagan storyteller had spent two weeks with them, crafting tales for hours until everyone in the lodge had fallen peacefully asleep despite the blizzard. Everyone but Ohneka.

Each night, when the storyteller would again ask *"Hoh?"* to the quiet room, eventually, only Ohneka replied with the customary *"Henh"* to declare he was still awake and listening. Then, the storyteller would always smile and tell Ohneka to sleep. There would be more stories the next night, he promised. Ohneka had not yet completely forgotten the feeling in the lodge those nights, the unreserved sounds of laughter and surprise, the unique warmth of all those people gathered, the smell of the fires, cornbread, and greasy skins, as they all listened to the stories together.

He remembered the thrill and terror of being invited to reach a hand into the man's storytelling pouch in front of everyone, then drawing out a shriveled owl claw that the storyteller took from his wobbly hand before starting two new tales. One about Owl and Crayfish that had the whole room laughing well into the night, and then another about the ghosts who lived backwards and traveled on the backs of old owls. The last story left the room silent, pleased and just a touch worried.

Ohneka thought it all magic. Since then, he'd always listened carefully each time one of the elders told one of the legends. Or when Bubeek, the medicine woman, told a tale of the Winds or the Turtle. He listened and remembered. While he knew he could never become a real *Hageota*, it was still fun inventing his own endings in his mind. Or ways to make them funnier, more scary. Surely, he told himself, this new storyteller would be worth the wait. Would teach him some new tale or trick.

"That's him!" he nudged Jino, and she looked up from the leather bracelet she was lacing together. "See? He's talking to the chief!"

"Amazing," she gasped. "I've never seen an old man before."

He lifted his fist in warning. "Jino, you better — "

"Hush," she said. "You might miss his first story." Then, she giggled and Ohneka recalled why we could never remain too mad at her teasing.

He turned to his other side where Dekni, his younger brother by two summers, waved and made faces at some friends across the room. Ohneka laid a hand across his brother's back to quiet him, and then turned back to the front of the room where the storyteller was at long last ready to start.

The storyteller's face appeared wrinkled and browned by many suns, like a field about to be planted, but much to Ohneka's relief, his deep black eyes still sparkled with life and intelligence. The stranger dressed quite plainly with long white hair which he kept tied in a beaded braid that ran down his gaunt back, and a buckskin shirt and leggings adorned with simple fringe. The only garment of note, Ohneka decided, was his breechcloth apron, which featured a woven multicolored image.

A dream catcher.

Ohneka still kept one near his own bed. A small tear-shaped hoop made of bent willow, strung like a web with sinew in the center and decorated with a single owl feather and some bits of shell. The dream catcher had been handmade by his mother years ago, and he'd been taught like the others that the charm would ensnare nightmares and allow only the good dreams through a small hole in the center each night. The trapped bad dreams, it was still believed by many, would then burn away on the dawn's first light. Most in the tribe still kept one near the bed out of habit or tradition. Ohneka had always thought it a good-enough story, and wondered if the *Hageota* would somehow work his apron's design into his performance.

The room had grown completely quiet as the storyteller lifted out his arms.

"*Hoh?*" he asked.

"*Henh!*" Ohneka shouted with a hundred others. The whole room then laughed at the thunderous outburst.

The storyteller smiled back and bowed. Waited for silence again. Then, he spoke. He first told of how "Bear Lost His Tail," to which Ohneka laughed with the crowd and shouted out the expected answers with the others when the storyteller invited them to participate.

The man reached next into his storyteller bag, a worn leather purse on a belt at his hip, and pulled out a small rock. He rolled the rock between his fingers while telling of a giant woman made of stone who'd been captured by one of the northern tribes. He next drew a rabbit's foot and told "Girl who Lived with Rabbits." Then an arrowhead, which prompted his account of the "Four Lost Hunters." Each story seemed more filled with a perfect blend of adventure, laughter and wonder than the last.

Throughout, Ohneka frequently turned to smile at Dekni or Jino, and pat Dekni's leg, to help him follow the stories. His brother, who'd lost most of his hearing one winter shortly after he could walk, always smiled back.

Ohneka watched in amazement as more tales were told long into the night and new songs were taught to everyone. The *Hageota* controlled the room completely now, every face watching him entirely, clinging to his every word and expression. Despite all the excitement, Ohneka found he'd become peacefully sleepy.

The storyteller then reached into his bag once more. This time, Ohneka could not see what he'd pulled out. It had been a wisp of something, ashes perhaps, that the old man waved over the dying blaze and then were lifted away on the fire's smoke.

The *Hageota* then told the story of the Giant Crow who carried away people beyond the stars and then dropped them when it was done. An odd story, horrifying at times, and Ohneka was surprisingly relieved when the storyteller said, "*Naho.*"

I have spoken.

Ohneka shook himself more awake, and even wondered if he'd dozed off for a minute. He looked about the rest of the room for the first time in awhile, and watched the others stir themselves slowly back to their feet too.

The night was over, and the crowd started moving slowly and quietly out of the longhouse back to their own lodges. Every face appeared pleased and satisfied, and Ohneka knew they were all thinking the same thing. *Here was a true storyteller! What would tomorrow night bring?*

"He was good, Ohneka," Jino said behind him.

"Wasn't he?" He tugged his brother's hand to keep him in the shifting crowd. "I told you he would be."

"Best hang your dream catcher close tonight," Jino said. "The last tale of the crow was quite horrible."

"I will," he smiled. "I had the same idea, actually. Though I would like a look at that crow for myself, I think."

She laughed. "Strange boy."

Just then, someone shoved past.

Ohneka fell back, pulling his brother to safety. "Hey," he shouted after the oddly shuffling form. "Careful!"

It was Ganyah's mother, Jejewa.

The squat woman continued to push through the crowd, forcing her way towards the outlet past the others amid complaints and some light laughter.

Ohneka shook his head and turned to talk again with Jino. He didn't think of Ganyah's mother again until the next morning.

When he first heard she'd vanished in the night.

Watching the village from afar, one would have assumed nothing unusual had happened the night before.

Chores were completed as they had been for a hundred years by mothers tending crops of corn and beans, and fathers and older boys going off to hunt deer and fish in the river. For the upcoming winter, some of the women fashioned new blankets and stretched deerskin to dry, and a group of men worked at steaming wood to craft two new sleds. Closer, however, the conversations were only about one thing.

The sudden disappearance of Ganyah's mother.

Ohneka joined some of the other children to harvest wild berries and herbs and stood over two baskets already half filled with deep red berries. Jino and Dekni worked beside him, filling their own baskets.

"She was probably eaten by wolves."

"That's disgusting." Jino kept picking. "And, you shouldn't be talking about it at all. It's disrespectful."

"Ganyah said he heard something outside their lodge last night. That he heard her screams lifting away on the wind."

"Ganyah's upset. He doesn't know what he's saying."

"Our father helped look by the river. But I heard someone found her beaded cape near Wundy Peak."

"Why would she be all the way up there?"

Ohneka shrugged. "That's the real mystery."

"The only mystery," Jino tossed a twig at him, "is why I waste my time with you two. Bubeek says she will not teach me to truly heal until I am done playing with silly boys."

Ohneka made a snarling wolf sound and she laughed. "Shouldn't you be with the other hunters?"

"I'll catch up with them later." His face quickly grew serious again and more thoughtful. "Everyone's saying how strangely she acted last night."

"Who? Ganyah's mother? They also say 'He who speaks of others burns his own tongue.' Stop gathering gossip and help us with these berries. It's probably nothing. Ganyah's mother will return again." She looked up. "But, we should still go to him, though, and see if we can do anything to help him."

"No. He and his father are with the chief."

That made Jino pause. "Something terrible might really have happened."

"I know," he said. "I didn't mean... I was just thinking."

"About what, now?"

"The crow."

"What crow?"

"The giant in the story."

"Why?"

"I just…"

She waited, her eyes suggesting that his next statement, no matter what it was, would be a stupid one.

"Nothing," he said. "I best be heading back now." He tapped his brother on the shoulder to let him know he was ready and then started back to the village.

Throughout the rest of the day, Ohneka hunted with the other boys and often found himself staring out west towards Wundy Peak, listening carefully to the tree-muffled wind for any hint of her cries for help. He'd heard none.

After all the chores were completed, the grimness of the situation settled some over village. Ganyah's mother was still missing. The adults gathered in various small clusters, speaking in hushed concerned tones. The children kept close to their own lodges, no games of lacrosse being played in the central square.

At dusk, he followed everyone back for another night of stories. "The chief feels it's just what we need," his father had grumbled at dinner. "Something to take our minds off poor Jejewa for awhile."

"What do you think?" Ohneka asked, already knowing what he'd say. The practical answer. The same sensible answer that led to his father's decision that Dekni should never learn how to become a hunter, that his hearing loss was a threat to himself and the tribe.

His father had shrugged. "Storytelling has its time and place, I suppose." He took a mouthful of stew. "Anyway, the chief wants us all there, so the real work can wait until morning."

Later, the longhouse again filled and the storyteller moved beside the front fire pit to ask "*Hoh?*" This night, it sounded more of a real question.

Did they want to hear such tales when one of their own was missing?

"*Henh,*" much of the room, including the chief, replied quietly, nodding that he should carry on. Ohneka nudged Jino beside him. He, certainly, was ready to hear more.

The storyteller spoke quietly and slowly, considerate of the room's more somber mood. First of the "Winter Wolves" and then the "Wife of the Thunderer." The stories proved thoughtful and lyrical, without needing any jokes or adventure to keep them moving. Ohneka peered over the crowd, his father looking on politely enough, and realized that the chief was probably right. It was pleasant to take your mind away from real worries for awhile. The made-up ones were always so much easier to solve.

The old man reached into his pouch and drew out the dried rattle of a snake. He shook it at the crowd, and there was a mixture of girlish shrieks and laughter. Then, he told the story of the "Giant Two-Headed Snake" and "The Day Snakes Made War on Man.'"

He dug into his bag again and Ohneka could not see what he'd drawn. Again, it was something dusty, which he sprinkled over the fire.

The *Hageota* then told the story "Hunting the Great Bear." *The experienced hunter preparing his arrows and strapping on his snowshoes …* Ohneka felt himself growing tired again, half lost in the story. *The huge bear possessed by evil spirits had glowed like the moon…*

Ohneka felt a tug at his arm and turned.

Dekni sat there, as before, and Ohneka's first thought of scolding him for interrupting went away as soon as he saw the look in his little brother's eyes.

Horror.

Dekni's eyes were wide with fear, his mouth frozen half open with trembling lips.

"What?" he asked sharply. Those around him shifted at the noise, annoyed now by his interruption. But, they never once, Ohneka noticed, took their eyes of the *Hageota*.

Ohneka knew his brother would not hear him well unless he yelled, so he lifted his hands in question. *What???* Dekni could not hear the tale either. *So, what had frightened him so?*

He noticed then that Dekni was pointing at something. One finger, trembling as if in a winter wind, was held out and low towards the front of the room. Ohneka turned to follow his brother's meaning.

He saw only the storyteller.

Just an old man speaking at the front of the lodge. His hands and mouth moving slowly, everyone gathered around his feet to listen. Ohneka didn't know what his brother had —

Dekni pointed stronger, more urgently.

Ohneka looked again.

He turned back to his brother and then forward again.

It was a trick of the lights, he thought. Something in the way the fires' flames were flickering in the shadowy room. Or, the moonlight somehow trickling through the smoke holes in the roof. But there was clearly now something there. Standing with them in the room.

He looked about to see if anyone else had seen the same thing.

Gegenh, one of the stronger hunters had risen from his mat. His hands were held to his head as if he had a terrible headache. *Did he see it too?*

Ohneka looked back at the storyteller.

The figure he'd seen had already vanished again. The flames in the blaze now swirled another direction. Whatever Ohneka had seen, whatever his brother had seen when everyone else had been listening to the tale, was now gone.

Ohneka thought of the bear story, and told himself it was some trick the storyteller had played. But, the thing he'd seen was not even a bear. It was something else.

Where he'd seen the storyteller standing all night, he'd seen something else. And for just an instant.

A hulking shaggy form with long tree trunk arms that drooped along the ground. Giant claws like daggers at the end of each. Yellow bulging eyes. And, the wide cavernous mouth, the jaw moving as he heard the *Hageot's* words, dripping many fangs within.

For an instant, he'd not seen the storyteller or a bear. But something else.

A nightmare.

"He's the one," Ohneka said again, looking about the dark and empty village. "I know it."

"You're ridiculous."

"Am I?" He waved her closer into the shadows just to make sure. "Then why are you here?"

"To prove you're ridiculous."

"You didn't see what I did," he whispered. "What Dekni saw too!" He clasped his brother's shoulder. "And now Gegenh is dead."

"Bears are dangerous," Jino whispered. "Gegenh was a daring hunter. These things happen. It's almost morning, Ohneka, Please …"

"Since when do hunters go out alone? Even Gegenh?"

She shrugged.

"And have you ever heard of a bear brave enough, hungry enough, to come into our village? Up to a lodge? That's what's ridiculous. I saw Gegenh last night. He was … He'd seen something, or heard something, in the story. Something that frightened him."

"The bear story?"

"Yes."

"We should tell the chief. Someone. Your father."

"No," Ohneka said, fighting to keep his eyes open against the approaching dawn. "They'd never believe us now."

"Your strange imagination is getting the best of you," she hissed in the darkness. "And I'm cold. Too many stories about giant crows and possessed bears, I think."

"Maybe." He waved a hand to hush her. "But, we'll find out soon enough. There he is now."

The three children froze in the darkness like deer, then watched as the storyteller emerged from his lodge, moving quickly and silently into the darkness. There'd been no stories that night, though they'd heard the storyteller would speak again the next. "Where is he going?" Jino whispered.

"That's what we're about to find out. Come on."

They kept to the shadows and silently moved after his retreating form. The rest of the village was likely asleep, though several fires burned bright around the outskirts to ward off any return of the bear. The men had spent the entire day looking for signs of the creature, but its marks had vanished into thin air just outside Juju's hut. They'd found nothing.

The storyteller crept to the right suddenly, staying to the shadows himself and vanishing behind one of the lodges.

"That's Moneton's hut?"

"Come on," he waved them forward. Just in time, to see the shadowy form push the flap aside and step into the lodge.

They tiptoed slowly behind, and from just outside the entrance, Ohneka could peak past the flap inside. "What's he doing?" Jino whispered behind him.

"I don't know. Wait …"

Inside, the storyteller stood directly above Moneton. His hands reached slowly over the sleeping man and Ohneka thought just then he should scream. Or something. Jump into the room and shout, "Got you!" But he waited …

The storyteller pulled back his hand. In it, he now held something. A dream catcher. Moneton's dream catcher.

Ohneka watched as he drew open his pouch. The storytelling pouch he used each night. And held the dream catcher over it.

Jino crept up behind him. "What's he doing?"

He held up a finger to still her.

Inside, the storyteller shook the catcher over his bag, his eyes closed, mouth quietly mumbling something they could not hear. Moneton's dream catcher shimmered briefly in the moonlight.

"What's he doing?" she asked.

Ohneka retreated quietly from the door, waving Jino and Dekni to follow just behind.

"What was that?" she asked. "What was he doing?"

Ohneka collected his thoughts, looked over the village from the shadows and watched the storyteller retreat from the lodge and return to his own. The full moon looked down upon them like a great eye watching from above.

The eye of a giant crow maybe, he thought.

"He's collecting dreams," he said. "Those trapped in the dream catchers."

"Dreams?"

"Nightmares."

Dekni nodded in understanding but Jino shook her head. "How? That's not possible."

"I don't know. What's possible anymore? What magics still walk the earth? I just — "

"But why," she asked. "Why would someone want a bagful of nightmares?"

"To open it," he said. "To sometimes let them out."

Ohneka did not listen to the story of "The Haunted Wood of Flying Heads" or the "Rabbit and the Fox." He paid no attention to "The No-Face Doll" and "The Moon Woman."

Hoh?

He simply watched and waited.

He tried hard not to think of the scaffold he'd passed earlier, or Gegenh's body within, stitched into its leather hide for burning later. Tried not to think of what he'd seen the night before, or carefully hiding their dream catchers when he and Dekni finally snuck back home. Of the frustration and disappointment in his father's face when he'd tried in vain to tell him what they'd discovered.

He just watched and waited.

The crowd all around him stared straight ahead at the storyteller as before. More quiet even than the night before, however. His hold on them grown stronger, Ohneka thought.

The *Hageota's* hair, pulled back again, appeared dark grey in the dancing firelight. No longer white, Ohneka thought. No longer even grey. The wrinkles less furrowed somehow. He simply looked younger. To Ohneka, the implication was somehow more horrible than the hulking beast he'd seen in the firelight the night before.

Eventually, the man reached into his storybag and came out with nothing Ohneka could see.

He felt Jino and Dekni stiffen next to him. They, too, had waited just for this moment.

He casually cast his hand over the fire again.

There was a brief shimmer of light in the blaze.

Hoh?

Moneton's nightmare.

Henh!

Cast into the hungry flames to somehow come to life later that night.

Was such a thing possible, Ohneka wondered. *Stone giants and ying heads? Talking turtles and tiny people living beneath the earth? Witches of evil? Brave heroes?*

Were such things truly possible?

The storyteller spoke softly.

His words this time told of the "Water People," a great tribe who lived beneath the sea, whose misshapen people had gills and scales like fish. How they'd invaded tribes who lived along the coastline for many ages, taken slaves to their undersea lairs.

But the three did not truly listen. They blocked most of the words from other minds with other thoughts: Memories of fishing and lacrosse and snowball fights, names for the different plants, ways of lashing down a snowshoe. They watched Moneton twist in his seat. The look of concern growing each moment on his face. His nightmare somehow captured and recast as a tale that the whole tribe now fed upon. Or nourished.

Making it stronger.

Making the *Hageota* stronger.

Sweat now dripped down Moneton's face and the man wiped his forehead, stepping up in the crowd among complaints and shouts to sit back down.

At the front of the longhouse, the storyteller's eyes shined red and gold like the fire's flames.

"This is real," Jino whispered. "Isn't it."

Ohneka looked at his brother, who nodded, and then turned back at her. "Yes," he said. "I believe so."

"So do I."

Then they got to work.

They'd not recognized Moneton when they first entered his lodge. His whole body was swollen and bloated, the stomach distended, arms and fingers plump with unseen water. His skin gleamed white in the fire's light, rotting with blue-tinged mold already along his neck and chin. Thick froth dribbled over his blackened lips. Though they'd only seen him hours before, he looked like he'd been dead, floating at the bottom of the river, for a week.

His wife and young daughter slept on woven mats just beside him. They too had already fallen into a deep sleep that was meant never to end. The storyteller's dark magic growing ever stronger. Reaching beyond the dreamer now. Their sleeping faces had gasped for air, frothed spit. Turning blue and cold with each passing moment.

Jino told him to go, to finish the rest. That she would be fine. Her voice had trembled some when she spoke, but Ohneka and Dekni went to their next stop. At dawn, when they returned, she was still working with the family.

Now, she sat across the room in the longhouse, her whole face heavy with exhaustion. Ohneka knuckled fatigue from his own eyes and then shook himself to attention. He'd moved to the back of the room this night, worried that his father might chase him out.

The *Hageota* looks angry tonight, Ohneka thought. No longer was he presenting himself as the old traveler. His features had grown shaper, eyes narrowed and searching over each face in the crowd.

Looking for someone …

Perhaps he already knows what we've done.

Ohneka carefully stepped behind some others to lose himself better in the crowd. He felt something cold run up along his spine. Across the room, he could see Jino cringing beside her mother. Something searching into her mind too, perhaps …

He's looking for us.

Ohneka's thoughts suddenly felt faint. Strange. As if a huge hairy spider was slowly crawling over them. He turned to find his brother in the crowd. The three of them needed to get out of that room. They all did.

But then the inner flap of lodge's entrance was pushed aside, and several latecomers stepped into the room.

Moneton and his family.

The three looked sick, certainly, and were swaddled in extra skins as they worked deeper into room. Moneton looked the worst. His face paler than usual, as others welcomed the family and cleared space for them to sit down.

Ohneka could not contain his smile. They'd done it, working together. It hadn't been another dream. Jino had really saved them.

"*Hoh?*" the storyteller shouted from the front of the room. His voice had sounded cross for the first time all week and it had not gone unnoticed by the crowd as the tribe hushed again awkwardly.

Glaring directly at Moneton, the *Hageota* did not wait for the customary reply to begin his night of tales.

He reached straight into his bag. The storyteller's face scrunched in confusion.

Then, he screamed and yanked his hand back.

The crowd broke into nervous whispers.

Something sprang from the bag, shooting out in a rush of light and what sounded like the howls of a hundred wolves.

The pit fires blew out instantly and Ohneka felt icy air blast across his face. The entire room now jumped to its feet amid countless frantic screams in the darkness.

Ohneka pushed free from his hiding spot and moved toward where, in the glow of the bag that now surrounded the storyteller, he could better see the man tearing at the belt on his hip. The bag glistened like starlight, and the things that grew out of it coiled in huge vines like blue smoke up and out of the back. They coiled like a great snake around the screeching storyteller. The man's whole form was lit up at the front of the longhouse now and everyone had turned to see.

The storyteller managed at last to tear the belt away and tossed it and the leather pouch to the floor. The long shimmering tendrils of light which had grown out of the bag bridged the space between and then clutched to the storyteller's legs and slithered promptly around his back and neck.

Ohneka continued to push through the eerily silent crowd, as only the sounds rushing from the bag and the storyteller's screams filled the longhouse now.

The *Hageota* had changed.

Between the swirling strands of light, Ohneka could again see the hulking thing he'd seen once before. Covered in matted grey hair, long blackened talons, feral eyes, and the horrible jaws.

Everyone saw it this time.

The rays of light that had sprung from the bag continued to enfold the creature, spinning it around and around. The thing that had been the storyteller writhed in the twisting light, and fought to pull away.

Away from the dreams.

Ohneka stumbled at last to Dekni and Jino's side.

He put an arm around his brother, who trembled some in the shimmering darkness.

It was Dekni, after all, who'd carefully crept into the storyteller's tent just before morning, then slowly snatched the pouch of his belt. Dekni, who'd worked beside Ohneka the rest of the night sneaking into the other lodges.

Collecting dreams.

Not shaking off the ones caught on the web, but positioning the bag over the hole in every dream catcher's center. Catching only the good ones.

Dekni, who'd then snuck back into the storyteller's tent and returned the pouch. Whatever nightmare the devil had stolen that night replaced with a dozen good dreams.

Ohneka felt Jino take hold of his other hand and the three watched together as the storyteller vanished.

One moment, he was there. His face warped in agony, the fang-filled mouth opened wide with disbelief and anguish, the spirals of shining light whirling about him completely, and then lifting through the smoke hole into the night.

The next moment, the light had vanished. And so had he.

Only ashes remained, the dark remains scattered across the floor on an unseen wind.

And the pouch.

Ohneka found himself moving towards it as the rest of the room broke into noise and movement. The fires were relit. Orders shouted by every adult in the room.

Ohneka picked up the pouch.

It felt cold. So cold it burned the tips of his fingers. Yet, he held onto it. He stared up through the smoke hole, looking at the white stars above.

Someone seized him. Squeezed his arm and shook him from his wandering thoughts.

"Ohneka," his father gaped down at him. "What happened here? What have you ..."

Ohneka feebly held up the storyteller's pouch as if that offered some explanation. His father looked at it and then into Ohneka's eyes.

"Father, I ..."

His father put a firm hand on Ohneka's shoulder. "I am sorry I did not listen before. Tell me now, son." He sat and held up a hand to quiet the others. "Tell us what happened here."

Ohneka looked about the longhouse, which had suddenly grown strangely quiet. The warmth of the fire now kissed his face as all the others slowly sat and grew completely silent.

He found Jino and Dekni, who smiled back at him in the crowd. Then, he looked over the rest of the faces. The chief. Gobo. Moneton and his family. His father. Everyone he'd ever known.

The eyes and ears of the entire tribe were upon him now.

He slowly lifted the storyteller's pouch high into the air so they could all see.

"*Hoh?*" Ohneka asked.

"*Henh,*" they replied.

NOTES: *Most scholars attribute the Ojibwa (Chippewa) tribe as the original designers of the dream catcher, an ancient Native American charm that quickly spread throughout the eastern tribes and later to the west. Also called "Spiderweb Charms," the catcher's weblike design is meant to capture the bad dreams oating above the sleeping person, while allowing the good dreams to escape through a small hole in the center of every charm. The bad dreams would then burn up in the sunrise. Dream catchers are typically decorated with scattered beads to represent the good dreams that may have been mistakenly caught during the night. A single bead towards the middle often represents the spider which made the web. The number of times the "web" connects to the wooden hoop has meaning as well, and there are dozens of variations (for instance, eight times to represent the eight legs of a spider, or thirteen times for the moons). Specific feathers are used to lure attributes such as courage (eagle) or wisdom (owl) into the dreams.*

Traveling storytellers were superstars, afforded the highest honors and hospitality. They moved from camp to camp trading stories and song for food and lodging. Most carried a story bag, which held small physical items to help them remember and tell their stories.

SELECTED
BIBLIOGRAPHY

America's Ancient Cities
   by Gene Stuart (National Geographic Society, 1988)

America's Fascinating Indian Heritage
   edited by James A. Maxwell (Readers Digest Books, 1995)

American Indians
   by William T. Hagan (University of Chicago Press, 1961)

A Native American Encyclopedia
   by Barry M. Pritzker (Oxford Press, 2000)

Growing Up Native American
   edited by Patricia Riley (William Morrow & Company, 1993)

Heroes & Heroines, Monsters & Magic: Native American Folktales
   as told by Joseph Bruchac (The Crossing Press, 1998)

In the Hands of the Great Spirit: The 20,000-Year History of American Indians
   by Jake Page (Free Press, 2003)
GG: "The most balanced and comprehensive book in the group,
   and an enjoyable read. Highly recommended!"

The American Indian Wars
   by John Tebbel & Keith Jennison (Castle Books, 2003)

The Earth Shall Weep: A History of Native America
  by James Wilson (Atlantic Monthly Press, 1999)

The European Discovery of America: The Northern Voyages
  by Samuel Eliot Morison (Oxford University Press, 1974)

The First Americans
  by Joy Hakim (Oxford University Press, 1993)
  GG: "The first in a recommended series of history books
  for younger readers."

The First Americans
  by Josepha Sherman (Smithmark, 1996)

The First Frontier
  by R. V. Coleman (Castle Books, 2005)

The Great Journey: The People of Ancient America
  by Brian M. Fagan (Thames and Hudson, 1987)
  GG: "Spectacular. For all fans of science and archeology."

The Indian Heritage of America
  by Alvin M. Josephy, Jr. (Houghton Mifflin Company, 1968)

The Indian in America's Past
  Edited by Jack D. Forbes (Prentice-Hall Inc., 1964)

The Viking Explorers
  by Frederick J. Pohl (Thomas Y. Crowell Company, 1966)

Ready for more

Tales?

Be sure to check out these other exciting
Tales Of ... books from Middle Atlantic Press!

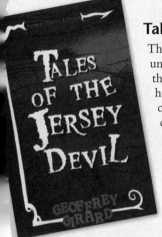

Tales of the Jersey Devil by Geoffrey Girard

The legend of the mysterious and terrifying Jersey Devil, a
unique American myth that has terrorized and captivated
the mysterious New Jersey Pine Barrens for more than two
hundred years, collected in thirteen original tales. From the
creature's birth in 1735 to a modern-day Jersey Devil hunt,
dare to follow this monster and those who have faced its
terror through more than two hundred years of American
history, folklore, and horror.

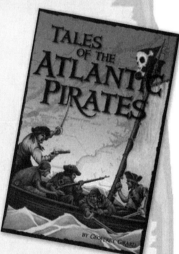

...les of the Atlantic Pirates by Geoffrey Girard

...nnon fire, swordplay and the ruthless pursuit of gold
...ve stalked the high seas from the decks of black-flagged
...ps for centuries. Here be thirteen original tales based
... the real-life pirates who once sailed and hunted along
...nerica's coast. From ghostly crews and cursed islands
... the capture of Blackbeard and modern-day treasure
...nts, join these seafaring outlaws for more than three
...ndred years of history, folklore, and adventure.

...e Thirteen: Tales of the American Colonies by Geoffrey Girard
...ilable 2008

Available at your local bookstore, shop,
or all major online book sellers.

Visit *www.MiddleAtlanticPress.com* or *www.GeoffreyGirard.com*
for more information.